BY CHARLES BUKOWSKI

Flower, Fist and Bestial Wail (1960)
Longshot Pomes for Broke Players (1962)
Run with the Hunted (1962)
It Catches My Heart in Its Hands (1963)
Crucifix in a Deathhand (1965)
Cold Dogs in the Courtyard (1965)
Confessions of a Man Insane Enough to Live with Beasts (1965)
All the Assholes in the World and Mine (1966)
At Terror Street and Agony Way (1968)
Poems Written Before Jumping out of an 8 Story Window (1968)
Notes of a Dirty Old Man (1969)
A Bukowski Sampler (1969)
The Days Run Away Like Wild Horses Over the Hills (1969)
Fire Station (1970)
Post Office (1971)
Mockingbird Wish Me Luck (1972)
*Erections, Ejaculations, Exhibitions and General Tales of
     Ordinary Madness* (1972)
South of No North (1973)
Burning in Water, Drowning in Flame: Selected Poems 1955–1973
     (1974)
Factotum (1975)
Love Is a Dog from Hell: Poems 1974–1977 (1977)
Women (1978)
*Play the Piano Drunk/Like a Percussion Instrument/Until the
     Fingers Begin to Bleed a Bit* (1979)
Shakespeare Never Did This (1979)
Dangling in the Tournefortia (1981)
Ham on Rye (1982)
Bring Me Your Love (1983)
Hot Water Music (1983)
There's No Business (1984)
War All the Time: Poems 1981–1984 (1984)
You Get So Alone at Times That It Just Makes Sense (1986)
The Movie: "Barfly" (1987)
The Roominghouse Madrigals: Early Selected Poems 1946-1966 (1988)

HAM ON RYE

A NOVEL BY

CHARLES BUKOWSKI

BLACK SPARROW PRESS   SANTA ROSA   1988

HAM ON RYE. Copyright © 1982 by Charles Bukowski.

All rights reserved. Printed in the United States of America. No part
of this book may be used or reproduced in any manner whatsoever
without written permission except in the case of brief quotations em-
bodied in critical articles and reviews. For information address Black
Sparrow Press, 24 Tenth Street, Santa Rosa, CA 95401.

LIBRARY OF CONGRESS CATALOGING IN PUBLICATION DATA

Bukowski, Charles.
  Ham on rye.

  I. Title.
PS3552.U4H3 1982   813'.54   82-9631
ISBN 0-87685-558-3
ISBN 0-87685-557-5 (pbk.)

eighth printing.

for all the fathers

Ham on Rye

1

The first thing I remember is being under something. It was a table, I saw a table leg, I saw the legs of the people, and a portion of the tablecloth hanging down. It was dark under there, I liked being under there. It must have been in Germany. I must have been between one and two years old. It was 1922. I felt good under the table. Nobody seemed to know that I was there. There was sunlight upon the rug and on the legs of the people. I liked the sunlight. The legs of the people were not interesting, not like the tablecloth which hung down, not like the table leg, not like the sunlight.

Then there is nothing . . . then a Christmas tree. Candles. Bird ornaments: birds with small berry branches in their beaks. A star. Two large people fighting, screaming. People eating, always people eating. I ate too. My spoon was bent so that if I wanted to eat I had to pick the spoon up with my right hand. If I picked it up with my left hand, the spoon bent away from my mouth. I wanted to pick the spoon up with my left hand.

Two people: one larger with curly hair, a big nose, a big mouth, much eyebrow; the larger person always seeming to be angry, often screaming; the smaller person quiet, round of face, paler, with large eyes. I was afraid of both of them. Sometimes there was a third, a fat one who wore dresses with lace at the throat. She wore a large brooch, and had many warts on her face with little hairs growing out of them. "Emily," they called her. These people didn't seem happy together. Emily was the grandmother, my father's mother. My father's name was "Henry." My mother's name was "Katherine." I never spoke to them by name. I was "Henry, Jr." These people spoke German most of the time and in the beginning I did too.

The first thing I remember my grandmother saying was, "I will bury *all* of you!" She said this the first time just before we began eating a meal, and she was to say it many times after that, just before we began to eat. Eating seemed very important. We ate mashed potatoes and gravy, especially on Sundays. We also ate roast beef, knockwurst and sauerkraut, green peas, rhubarb, carrots, spinach, string beans, chicken, meatballs and spaghetti, sometimes mixed with ravioli; there were boiled onions, asparagus, and every Sunday there was strawberry shortcake with vanilla ice cream. For breakfasts we had french toast and sausages, or there were hotcakes or waffles with bacon and scrambled eggs on the side. And there was always coffee. But what I remember best is all the mashed potatoes and gravy and my grandmother, Emily, saying, "I will bury *all* of you!"

She visited us often after we came to America, taking the red trolley in from Pasadena to Los Angeles. We only went to see her occasionally, driving out in the Model-T Ford.

I liked my grandmother's house. It was a small house under an overhanging mass of pepper trees. Emily had all her canaries in different cages. I remember one visit best. That evening she went about covering the cages with white hoods so that the birds could sleep. The people sat in chairs and talked. There was a piano and I sat at the piano and hit the keys and listened to the sounds as the people talked. I liked the sound of the keys best up at one end of the piano where there was hardly any sound at all—the sound the keys made was like chips of ice striking against one another.

"Will you stop that?" my father said loudly.

"Let the boy play the piano," said my grandmother.

My mother smiled.

"That boy," said my grandmother, "when I tried to pick him up out of the cradle to kiss him, he reached up and hit me in the nose!"

They talked some more and I went on playing the piano.

"Why don't you get that thing tuned?" asked my father.

Then I was told that we were going to see my grandfather. My grandfather and grandmother were not living together. I was told that my grandfather was a bad man, that his breath stank.

"Why does his breath stink?"

They didn't answer.

"Why does his breath stink?"

"He drinks."

We got into the Model-T and drove over to see my Grandfather Leonard. As we drove up and stopped he was standing on the porch of his house. He was old but he stood very straight. He had been an army officer in Germany and had come to America when he heard that the streets were paved with gold. They weren't, so he became the head of a construction firm.

The other people didn't get out of the car. Grandfather wiggled a finger at me. Somebody opened a door and I climbed out and walked toward him. His hair was pure white and long and his beard was pure white and long, and as I got closer I saw that his eyes were brilliant, like blue lights watching me. I stopped a little distance away from him.

"Henry," he said, "you and I, we know each other. Come into the house."

He held out his hand. As I got closer I could smell the stink of his breath. It was very strong but he was the most beautiful man I had ever seen and I wasn't afraid.

I went into his house with him. He led me to a chair.

"Sit down, please. I'm very happy to see you."

He went into another room. Then he came out with a little tin box.

"It's for you. Open it."

I had trouble with the lid, I couldn't open the box.

"Here," he said, "let me have it."

He loosened the lid and handed the tin box back to me. I lifted the lid and here was this cross, a German cross with a ribbon.

"Oh no," I said, "you keep it."

"It's yours," he said, "it's just a gummy badge."

"Thank you."

"You better go now. They will be worried."

"All right. Goodbye."

"Goodbye, Henry. No, wait . . ."

I stopped. He reached into a small front pocket of his pants with a couple of fingers, and tugged at a long gold chain with his other hand. Then he handed me his gold pocket watch, with the chain.

11

"Thank you, Grandfather . . ."

They were waiting outside and I got into the Model-T and we drove off. They all talked about many things as we drove along. They were always talking, and they talked all the way back to my grandmother's house. They spoke of many things but never, once, of my grandfather.

2

I remember the Model-T. Sitting high, the running boards seemed friendly, and on cold days, in the mornings, and often at other times, my father had to fit the hand-crank into the front of the engine and crank it many times in order to start the car.

"A man can get a broken arm doing this. It kicks back like a horse."

We went for Sunday rides in the Model-T when grandmother didn't visit. My parents liked the orange groves, miles and miles of orange trees always either in blossom or full of oranges. My parents had a picnic basket and a metal chest. In the metal chest were frozen cans of fruit on dry ice, and in the picnic basket were weenie and liverwurst and salami sandwiches, potato chips, bananas and soda-pop. The soda-pop was shifted continually back and forth between the metal box and the picnic basket. It froze quickly, and then had to be thawed.

My father smoked Camel cigarettes and he knew many tricks and games which he showed us with the packages of Camel cigarettes. How many pyramids were there? Count them. We would count them and then he would show us more of them.

There were also tricks about the humps on the camels and about the written words on the package. Camel cigarettes were magic cigarettes.

There was a particular Sunday I can recall. The picnic basket was empty. Yet we still drove along through the orange groves, further and further away from where we lived.

"Daddy," my mother asked, "aren't we going to run out of gas?"

"No, there's plenty of god-damned gas."

"Where are we going?"

"I'm going to get me some god-damned oranges!"

My mother sat very still as we drove along. My father pulled up alongside the road, parked near a wire fence and we sat there, listening. Then my father kicked the door open and got out.

"Bring the basket."

We all climbed through the strands of the fence.

"Follow me," said my father.

Then we were between two rows of orange trees, shaded from the sun by the branches and the leaves. My father stopped and reaching up began yanking oranges from the lower branches of the nearest tree. He seemed angry, yanking the oranges from the tree, and the branches seemed angry, leaping up and down. He threw the oranges into the picnic basket which my mother held. Sometimes he missed and I chased the oranges and put them into the basket. My father went from tree to tree, yanking at the lower branches, throwing the oranges into the picnic basket.

"Daddy, we have enough," said my mother.

"Like hell."

He kept yanking.

Then a man stepped forward, a very tall man. He held a shotgun.

"All right, buddy, what do you think you're doing?"

"I'm picking oranges. There are plenty of oranges."

"These are my oranges. Now, listen to me, tell your woman to dump them."

"There are plenty of god-damned oranges. You're not going to miss a few god-damned oranges."

"I'm not going to miss *any* oranges. Tell your woman to dump them."

The man pointed his shotgun at my father.

"Dump them," my father told my mother.

The oranges rolled to the ground.

"Now," said the man, "get out of my orchard."

"You don't need all these oranges."

"I know what I need. Now get out of here."

"Guys like you ought to be hung!"

"I'm the law here. Now move!"

The man raised his shotgun again. My father turned and began walking out of the orange grove. We followed him and the man trailed us. Then we got into the car but it was one of those times when it wouldn't start. My father got out of the car to crank it. He cranked it twice and it wouldn't start. My father was beginning to sweat. The man stood at the edge of the road.

"Get that god-damned cracker box started!" he said.

My father got ready to twist the crank again. "We're not on your property! We can stay here as long as we damn well please!"

"Like hell! Get that thing *out* of here, and fast!"

My father cranked the engine again. It sputtered, then stopped. My mother sat with the empty picnic box on her lap. I was afraid to look at the man. My father whirled the crank again and the engine started. He leaped into the car and began working the levers on the steering wheel.

"Don't come back," said the man, "or next time it might not go so easy for you."

My father drove the Model-T off. The man was still standing near the road. My father was driving very fast. Then he slowed the car and made a U-turn. He drove back to where the man had stood. The man was gone. We speeded back on the way out of the orange groves.

"I'm coming back some day and get that bastard," said my father.

"Daddy, we'll have a nice dinner tonight. What would you like?" my mother asked.

"Pork chops," he answered.

I had never seen him drive the car that fast.

3

My father had two brothers. The younger was named Ben and the older was named John. Both were alcoholics and ne'er-do-wells. My parents often spoke of them.

"Neither of them amount to anything," said my father.

"You just come from a bad family, Daddy," said my mother.

"And *your* brother doesn't amount to a damn either!"

My mother's brother was in Germany. My father often spoke badly of him.

I had another uncle, Jack, who was married to my father's sister, Elinore. I had never seen my Uncle Jack or my Aunt Elinore because there were bad feelings between them and my father.

"See this scar on my hand?" asked my father. "Well, that's where Elinore stuck me with a sharp pencil when I was very young. That scar has never gone away."

My father didn't like people. He didn't like me. "Children should be seen and not heard," he told me.

It was an early Sunday afternoon without Grandma Emily.

"We should go see Ben," said my mother. "He's dying."

"He borrowed all that money from Emily. He pissed it away on gambling and women and booze."

"I know, Daddy."

"Emily won't have any money left when she dies."

"We should still go see Ben. They say he has only two weeks left."

"All right, all right! We'll go!"

So we went and got into the Model-T and started driving. It took some time, and my mother had to stop for flowers. It was a long drive toward the mountains. We reached the foothills and took the little winding mountain road upwards. Uncle Ben was in a sanitarium up there, dying of TB.

"It must cost Emily a lot of money to keep Ben up here," said my father.

"Maybe Leonard is helping."

"Leonard doesn't have anything. He drank it up and he gave it away."

"I like Grandpa Leonard," I said.

"Children should be seen and not heard," said my father. Then he continued, "Ah, that Leonard, the only time he was good to us children was when he was drunk. He'd joke with us and give us money. But the next day when he was sober he was the meanest man in the world."

The Model-T was climbing the mountain road nicely. The air was clear and sunny.

"Here it is," said my father. He guided the car into the parking lot of the sanitarium and we got out. I followed my mother and father into the building. As we entered his room, my Uncle Ben was sitting upright in bed, staring out the window. He turned and looked at us as we entered. He was a very handsome man, thin, with black hair, and he had dark eyes which glittered, were brilliant with glittering light.

"Hello, Ben," said my mother.

"Hello, Katy." Then he looked at me. "Is this Henry?"

"Yes."

"Sit down."

My father and I sat down.

My mother stood there. "These flowers, Ben. I don't see a vase."

"They're nice flowers, thanks, Katy. No, there isn't a vase."

"I'll go get a vase," said my mother.

She left the room, holding the flowers.

"Where are all your girlfriends now, Ben?" asked my father.

"They come around."

"I'll bet."

"They come around."

"We're here because Katherine wanted to see you."

"I know."

"I wanted to see you too, Uncle Ben. I think you're a real pretty man."

"Pretty like my ass," said my father.

My mother entered the room with the flowers in a vase.

"Here, I'll put them on this table by the window."

"They're nice flowers, Katy."

My mother sat down.

"We can't stay too long," said my father.

Uncle Ben reached under the mattress and his hand came out holding a pack of cigarettes. He took one out, struck a match and lit it. He took a long drag and exhaled.

"You know you're not allowed cigarettes," said my father. "I know how you get them. Those prostitutes bring them to you. Well, I'm going to tell the doctors about it and I'm going to get them to stop letting those prostitutes in here!"

"You're not going to do shit," said my uncle.

"I got a good mind to rip that cigarette out of your mouth!" said my father.

"You never had a good mind," said my uncle.

"Ben," my mother said, "you shouldn't smoke, it will kill you."

"I've had a good life," said my uncle.

"You never had a good life," said my father. "Lying, boozing, borrowing, whoring, drinking. You never worked a day in your life! And now you're dying at the age of 24!"

"It's been all right," said my uncle. He took another heavy drag on the Camel, then exhaled.

"Let's get out of here," said my father. "This man is insane!"

My father stood up. Then my mother stood up. Then I stood up.

"Goodbye, Katy," said my uncle, "and goodbye, Henry." He looked at me to indicate which Henry.

We followed my father through the sanitarium halls and out into the parking lot to the Model-T. We got in, it started, and we began down the winding road out of the mountains.

"We should have stayed longer," said my mother.

"Don't you know that TB is catching?" asked my father.

18

"I think he was a very pretty man," I said.

"It's the disease," said my father. "It makes them look like that. And besides the TB, he's caught many other things too."

"What kind of things?" I asked.

"I can't tell you," my father answered. He steered the Model-T down the winding mountain road as I wondered about that.

4

It was another Sunday that we got into the Model-T in search of my Uncle John.

"He has no ambition," said my father. "I don't see how he can hold his god-damned head up and look people in the eye."

"I wish he wouldn't chew tobacco," said my mother. "He spits the stuff everywhere."

"If this country was full of men like him the Chinks would take over and *we'd* be running the laundries . . ."

"John never had a chance," said my mother. "He ran away from home early. At least you got a high school education."

"College," said my father.

"Where?" asked my mother.

"The University of Indiana."

"Jack said you only went to high school."

"*Jack* only went to high school. That's why he gardens for the rich."

"Am I ever going to see my Uncle Jack?" I asked.

"First let's see if we can find your Uncle John," said my father.

"Do the Chinks really want to take over this country?" I asked.

"Those yellow devils have been waiting for centuries to do it. What's stopped them is that they have been kept busy fighting the Japs."

"Who are the best fighters, the Chinks or the Japs?"

"The Japs. The trouble is that there are too many Chinks. When you kill a Chink he splits in half and becomes two Chinks."

"How come their skin is yellow?"

"Because instead of drinking water they drink their own pee-pee."

"Daddy, *don't* tell the boy that!"

"Then tell him to stop asking questions."

We drove along through another warm Los Angeles day. My mother had on one of her pretty dresses and fancy hats. When my mother was dressed up she always sat straight and held her neck very stiff.

"I wish we had enough money so we could help John and his family," said my mother.

"It's not my fault if they don't have a pot to piss in," answered my father.

"Daddy, John was in the war just like you were. Don't you think he deserves something?"

"He never rose in the ranks. I became a master sergeant."

"Henry, all your brothers can't be like you."

"They don't have any god-damned *drive!* They think they can live off the land!"

We drove along a bit further. Uncle John and his family lived in a small court. We went up the cracked sidewalk to a sagging porch and my father pushed the bell. The bell didn't ring. He knocked, loudly.

"Open up! It's the cops!" my father yelled.

"Daddy, stop it!" said my mother.

After what seemed a long time, the door opened a crack. Then it opened further. And we could see my Aunt Anna. She was very thin, her cheeks were hollow and her eyes had pouches, dark pouches. Her voice was thin, too.

"Oh, Henry . . . Katherine . . . come in, please . . ."

We followed her in. There was very little furniture. There was a breakfast nook with a table and four chairs and there were two beds. My mother and father sat in the chairs. Two girls, Katherine and Betsy (I learned their names later) were at the sink taking turns trying to scrape peanut butter out of a nearly empty peanut butter jar.

"We were just having lunch," said my Aunt Anna.

The girls came over with tiny smears of peanut butter which

21

they spread on dry pieces of bread. They kept looking into the jar and scraping with the knife.

"Where's John?" asked my father.

My aunt sat down wearily. She looked very weak, very pale. Her dress was dirty, her hair uncombed, tired, sad.

"We've been waiting for him. We haven't seen him for quite some time."

"Where did he go?"

"I don't know. He just left on his motorcycle."

"All he does," said my father, "is think about his motorcycle."

"Is this Henry, Jr.?"

"Yes."

"He just stares. He's so quiet."

"That's the way we want him."

"Still water runs deep."

"Not with this one. The only thing that runs deep with him are the holes in his ears."

The two girls took their slices of bread and walked outside and sat on the stoop to eat them. They hadn't spoken to us. I thought they were quite nice. They were thin like their mother but they were still quite pretty.

"How are you, Anna?" asked my mother.

"I'm all right."

"Anna, you don't look well. I think you need food."

"Why doesn't your boy sit down? Sit down, Henry."

"He likes to stand," said my father. "It makes him strong. He's getting ready to fight the Chinks."

"Don't you like the Chinese?" my aunt asked me.

"No," I answered.

"Well, Anna," my father asked, "how are things going?"

"Awful, really. . . . The landlord keeps asking for the rent. He gets very nasty. He frightens me. I don't know what to do."

"I hear the cops are after John," said my father.

"He didn't do very much."

"What did he do?"

"He made some counterfeit dimes."

"*Dimes?* Jesus Christ, what kind of ambition is *that?*"

"John really doesn't want to be bad."

"Seems to me he doesn't want to be *anything*."

"He would if he could."

"Yeah. And if a frog had wings he wouldn't wear his ass out a-hoppin'!"

There was silence then and they sat there. I turned and looked outside. The girls were gone from the porch, they had gone off somewhere.

"Come, sit down, Henry," said my Aunt Anna.

I stood there. "Thank you, it's all right."

"Anna," my mother asked, "are you sure that John will come back?"

"He'll come back when he gets tired of the hens," said my father.

"John loves his children . . ." said Anna.

"I hear the cops are after him for something else."

"What?"

"Rape."

"Rape?"

"Yes, Anna, I heard about it. He was riding his motorcycle one day. This young girl was hitch-hiking. She got onto the back of his motorcycle and as they rode along all of a sudden John saw an empty garage. He drove in there, closed the door and raped the girl."

"How did you find out?"

"Find out? The cops came and told me, they asked me where he was."

"Did you tell them?"

"What for? To have him go to jail and evade his responsibilities? That's just what he'd want."

"I never thought of it that way."

"Not that I'm for rape . . ."

"Sometimes a man can't help what he does."

"What?"

"I mean, after having the children, and with this type of life, the worry and all . . . I don't look so good anymore. He saw a young girl, she looked good to him . . . she got on his bike, you know, she put her arms around him . . ."

"What?" asked my father. "How would *you* like to be raped?"

"I guess I wouldn't like it."

"Well, I'm sure the young girl didn't like it either."

A fly appeared and whirled around and around the table. We watched it.

"There's nothing to eat here," said my father. "The fly has come to the wrong place."

The fly became more and more bold. It circled closer and made buzzing sounds. The closer it circled the louder the buzzing became.

"You're not going to tell the cops that John might come home?" my aunt asked my father.

"I am not going to let him off the hook so easily," said my father.

My mother's hand leaped quickly. It closed and she brought her hand back down to the table.

"I got him," she said.

"Got what?" asked my father.

"The fly," she smiled.

"I don't believe you . . ."

"You see the fly anywhere? The fly is gone."

"It flew off."

"No, I have it in my hand."

"Nobody is that quick."

"I have it in my hand."

"Bullshit."

"You don't believe me?"

"No."

"Open your mouth."

"All right."

My father opened his mouth and my mother cupped her hand over it. My father leaped up, grabbing at his throat.

"JESUS CHRIST!"

The fly came out of his mouth and began circling the table again.

"That's enough," said my father, "we're going home!"

He got up and walked out the door and down the walk and got into the Model-T and just sat there very stiffly, looking dangerous.

"We brought you a few cans of food," my mother said to my aunt. "I'm sorry it can't be money but Henry is afraid John will use it for gin, or for gasoline for his motorcycle. It isn't much: soup, hash, peas . . ."

24

"Oh, Katherine, thank you! Thank you, both . . ."

My mother got up and I followed her. There were two boxes of canned food in the car. I saw my father sitting there rigidly. He was still angry.

My mother handed me the smaller box of cans and she took the large box and I followed her back into the court. We set the boxes down in the breakfast nook. Aunt Anna came over and picked up a can. It was a can of peas, the label on it covered with little round green peas.

"This is lovely," said my aunt.

"Anna, we have to go. Henry's dignity is upset."

My aunt threw her arms around my mother. "Everything has been so awful. But this is like a dream. Wait until the girls come home. Wait until the girls see all these cans of food!"

My mother hugged my aunt back. Then they separated.

"John is not a bad man," my aunt said.

"I know," my mother answered. "Goodbye, Anna."

"Goodbye, Katherine. Goodbye, Henry."

My mother turned and walked out the door. I followed her. We walked to the car and got in. My father started the car.

As we were driving off I saw my aunt at the door waving. My mother waved back. My father didn't wave back. I didn't either.

5

I had begun to dislike my father. He was always angry about something. Wherever we went he got into arguments with people. But he didn't appear to frighten most people; they often just stared at him, calmly, and he became more furious. If we ate out, which was seldom, he always found something wrong with the food and sometimes refused to pay. "There's flyshit in this whipped cream! What the hell kind of a place is this?"

"I'm sorry, sir, you needn't pay. Just leave."

"I'll leave, all right! But I'll be back! I'll burn this god-damned place down!"

Once we were in a drug store and my mother and I were standing to one side while my father yelled at a clerk. Another clerk asked my mother, "Who *is* that horrible man? Every time he comes in here there's an argument."

"That's my husband," my mother told the clerk.

Yet, I remember another time. He was working as a milkman and made early morning deliveries. One morning he awakened me. "Come on, I want to show you something." I walked outside with him. I was wearing my pajamas and slippers. It was still dark, the moon was still up. We walked to the milk wagon which was horsedrawn. The horse stood very still. "Watch," said my father. He took a sugar cube, put it in his hand and held it out to the horse. The horse ate it out of his palm. "Now you try it . . ." He put a sugar cube in my hand. It was a very large horse. "Get closer! Hold out your hand!" I was afraid the horse would bite my hand off. The head came down; I saw the nostrils; the lips pulled back, I saw the tongue and the teeth, and then the sugar cube was gone. "Here. Try it again . . ." I tried it again. The horse took the sugar cube and waggled his head. "Now," said my father, "I'll take you back inside before the horse shits on you."

I was not allowed to play with other children. "They are bad children," said my father, "their parents are poor." "Yes," agreed my mother. My parents wanted to be rich so they imagined themselves rich.

The first children of my age that I knew were in kindergarten. They seemed very strange, they laughed and talked and seemed happy. I didn't like them. I always felt as if I was going to be sick, to vomit, and the air seemed strangely still and white. We painted with watercolors. We planted radish seeds in a garden and some weeks later we ate them with salt. I liked the lady who taught kindergarten, I liked her better than my parents. One problem I had was going to the bathroom. I always needed to go to the bathroom, but I was ashamed to let the others know that I had to go, so I held it. It was really terrible to hold it. And the air was white, I felt like vomiting, I felt like shitting and pissing, but I didn't say anything. And when some of the others came back from the bathroom I'd think, you're dirty, you did something in there . . .

The little girls were nice in their short dresses, with their long hair and their beautiful eyes, but I thought, they do things in there too, even though they pretend they don't.

Kindergarten was mostly white air . . .

Grammar school was different, first grade to sixth grade, some of the kids were twelve years old, and we all came from poor neighborhoods. I began to go to the bathroom, but only to piss. Coming out once I saw a small boy drinking at a water fountain. A larger boy walked up behind him and jammed his face down into the water jet. When the small boy raised his head, some of his teeth were broken and blood came out of his mouth, there was blood in the fountain. "You tell anyone about this," the older boy told him, "and I'll really get you." The boy took out a handkerchief and held it to his mouth. I walked back to class where the teacher was telling us about George Washington and Valley

Forge. She wore an elaborate white wig. She often slapped the palms of our hands with a ruler when she thought we were being disobedient. I don't think she ever went to the bathroom. I hated her.

Each afternoon after school there would be a fight between two of the older boys. It was always out by the back fence where there was never a teacher about. And the fights were never even; it was always a larger boy against a smaller boy and the larger boy would beat the smaller boy with his fists, backing him into the fence. The smaller boy would attempt to fight back but it was useless. Soon his face was bloody, the blood running down into his shirt. The smaller boys took their beatings wordlessly, never begging, never asking mercy. Finally, the larger boy would back off and it would be over and all the other boys would walk home with the winner. I'd walk home quickly, alone, after holding my shit all through school and all through the fight. Usually by the time I got home I would have lost the urge to relieve myself. I used to worry about that.

6

I didn't have any friends at school, didn't want any. I felt better being alone. I sat on a bench and watched the others play and they looked foolish to me. During lunch one day I was approached by a new boy. He wore knickers, was cross-eyed and pigeon-toed. I didn't like him, he didn't look good. He sat on the bench next to me.

"Hello, my name's David."

I didn't answer.

He opened his lunch bag. "I've got peanut butter sandwiches," he said. "What do you have?"

"Peanut butter sandwiches."

"I've got a banana, too. And some potato chips. Want some potato chips?"

I took some. He had plenty, they were crisp and salty, the sun shone right through them. They were good.

"Can I have some more?"

"All right."

I took some more. He even had jelly on his peanut butter sandwiches. It dripped out and ran over his fingers. David didn't seem to notice.

"Where do you live?" he asked.

"Virginia Road."

"I live on Pickford. We can walk home together after school. Take some more potato chips. Who's your teacher?"

"Mrs. Columbine."

"I have Mrs. Reed. I'll see you after class, we'll walk home together."

Why did he wear those knickers? What did he want? I really didn't like him. I took some more of his potato chips.

That afternoon, after school, he found me and began walking along beside me. "You never told me your name," he said.

"Henry," I answered.

As we walked along I noticed a whole gang of boys, first graders, following us. At first they were half a block behind us, then they closed the gap to several yards behind us.

"What do they want?" I asked David.

He didn't answer, just kept walking.

"Hey, knicker-shitter!" one of them yelled. "Your mother make you shit in your knickers?"

"Pigeon-toe, ho-ho, pigeon-toe!"

"Cross-eye! Get ready to die!"

Then they circled us.

"Who's your friend? Does he kiss your rear end?"

One of them had David by the collar. He threw him onto a lawn. David stood up. A boy got down behind him on his hands and knees. The other boy shoved him and David fell over backwards. Another boy rolled him over and rubbed his face in the grass. Then they stepped back. David got up again. He didn't make a sound but the tears were rolling down his face. The largest boy walked up to him. "We don't want you in our school, sissy. Get out of our school!" He punched David in the stomach. David bent over and as he did, the boy brought his knee up into David's face. David fell. He had a bloody nose.

Then the boys circled me. "Your turn now!" They kept circling and as they did I kept turning. There were always some of them behind me. Here I was loaded with shit and I had to fight. I was terrified and calm at the same time. I didn't understand their motive. They kept circling and I kept turning. It went on and on. They screamed things at me but I didn't hear what they said. Finally they backed off and went away down the street. David was waiting for me. We walked down the sidewalk toward his place on Pickford Street.

Then we were in front of his house.

"I've got to go in now. Goodbye."

"Goodbye, David."

He went in and then I heard his mother's voice. *"David!* Look at your knickers and shirt! They're torn and full of grass stains! You do this almost every day! Tell me, why do you do it?"

David didn't answer.

"I asked you a question! Why do you do this to your clothes?"

"I can't help it, Mom . . ."

"You can't *help* it? You stupid boy!"

I heard her beating him. David began to cry and she beat him harder. I stood on the front lawn and listened. After a while the beating stopped. I could hear David sobbing. Then he stopped.

His mother said, "Now, I want you to practice your violin lesson."

I sat down on the lawn and waited. Then I heard the violin. It was a very sad violin. I didn't like the way David played. I sat and listened for some time but the music didn't get any better. The shit had hardened inside of me. I no longer felt like shitting. The afternoon light hurt my eyes. I felt like vomiting. I got up and walked home.

7

There were continual fights. The teachers didn't seem to know anything about them. And there was always trouble when it rained. Any boy who brought an umbrella to school or wore a raincoat was singled out. Most of our parents were too poor to buy us such things. And when they did, we hid them in the bushes. Anybody seen carrying an umbrella or wearing a raincoat was considered a sissy. They were beaten after school. David's mother had him carry an umbrella whenever it was the least bit cloudy.

There were two recess periods. The first graders gathered at their own baseball diamond and the teams were chosen. David and I stood together. It was always the same. I was chosen next to last and David was chosen last, so we always played on different teams. David was worse than I was. With his crossed eyes, he couldn't even see the ball. I needed lots of practice. I had never played with the kids in the neighborhood. I didn't know how to catch a ball or how to hit one. But I wanted to, I liked it. David was afraid of the ball, I wasn't. I swung hard, I swung harder than anybody but I could never hit the ball. I always struck out. Once I fouled a ball off. That felt good. Another time I drew a walk. When I got to first, the first baseman said, "That's the only way you'll ever get here." I stood and looked at him. He was chewing gum and he had long black hairs coming out of his nostrils. His hair was thick with vaseline. He wore a perpetual sneer.

"What are you looking at?" he asked me.

I didn't know what to say. I wasn't used to conversation.

"The guys say you're crazy," he told me, "but you don't scare me. I'll be waiting for you after school some day."

32

I kept looking at him. He had a terrible face. Then the pitcher wound up and I broke for second. I ran like crazy and slid into second. The ball arrived late. The tag was late.

"You're *out!*" screamed the boy whose turn it was to umpire. I got up, not believing it.

"I said, 'YOU'RE OUT!'" the umpire screamed.

Then I knew that I was not accepted. David and I were not accepted. The others wanted me "out" because I was *supposed* to *be* "out." They knew David and I were friends. It was because of David that I wasn't wanted. As I walked off the diamond I saw David playing third base in his knickers. His blue and yellow stockings had fallen down around his feet. Why had he chosen me? I was a marked man. That afternoon after school I quickly left class and walked home alone, without David. I didn't want to watch him beaten again by our classmates or by his mother. I didn't want to listen to his sad violin. But the next day at lunch time, when he sat down next to me I ate his potato chips.

My day came. I was tall and I felt very powerful at the plate. I couldn't believe that I was as bad as they wished me to be. I swung wildly but with force. I knew I was strong, and maybe like they said, "crazy." But I had this feeling inside of me that something real was there. Just hardened shit, maybe, but that was more than they had. I was up at bat. "Hey, it's the STRIKEOUT KING! MR. WINDMILL!" The ball arrived. I swung and I felt the bat connect like I had wanted it to do for so long. The ball went up, up and HIGH, into left field, 'way OVER the left fielder's head. His name was Don Brubaker and he stood and watched it fly over his head. It looked like it was never going to come down. Then Brubaker started running after the ball. He wanted to throw me out. He would never do it. The ball landed and rolled onto a diamond where some 5th graders were playing. I ran slowly to first, hit the bag, looked at the guy on first, ran slowly to second, touched it, ran to third where David stood, ignored him, tagged third and walked to home plate. Never such a day. Never such a home run by a first grader! As I stepped on home plate I heard one of the players, Irving Bone, say to the team captain, Stanley Greenberg, "Let's put him on the regular team." (The regular team played teams from other schools.)

"No," said Stanley Greenberg.

Stanley was right. I never hit another home run. I struck out most of the time. But they always remembered that home run and while they still hated me, it was a better kind of hatred, like they weren't quite sure *why*.

Football season was worse. We played touch football. I couldn't catch the football or throw it but I got into one game. When the runner came through I grabbed him by the shirt collar and threw him on the ground. When he started to get up, I kicked him. I didn't like him. It was the first baseman with vaseline in his hair and the hair in his nostrils. Stanley Greenberg came over. He was larger than any of us. He could have killed me if he'd wanted to. He was our leader. Whatever he said, that was it. He told me, "You don't understand the rules. No more football for you."

I was moved into volleyball. I played volleyball with David and the others. It wasn't any good. They yelled and screamed and got excited, but the *others* were playing football. I wanted to play football. All I needed was a little practice. Volleyball was shameful. Girls played volleyball. After a while I wouldn't play. I just stood in the center of the field where nobody was playing. I was the only one who would not play anything. I stood there each day and waited through the two recess sessions, until they were over.

One day while I was standing there, more trouble came. A football sailed from high behind me and hit me on the head. It knocked me to the ground. I was very dizzy. They stood around snickering and laughing. "Oh, look, Henry fainted! Henry fainted like a lady! Oh, look at Henry!"

I got up while the sun spun around. Then it stood still. The sky moved closer and flattened out. It was like being in a cage. They stood around me, faces, noses, mouths and eyes. Because they were taunting me I thought they had deliberately hit me with the football. It was unfair.

"Who kicked that ball?" I asked.

"You wanna know who kicked the ball?"

"Yes."

"What are you going to do when you find out?"

I didn't answer.

"It was Billy Sherril," somebody said.

Billy was a round fat boy, really nicer than most, but he was one of them. I began walking toward Billy. He stood there. When I got close he swung. I almost didn't feel it. I hit him behind his left ear and when he grabbed his ear I hit him in the stomach. He fell to the ground. He stayed down. "Get up and fight him, Billy," said Stanley Greenberg. Stanley lifted Billy up and pushed him toward me. I punched Billy in the mouth and he grabbed his mouth with both hands.

"O.K.," said Stanley, "I'll take his place!"

The boys cheered. I decided to run, I didn't want to die. But then a teacher came up. "What's going on here?" It was Mr. Hall.

"Henry picked on Billy," said Stanley Greenberg.

"Is that right, boys?" asked Mr. Hall.

"Yes," they said.

Mr. Hall took me by the ear all the way to the principal's office. He pushed me into a chair in front of an empty desk and then knocked on the principal's door. He was in there for some time and when he came out he left without looking at me. I sat there five or ten minutes before the principal came out and sat behind the desk. He was a very dignified man with a mass of white hair and a blue bow tie. He looked like a real gentleman. His name was Mr. Knox. Mr. Knox folded his hands and looked at me without speaking. When he did that I was not so sure that he was a gentleman. He seemed to want to humble me, treat me like the others.

"Well," he said at last, "tell me what happened."

"Nothing happened."

"You hurt that boy, Billy Sherril. His parents are going to want to know why."

I didn't answer.

"Do you think you can take matters into your own hands when something happens you don't like?"

"No."

"Then why did you do it?"

I didn't answer.

"Do you think you're better than other people?"

"No."

Mr. Knox sat there. He had a long letter opener and he slid it back and forth on the green felt padding of the desk. He had a large bottle of green ink on his desk and a pen holder with four pens. I wondered if he would beat me.

"Then why did you do what you did?"

I didn't answer. Mr. Knox slid the letter opener back and forth. The phone rang. He picked it up.

"Hello? Oh, Mrs. Kirby? He what? What? Listen, can't *you* administer the discipline? I'm busy now. All right, I'll phone you when I'm done with this one . . ."

He hung up. He brushed his fine white hair back out of his eyes with one hand and looked at me.

"Why do you cause me all this trouble?"

I didn't answer him.

"You think you're tough, huh?"

I kept silent.

"Tough kid, huh?"

There was a fly circling Mr. Knox's desk. It hovered over his green ink bottle. Then it landed on the black cap of the ink bottle and sat there rubbing its wings.

"O.K., kid, you're tough and I'm tough. Let's shake hands on that."

I didn't think I was tough so I didn't give him my hand.

"Come on, give me your hand."

I stretched my hand out and he took it and began shaking it. Then he stopped shaking it and looked at me. He had blue clear eyes lighter than the blue of his bow tie. His eyes were almost beautiful. He kept looking at me and holding my hand. His grip began to tighten.

"I want to congratulate you for being a tough guy."

His grip tightened some more.

"Do you think I'm a tough guy?"

I didn't answer.

He crushed the bones of my fingers together. I could feel the bone of each finger cutting like a blade into the flesh of the finger next to it. Shots of red flashed before my eyes.

"Do you think I'm a tough guy?" he asked.

"I'll kill you," I said.

"You'll what?"

36

Mr. Knox tightened his grip. He had a hand like a vise. I could see every pore in his face.

"Tough guys don't scream, do they?"

I couldn't look at his face anymore. I put my face down on the desk.

"Am I a tough guy?" asked Mr. Knox.

He squeezed harder. I had to scream, but I kept it as quiet as possible so no one in the classes could hear me.

"Now, am I a tough guy?"

I waited. I hated to say it. Then I said, "Yes."

Mr. Knox let go of my hand. I was afraid to look at it. I let it hang by my side. I noticed that the fly was gone and I thought, it's not so bad to be a fly. Mr. Knox was writing on a piece of paper.

"Now, Henry, I'm writing a little note to your parents and I want you to deliver it to them. And you *will* deliver it to them, won't you?"

"Yes."

He folded the note into an envelope and handed it to me. The envelope was sealed and I had no desire to open it.

8

I took the envelope home to my mother and handed it to her and walked into the bedroom. My bedroom. The best thing about the bedroom was the bed. I liked to stay in bed for hours, even during the day with the covers pulled up to my chin. It was good in there, nothing ever occurred in there, no people, nothing. My mother often found me in bed in the daytime.

"Henry, get up! It's not good for a young boy to lay in bed all day! Now, get up! *Do* something!"

But there was nothing to do.

I didn't go to bed that day. My mother was reading the note. Soon I heard her crying. Then she was wailing. "Oh, my god! You've disgraced your father and myself! It's a disgrace! Suppose the neighbors find out? What will the neighbors think?"

They never spoke to their neighbors.

Then the door opened and my mother came running into the room: *"How could you have done this to your mother?"*

The tears were running down her face. I felt guilty.

"Wait until your father gets home!"

She slammed the bedroom door and I sat in the chair and waited. Somehow I felt guilty . . .

I heard my father come in. He always slammed the door, walked heavily, and talked loudly. He was home. After a few moments the bedroom door opened. He was six feet two, a large man. Everything vanished, the chair I was sitting in, the wallpaper, the walls, all of my thoughts. He was the dark covering the sun, the violence of him made everything else utterly disappear. He was all ears, nose, mouth, I couldn't look at his eyes, there was only his red angry face.

"All right, Henry. Into the bathroom."

I walked in and he closed the door behind us. The walls were white. There was a bathroom mirror and a small window, the screen black and broken. There was the bathtub and the toilet and the tiles. He reached and took down the razor strop which hung from a hook. It was going to be the first of many such beatings, which would recur more and more often. Always, I felt, without real reason.

"All right, take down your pants."

I took my pants down.

"Pull down your shorts."

I pulled them down.

Then he laid on the strop. The first blow inflicted more shock than pain. The second hurt more. Each blow which followed increased the pain. At first I was aware of the walls, the toilet, the tub. Finally I couldn't see anything. As he beat me, he berated me, but I couldn't understand the words. I thought about his roses, how he grew roses in the yard. I thought about his automobile in the garage. I tried not to scream. I knew that if I did scream he might stop, but knowing this, and knowing his desire for me to scream, prevented me. The tears ran from my eyes as I remained silent. After a while it all became just a whirlpool, a jumble, and there was only the deadly possibility of being there forever. Finally, like something jerked into action, I began to sob, swallowing and choking on the salt slime that ran down my throat. He stopped.

He was no longer there. I became aware of the little window again and the mirror. There was the razor strop hanging from the hook, long and brown and twisted. I couldn't bend over to pull up my pants or my shorts and I walked to the door, awkwardly, my clothes around my feet. I opened the bathroom door and there was my mother standing in the hall.

"It wasn't right," I told her. "Why didn't you help me?"

"The father," she said, "is always right."

Then my mother walked away. I went to my bedroom, dragging my clothing around my feet and sat on the edge of the bed. The mattress hurt me. Outside, through the rear screen I could see my father's roses growing. They were red and white and yellow, large and full. The sun was very low but not yet set and the last of it slanted through the rear window. I felt that even the sun belonged to my father, that I had no right to it because it was shining upon my father's house. I was like his roses, something that belonged to him and not to me . . .

9

By the time they called me to dinner I was able to pull up my clothing and walk to the breakfast nook where we ate all our meals except on Sunday. There were two pillows on my chair. I sat on them but my legs and ass still burned. My father was talking about his job, as always.

"I told Sullivan to combine three routes into two and let one man go from each shift. Nobody is really pulling their weight around there . . ."

"They ought to listen to you, Daddy," said my mother.

"Please," I said, "please excuse me but I don't feel like eating . . .

"You'll eat your FOOD!" said my father. "Your mother prepared this food!"

"Yes," said my mother, "carrots and peas and roast beef."

"And the mashed potatoes and gravy," said my father.

"I'm not hungry."

"You will eat every carrot, and pee on your plate!" said my father.

He was trying to be funny. That was one of his favorite remarks.

"DADDY!" said my mother in shocked disbelief.

I began eating. It was terrible. I felt as if I were eating *them*, what they believed in, what they were. I didn't chew any of it, I just swallowed it to get rid of it. Meanwhile my father was talking about how good it all tasted, how lucky we were to be eating good food when most of the people in the world, and many even in

America, were starving and poor.

"What's for dessert, Mama?" my father asked.

His face was horrible, the lips pushed out, greasy and wet with pleasure. He acted as if nothing had happened, as if he hadn't beaten me. When I was back in my bedroom I thought, these people are not my parents, they must have adopted me and now they are unhappy with what I have become.

10

Lila Jane was a girl my age who lived next door. I still wasn't allowed to play with the children in the neighborhood, but sitting in the bedroom often got dull. I would go out and walk around in the backyard, looking at things, bugs mostly. Or I would sit on the grass and imagine things. One thing I imagined was that I was a great baseball player, so great that I could get a hit every time at bat, or a home run anytime I wanted to. But I would deliberately make outs just to trick the other team. I got my hits when I felt like it. One season, going into July, I was hitting only .139 with one home run. HENRY CHINASKI IS FINISHED, the newspapers said. Then I began to hit. And how I hit! At one time I allowed myself 16 home runs in a row. Another time I batted in 24 runs in one game. By the end of the season I was hitting .523.

Lila Jane was one of the pretty girls I'd seen at school. She was one of the nicest, and she was living right next door. One day when I was in the yard she came up to the fence and stood there looking at me.

"You don't play with the other boys, do you?"

I looked at her. She had long red-brown hair and dark brown eyes.

"No," I said, "no, I don't."

"Why not?"

"I see them enough at school."

"I'm Lila Jane," she said.

"I'm Henry."

She kept looking at me and I sat there on the grass and looked at her. Then she said, "Do you want to see my panties?"

"Sure," I said.

She lifted her dress. The panties were pink and clean. They looked good. She kept holding her dress up and then turned around so that I could see her behind. Her behind looked nice. Then she pulled her dress down. "Goodbye," she said and walked off.

"Goodbye," I said.

It happened each afternoon. "Do you want to see my panties?"

"Sure."

The panties were nearly always a different color and each time they looked better.

One afternoon after Lila Jane showed me her panties I said, "Let's go for a walk."

"All right," she said.

I met her in front and we walked down the street together. She was really pretty. We walked along without saying anything until we came to a vacant lot. The weeds were tall and green.

"Let's go into the vacant lot," I said.

"All right," said Lila Jane.

We walked out into the tall weeds.

"Show me your panties again."

She lifted her dress. Blue panties.

"Let's stretch out here," I said.

We got down in the weeds and I grabbed her by the hair and kissed her. Then I pulled up her dress and looked at her panties. I put my hand on her behind and kissed her again. I kept kissing her and grabbing at her behind. I did this for quite a long time. Then I said, "Let's do it." I wasn't sure what there was to do but I felt there was more.

"No, I can't," she said.

"Why not?"

"Those men will see."

"What men?"

"There!" she pointed.

I looked between the weeds. Maybe half a block away some

44

men were working repairing the street.

"They can't see us!"

"Yes, they can!"

I got up. "God damn it!" I said and I walked out of the lot and went back home.

I didn't see Lila Jane again for a while in the afternoons. It didn't matter. It was football season and I was—in my imagination—a great quarterback. I could throw the ball 90 yards and kick it 80. But we seldom had to kick, not when I carried the ball. I was best running into grown men. I crushed them. It took five or six men to tackle me. Sometimes, like in baseball, I felt sorry for everybody and I allowed myself to be tackled after only gaining 8 or 10 yards. Then I usually got injured, badly, and they had to carry me off the field. My team would fall behind, say 40 to 17, and with 3 or 4 minutes left to play I'd return, angry that I had been injured. Every time I got the ball I ran all the way to a touchdown. How the crowd screamed! And on defense I made every tackle, intercepted every pass. I was everywhere. Chinaski, the Fury! With the gun ready to go off I took the kickoff deep in my own end zone. I ran forward, sideways, backwards. I broke tackle after tackle, I leaped over fallen tacklers. I wasn't getting any blocking. My team was a bunch of sissies. Finally, with five men hanging on to me I refused to fall and dragged them over the goal line for the winning touchdown.

I looked up one afternoon as a big guy entered our yard through the back gate. He walked in and just stood there looking at me. He was a year or so older than I was and he wasn't from my grammar school. "I'm from Marmount Grammar School," he said.

"You better get out of here," I told him. "My father will be coming home soon."

"Is that right?" he asked.

I stood up. "What are you doing here?"

"I hear you guys from Delsey Grammar think you're tough."

"We win all the inter-school games."

"That's because you cheat. We don't like cheaters at Marmount."

He had on an old blue shirt, half unbuttoned in front. He had a leather thong on his left wrist.

"You think you're tough?" he asked me.

"No."

"What do you have in your garage? I think I'll take something from your garage."

"Stay out of there."

The garage doors were open and he walked past me. There wasn't much in there. He found an old deflated beach ball and picked it up.

"I think I'll take this."

"Put it down."

"Down your throat!" he said and then he threw it at my head. I ducked. He came out of the garage toward me. I backed up.

He followed me into the yard. "Cheaters never prosper!" he said. He swung at me. I ducked. I could feel the wind from his swing. I closed my eyes, rushed him and started punching. I was hitting something, sometimes. I could feel myself getting hit but it didn't hurt. Mostly I was scared. There was nothing to do but to keep punching. Then I heard a voice: "Stop it!" It was Lila Jane. She was in my backyard. We both stopped fighting. She took an old tin can and threw it. It hit the boy from Marmount in the middle of the forehead and bounced off. He stood there a moment and then ran off, crying and howling. He ran out the rear gate and down the alley and was gone. A little tin can. I was surprised, a big guy like him crying like that. At Delsey we had a code. We never made a sound. Even the sissies took their beatings silently. Those guys from Marmount weren't much.

"You didn't have to help me," I told Lila Jane.

"He was hitting you!"

"He wasn't hurting me."

Lila Jane ran off through the yard, out the rear gate, then into her yard and into her house.

Lila Jane still likes me, I thought.

11

During the second and third grades I still didn't get a chance to play baseball but I knew that somehow I was developing into a player. If I ever got a bat in my hands again I knew I would hit it over the school building. One day I was standing around and a teacher came up to me.

"What are you doing?"

"Nothing."

"This is Physical Education. You should be participating. Are you disabled?"

"What?"

"Is there anything wrong with you?"

"I don't know."

"Come with me."

He walked me over to a group. They were playing kickball. Kickball was like baseball except they used a soccer ball. The pitcher rolled it to the plate and you kicked it. If it went on a fly and was caught you were out. If it rolled on through the infield or you kicked it high between the fielders you took as many bases as you could.

"What's your name?" the teacher asked me.

"Henry."

He walked up to the group. "Now," he said, "Henry is going to play shortstop."

They were from my grade. They all knew me. Shortstop was the toughest position. I went out there. I knew they were going to gang up on me. The pitcher rolled the ball real slow and the first guy kicked it right at me. It came hard, chest high, but it was no problem. The ball was big and I stuck out my hands and caught it. I threw the ball to the pitcher. The next guy did the same thing. It came a little higher this time. And a little faster. No problem. Then Stanley Greenberg walked up to the plate. That was it. I was out of luck. The pitcher rolled the ball and Stanley kicked it. It came at me like a cannonball, head high. I wanted to duck but didn't. The ball smashed into my hands and I held it. I took the ball and rolled it to the pitcher's mound. Three outs. I trotted to the sideline. As I did, some guy passed me and said, "Chinaski, the great shitstop!"

It was the boy with the vaseline in his hair and the long black nostril hairs. I spun around. "Hey!" I said. He stopped. I looked at him. "Don't ever say anything to me again." I saw the fear in his eyes. He walked out to his position and I went and leaned against the fence while our team came to the plate. Nobody stood near me but I didn't care. I was gaining ground.

It was difficult to understand. We were the children in the poorest school, we had the poorest, least educated parents, most of us lived on terrible food, and yet boy for boy we were much bigger than the boys from other grammar schools around the city. Our school was famous. We were feared.

Our 6th grade team beat the other 6th grade teams in the city very badly. Especially in baseball. Scores like 14 to 1, 24 to 3, 19 to 2. We just could hit the ball.

One day the City Champion Junior High School team, Miranda Bell, challenged us. Somehow money was raised and each of our players was given a new blue cap with a white "D" in front. Our team looked good in those caps. When the Miranda Bell guys showed up, the 7th grade champs, our 6th grade guys just looked at them and laughed. We were bigger, we looked tougher, we walked differently, we knew something that they didn't know. We younger guys laughed too. We knew we had them where we wanted them.

The Miranda guys looked too polite. They were very quiet. Their pitcher was their biggest player. He struck out our first three batters, some of our best hitters. But we had Lowball

Johnson. Lowball did the same to them. It went on like that, both sides striking out, or hitting little grounders and an occasional single, but nothing else. Then we were at bat in the bottom of the 7th. Beefcake Cappalletti nailed one. God, you could hear the shot! The ball looked like it was going to hit the school building and break a window. Never had I seen a ball take off like that! It hit the flagpole near the top and bounced back in. Easy home run. Cappalletti rounded the bases and our guys looked *good* in their new blue caps with the white "D."

The Miranda guys just quit after that. They didn't know how to come back. They came from a wealthy district, they didn't know what it meant to fight back. Our next guy doubled. How we screamed! It was over. There was nothing they could do. The next batter tripled. They changed pitchers. He walked the next guy. The next batter singled. Before the inning was over we had scored nine runs.

Miranda never got a chance to bat in the 8th. Our 5th graders went over and challenged them to fight. Even one of the 4th graders ran over and picked a fight with one of them. The Miranda guys took their equipment and left. We ran them off, up the street.

There was nothing left to do so a couple of our guys got into a fight. It was a good one. They both had bloody noses but were swinging good when one of the teachers who had stayed to watch the game broke it up. He didn't know how close he came to getting jumped himself.

12

One night my father took me on his milk route. There were no longer any horsedrawn wagons. The milk trucks now had engines. After loading up at the milk company we drove off on his route. I liked being out in the very early morning. The moon was up and I could see the stars. It was cold but it was exciting. I wondered why my father had asked me to come along since he had taken to beating me with the razor strop once or twice a week and we weren't getting along.

At each stop he would jump out and deliver a bottle or two of milk. Sometimes it was cottage cheese or buttermilk or butter and now and then a bottle of orange juice. Most of the people left notes in the empty bottles explaining what they wanted.

My father drove along, stopping and starting, making deliveries.

"O.K., kid, which direction are we driving in now?"

"North."

"You're right. We're going north."

We went up and down streets, stopping and starting.

"O.K., which way are we going now?"

"West."

"No, we're going south."

We drove along in silence some more.

"Suppose I pushed you out of the truck now and left you on the sidewalk, what would you do?"

"I don't know."

"I mean, how would you live?"

50

"Well, I guess I'd go back and drink the milk and orange juice you just left on the porch steps."

"Then what would you do?"

"I'd find a policeman and tell him what you did."

"You would, huh? And what would you tell him?"

"I'd tell him that you told me that 'west' was 'south' because you wanted me to get lost."

It began to get light. Soon all the deliveries were made and we stopped at a cafe to have breakfast. The waitress walked over. "Hello, Henry," she said to my father. "Hello, Betty." "Who's the kid?" asked Betty. "That's little Henry." "He looks just like you." "He doesn't have my brains, though." "I hope not."

We ordered. We had bacon and eggs. As we ate my father said, "Now comes the hard part."

"What is that?"

"I have to collect the money people owe me. Some of them don't want to pay."

"They ought to pay."

"That's what I tell them."

We finished eating and started driving again. My father got out and knocked on doors. I could hear him complaining loudly, "HOW THE HELL DO YOU THINK *I'M* GOING TO EAT? YOU'VE SUCKED UP THE MILK, NOW IT'S TIME FOR YOU TO SHIT OUT THE MONEY!"

He used a different line each time. Sometimes he came back with the money, sometimes he didn't.

Then I saw him enter a court of bungalows. A door opened and a woman stood there dressed in a loose silken kimono. She was smoking a cigarette. "Listen, baby, I've got to have the money. You're into me deeper than anybody!"

She laughed at him.

"Look, baby, just give me half, give me a payment, something to show."

She blew a smoke ring, reached out and broke it with her finger.

"Listen, you've got to pay me," my father said. "This is a desperate situation."

"Come on in. We'll talk about it," said the woman.

My father went in and the door closed. He was in there for a long time. The sun was really up. When my father came out his hair was hanging down around his face and he was pushing his shirt tail into his pants. He climbed into the truck.

"Did that woman give you the money?" I asked.

"That was the last stop," said my father. "I can't take it any more. We'll return the truck and go home . . ."

I was to see that woman again. One day I came home after school and she was sitting on a chair in the front room of our house. My mother and father were sitting there too and my mother was crying. When my mother saw me she stood up and ran toward me, grabbed me. She took me into the bedroom and sat me on the bed. "Henry, do you love your mother?" I really didn't but she looked so sad that I said, "Yes." She took me back into the other room.

"Your father says he loves this woman," she said to me.

"I love *both* of you! Now get that kid out of here!"

I felt that my father was making my mother very unhappy.

"I'll kill you," I told my father.

"Get that kid out of here!"

"How can you love that woman?" I asked my father. "Look at her nose. She has a nose like an elephant!"

"Christ!" said the woman, "I don't have to take this!" She looked at my father: "*Choose*, Henry! One or the other! Now!"

"But I can't! I love you both!"

"I'll kill you!" I told my father.

He walked over and slapped me on the ear, knocking me to the floor. The woman got up and ran out of the house and my father went after her. The woman leaped into my father's car, started it and drove off down the street. It happened very quickly. My father ran down the street after her and the car. "EDNA! EDNA, COME BACK!" My father actually caught up with the car, reached into the front seat and grabbed Edna's purse. Then the car speeded up and my father was left with the purse.

"I knew something was going on," my mother told me. "So I hid in the car trunk and I caught them together. Your father drove me back here with that horrible woman. Now she's got his car."

My father walked back with Edna's purse. "Everybody into the house!" We went inside and my father locked me in the bedroom and my mother and father began arguing. It was loud and very ugly. Then my father began beating my mother. She screamed and he kept beating her. I climbed out a window and tried to get in the front door. It was locked. I tried the rear door, the windows. Everything was locked. I stood in the backyard and listened to the screaming and the beating.

Then the beating and the screaming stopped and all I could hear was my mother sobbing. She sobbed a long time. It gradually grew less and less and then she stopped.

13

I was in the 4th grade when I found out about it. I was probably one of the last to know, because I still didn't talk to anybody. A boy walked up to me while I was standing around at recess.

"Don't you know how it happens?" he asked.

"What?"

"Fucking."

"What's that?"

"Your mother has a hole . . ."—he took the thumb and forefinger of his right hand and made a circle—"and your father has a dong . . ."—he took his left forefinger and ran it back and forth through the hole. "Then your father's dong shoots juice and sometimes your mother has a baby and sometimes she doesn't."

"God makes babies," I said.

"Like shit," the kid said and walked off.

It was hard for me to believe. When recess was over I sat in class and thought about it. My mother had a hole and my father had a dong that shot juice. How could they have things like that and walk around as if everything was normal, and talk about things, and then do it and not tell anybody? I really felt like puking when I thought that I had started off as my father's juice.

That night after the lights were out I stayed awake in bed and listened. Sure enough, I began to hear sounds. Their bed began creaking. I could hear the springs. I got out of bed and tiptoed down to their door and listened. The bed kept making sounds.

Then it stopped. I hurried back down the hall and into my bedroom. I heard my mother go into the bathroom. I heard the toilet flush and then she walked out.

What a terrible thing! No wonder they did it in secret! And to think, everybody did it! The teachers, the principal, everybody! It was pretty stupid. Then I thought about doing it with Lila Jane and it didn't seem so dumb.

The next day in class I thought about it all day. I looked at the little girls and imagined myself doing it with them. I would do it with all of them and make babies, I'd fill the world with guys like me, great baseball players, home run hitters. That day just before class ended the teacher, Mrs. Westphal, said: "Henry, will you stay after class?"

The bell rang and the other children left. I sat at my desk and waited. Mrs. Westphal was correcting papers. I thought, maybe she wants to do it with me. I imagined pulling her dress up and looking at her hole. "All right, Mrs. Westphal, I'm ready."

She looked up from her papers. "All right, Henry, first erase all the blackboards. Then take the erasers outside and dust them."

I did as I was told, then sat back down at my desk. Mrs. Westphal just sat there correcting papers. She had on a tight blue dress, she wore large golden earrings, had a tiny nose and wore rimless glasses. I waited and waited. Then I said, "Mrs. Westphal, why did you keep me after school?"

She looked up and stared at me. Her eyes were green and deep. "I kept you after school because sometimes you're bad."

"Oh, yeah?" I smiled.

Mrs. Westphal looked at me. She took her glasses off and kept staring. Her legs were behind the desk. I couldn't look up her dress.

"You were *very* inattentive today, Henry."

"Yeah?"

"'Yes' is the word. You're addressing a lady!"

"Oh, I know . . ."

"Don't get sassy with me!"

"Whatever you say."

Mrs. Westphal stood up and came out from behind her desk.

She walked down the aisle and sat on the top of the desk across from me. She had nice long legs in silk stockings. She smiled at me, reached out a hand and touched one of my wrists.

"Your parents don't give you much love, do they?"

"I don't need that stuff," I told her.

"Henry, everybody needs love."

"I don't need anything."

"You poor boy."

She stood up, came to my desk and slowly took my head in her hands. She bent over and pressed it against her breasts. I reached around and grabbed her legs.

"Henry, you must stop fighting everybody! We want to help you."

I grabbed Mrs. Westphal's legs harder. "All right," I said, "let's fuck!"

Mrs. Westphal pushed me away and stood back.

"What did you say?"

"I said, 'let's fuck!'"

She looked at me a long time. Then she said, "Henry, I am *never* going to tell anybody what you said, not the principal or your parents or anybody. But I never, *never* want you to say that to me again, do you understand?"

"I understand."

"All right. You can go home now."

I got up and walked toward the door. When I opened it, Mrs. Westphal said, "Good afternoon, Henry."

"Good afternoon, Mrs. Westphal."

I walked down the street wondering about it. I felt she wanted to fuck but was afraid because I was too young for her and that my parents or the principal might find out. It had been exciting being in the room with her alone. This thing about fucking was nice. It gave people extra things to think about.

There was one large boulevard to cross on the way home. I entered the crosswalk. Suddenly there was a car coming right at me. It didn't slow down. It was weaving wildly. I tried to run out of its path but it appeared to follow me. I saw headlights, wheels, a bumper. The car hit me and then there was blackness . . .

56

14

Later in the hospital they were dabbing at my knees with pieces of cotton that had been soaked in something. It burned. My elbows burned too.

The doctor was bending over me with a nurse. I was in bed and the sun came through the window. It seemed very pleasant. The doctor smiled at me. The nurse straightened up and smiled at me. It was nice there.

"Do you have a name?" the doctor asked.

"Henry."

"Henry what?"

"Chinaski."

"Polish, eh?"

"German."

"How come nobody wants to be Polish?"

"I was born in Germany."

"Where do you live?" asked the nurse.

"With my parents."

"Really?" asked the doctor. "And where is that?"

"What happened to my elbows and knees?"

"A car ran you over. Luckily, the wheels missed you. Witnesses said he appeared to be drunk. Hit and run. But they got his license. They'll get him."

"You have a pretty nurse . . ." I said.

"Well, thank you," she said.

"Do you want a date with her?" asked the doctor.

"What's that?"

"Do you want to go out with her?" the doctor asked.

"I don't know if I could do it with her. I'm too young."

"Do what?"

"You know."

"Well," the nurse smiled, "come see me after your knees heal up and we'll see what we can do."

"Pardon me," said the doctor, "but I have to see another accident case." He left the room.

"Now," said the nurse, "what street do you live on?"

"Virginia Road."

"Give me the number, sweetie."

I told her the house number. She asked if there was a telephone. I told her that I didn't know the number.

"That's all right," she said, "we'll get it. And don't worry. You were lucky. You just got a bump on the head and skinned up a little."

She was nice but I knew that after my knees healed, she wouldn't want to see me again.

"I want to stay here," I told her.

"What? You mean, you don't want to go home to your parents?"

"No. Let me stay here."

"We can't do that, sweetie. We need these beds for people who are really sick and injured."

She smiled and walked out of the room.

When my father came he walked straight into the room and without a word scooped me out of bed. He carried me out of the room and down the hallway.

"You little bastard! Didn't I teach you to look BOTH ways before you cross the street?"

He rushed me down the hall. We passed the nurse.

"Goodbye, Henry," she said.

"Goodbye."

We got into an elevator with an old man in a wheelchair. A nurse was standing behind him. The elevator began to descend.

"I think I'm going to die," the old man said. "I don't want to die. I'm afraid to die . . ."

"You've lived long enough, you old fart!" muttered my father.

The old man looked startled. The elevator stopped. The door remained closed. Then I noticed the elevator operator. He sat on a small stool. He was a dwarf dressed in a bright red uniform with a red cap.

The dwarf looked at my father. "Sir," he said, "you are a repugnant fool!"

"Shortcake," replied my father, "open the fucking door or it's your ass."

The door opened. We went out the entrance. My father carried me across the hospital lawn. I still had on a hospital gown. My father carried my clothes in a bag in one hand. The wind blew back my gown and I saw my skinned knees which were not bandaged and were painted with iodine. My father was almost running across the lawn.

"When they catch that son-of-a-bitch," he said, "I'll sue him! I'll sue him for his last penny! He'll support me the rest of his life! I'm sick of that god-damned milk truck! *Golden State Creamery!* Golden State, my hairy ass! We'll move to the South Seas. We'll live on coconuts and pineapples!"

My father reached the car and put me in the front seat. Then he got in on his side. He started the car.

"I hate drunks! My father was a drunk. My brothers are drunks. Drunks are *weak*. Drunks are *cowards*. And hit-and-run drunks should be jailed for the rest of their lives!"

As we drove toward home he continued to talk to me.

"Do you know that in the South Seas the natives live in grass shacks? They get up in the morning and the food falls from the trees to the ground. They just pick it up and eat it, coconuts and pineapple. And the natives think that white men are gods! They catch fish and roast boar, and their girls dance and wear grass skirts and rub their men behind the ears. Golden State Creamery, my hairy *ass!*"

But my father's dream was not to be. They caught the man who hit me and put him in jail. He had a wife and three children and didn't have a job. He was a penniless drunkard. The man sat in jail for some time but my father didn't press charges. As he said, "You can't get blood out of a fucking turnip!"

15

My father always ran the neighborhood kids away from our house. I was told not to play with them but I walked down the street and watched them anyhow.

"Hey, Heinie!" they yelled, "Why don't you go back to Germany?"

Somehow they had found out about my birthplace. The worst thing was that they were all about my age and they not only hung together because they lived in the same neighborhood but because they went to the same Catholic school. They were tough kids, they played tackle football for hours and almost every day a couple of them got into a fist fight. The four main guys were Chuck, Eddie, Gene and Frank.

"Hey, Heinie, go back to Krautland!"

There was no getting in with them . . .

Then a red-headed kid moved in next door to Chuck. He went to some kind of special school. I was sitting on the curb one day when he came out of his house. He sat on the curb next to me. "Hi, my name's Red."

"I'm Henry."

We sat there and watched the guys play football. I looked at Red.

"How come you got a glove on your left hand?" I asked.

"I've only got one arm," he said.

"That hand looks real."

60

"It's fake. It's a fake arm. Touch it."

"What?"

"Touch it. It's fake."

I felt it. It was hard, rock hard.

"How'd that happen?"

"I was born that way. The arm's fake all the way up to the elbow. I've got to strap it on. I've got little fingers at the end of my elbow, fingernails and all, but the fingers aren't any good."

"You got any friends?" I asked.

"No."

"Me neither."

"Those guys won't play with you?"

"No."

"I got a football."

"Can you catch it?"

"Straight shit," said Red.

"Go get it."

"O.K. . . ."

Red went back to his father's garage and came out with a football. He tossed it to me. Then he backed across his front lawn.

"Go on, throw it . . ."

I let it go. His good arm came around and his bad arm came around and he caught it. The arm made a slight squeaking sound as he caught the football.

"Nice catch," I said. "Now wing me one!"

He cocked his arm and let it fly; it came like a bullet and I managed to hold onto it as it dug into my stomach.

"You're standing too close," I told him. "Step back some more."

At last, I thought, some practice catching and throwing. It felt real good.

Then I was the quarterback. I rolled back, straight-armed an invisible tackler, and let go a spiral fly. It fell short. Red ran forward, leaped, caught the ball, rolled over three or four times and still held onto it.

"You're good, Red. How'd you get so good?"

"My father taught me. We practice a lot."

Then Red walked back and let one sail. It looked to be over my head as I ran back for it. There was a hedge between Red's house and Chuck's house and I fell into the hedge going for the ball. The ball hit the top of the hedge and bounced over. I went around to Chuck's yard to get the ball. Chuck passed the ball to me. "So you got yourself a freak friend, hey, Heinie?"

It was a couple of days later and Red and I were on his front lawn passing and kicking the football. Chuck and his friends weren't around. Red and I were getting better and better. Practice, that's all it took. All a guy needed was a chance. Somebody was always controlling who got a chance and who didn't.

I caught one over the shoulder, whirled and winged it back to Red who leaped high and came down with it. Maybe some day we'd play for U.S.C. Then I saw five boys walking down the sidewalk toward us. They weren't guys from my grammar school. They were our age and looked like trouble. Red and I kept throwing the ball and they stood watching us.

Then one of the guys stepped onto the lawn. The biggest.

"Throw me the ball," he said to Red.

"Why?"

"I wanna see if I can catch it."

"I don't care if you can catch it or not."

"Throw me the ball!"

"He's got one arm," I said. "Leave him alone."

"Stay out of this, monkey-face!" Then he looked at Red. "Throw me the ball."

"Go to hell!" said Red.

"Get the ball!" the big guy said to the others. They ran at us. Red turned and threw the ball on the roof of his house. The roof was slanted and the ball rolled back down but managed to stick behind a drain pipe. Then they were on us. Five to two, I thought, there's no chance. I caught a fist on the temple, swung and missed. Somebody kicked me in the ass. It was a good one and burned all the way up the spine. Then I heard a cracking sound, it was almost like a rifle shot and one of them was down on the ground holding his forehead.

"Oh shit," he said, "my skull is crushed!"

I saw Red and he was standing in the center of the lawn. He was holding the hand of his fake arm with the hand of his good arm. It was like a club. Then he swung again. There was another loud crack and another of them was down on the lawn. I began to feel brave and I landed a punch right on a guy's mouth. I saw the lip split and the blood began to dribble down his chin. The other two ran off. Then the big guy who had gone down first got up and the other one got up. They held their heads. The guy with the bloody mouth stood there. Then they retreated down the street together. When they got quite a way down the big guy turned around and said, "We'll be back!"

Red began running toward them and I ran behind Red. They started running and Red and I stopped chasing them after they turned the corner. We walked back, found a ladder in the garage. We got the football down and began throwing it back and forth . . .

One Saturday Red and I decided to go swimming at the public pool down on Bimini Street. Red was a strange guy. He didn't talk much but I didn't talk much either and we got along. There was nothing to say anyhow. The only thing I ever really asked him about was his school but he just said it was a special school and that it cost his father some money.

We arrived at the pool in the early afternoon, got our lockers, and took our clothes off. We had our swimming trunks on underneath. Then I saw Red unhitch his arm and put it in his locker. It was the first time since the fight I had seen him without his fake arm. I tried not to look at his arm which ended at the elbow. We walked to the place where you had to soak your feet in a chlorine solution. It stank but it stopped the spread of athlete's foot or something. Then we walked to the pool and got in. The water stank too and after I was in I pissed in it. There were people of all ages in the pool, men and women, boys and girls. Red really liked the water. He leaped up and down in it. Then he ducked under and came up. He spit water out of his mouth. I tried to swim. I couldn't help noticing Red's half-arm, couldn't help looking at it. I always made sure to look at it when I thought he was occupied with something else. It ended at the elbow, sort of rounded off, and I saw the little fingers. I didn't want to stare real hard, but it seemed as if there were only three or four of them, very tiny, curled up there. They were very *red* and each of the tiny fingers had a little fingernail. Nothing was going to grow anymore; it had all stopped. I didn't want to think about it. I dove under. I was going to scare Red. I was going to grab his legs from behind. I came up against something soft. My face went right into it. It was a fat woman's ass. I felt her grab me by the hair and she pulled me up out of the water. She had on a blue bathing cap and the strap was tight around her chin, digging into her flesh. Her front feeth were capped with silver and her breath smelled of garlic.

"You dirty little pervert! Trying for free grabs, are you?"

I pushed away from her and backed off. As I moved backwards she followed me through the water, her sagging breasts pushing a tidal wave in front of her.

"You dirty little prick. You wanna suck my titties? You got a dirty mind, huh? You wanna eat my shit? How about some of my shit, little prick?"

I backed up further into the deeper water. I was now standing on my toes, moving backwards. I swallowed some water. She kept coming, a steamship of a woman. I couldn't retreat any further. She moved right up to me. Her eyes were pale and blank, there wasn't any color in them. I felt her body touching mine.

"Touch my cunt," she said. "I know you want to touch it, so go ahead, touch my cunt. Touch it, touch it!"

She waited.

"If you don't, I'm going to tell the lifeguard you molested me and you'll be put in jail! Now, touch it!"

I couldn't do it. Suddenly she reached under and grabbed my parts and yanked. She almost tore my dong off. I fell backwards into the deep water, sank, struggled, and came to the top. I was six feet away from her and began swimming toward shallow water.

"I'm going to tell the lifeguard you molested me!" she screamed.

Then a man swam between us. "That little son-of-a-bitch!" she pointed at me and screamed at the man. "He grabbed my *cunt!*"

"Lady," said the man, "the boy probably thought it was the grate over the drain."

I swam over to Red.

"Listen," I said, "we've got to get out of here! That fat lady is going to tell the lifeguard that I touched her cunt!"

"What'd you do that for?" Red asked.

"I wanted to see what it felt like."

"What'd it feel like?"

64

We got out of the pool, showered. Red put his arm back on and we dressed. "Did you really do it?" he asked.

"A guy's got to get started sometime."

It was a month or so later that Red's family moved. One day they were gone. Just like that. Red never said anything in advance to me. He was gone, the football was gone, and those tiny red fingers with fingernails, they were gone. He was a good guy.

16

I didn't know exactly why but Chuck, Eddie, Gene and Frank let me join them in some of their games. I think it started when another guy showed up and they needed three on a side. I still required more practice to get really good but I was getting better. Saturday was the best day. That's when we had our big games, other guys joined in, and we played football in the street. We played tackle on the lawns but when we played in the street we played touch. There was more passing then because you couldn't get far with a run in touch.

There was trouble at the house, much fighting between my mother and my father, and as a consequence, they kind of forgot about me. I got to play football each Saturday. During one game I broke into the open behind the last pass defender and I saw Chuck wing the ball. It was a long high spiral and I kept running. I looked back over my shoulder, I saw it coming, it fell right into my hands and I held it and was in for the touchdown.

Then I heard my father's voice yell "HENRY!" He was standing in front of his house. I lobbed the ball to one of the guys on my team so they could kick off and I walked down to where my father stood. He looked angry. I could almost feel his anger. He always stood with one foot a little bit forward, his face flushed, and I could see his pot belly going up and down with his breathing. He was six feet two and like I said, he looked to be all ears, mouth and nose when angry. I couldn't look at his eyes.

"All right," he said, "you're old enough to mow the lawn now. You're big enough to mow it, edge it, water it, and water the flowers. It's time you did something around here. It's time you got off your dead ass!"

"But I'm playing football with the guys. Saturday is the only real chance I have."

"Are you talking back to me?"

"No."

I could see my mother watching from behind a curtain. Every Saturday they cleaned the whole house. They vacuumed the rugs and polished the furniture. They took up the rugs and waxed the hardwood floors and then covered the floors with the rugs again. You couldn't even see where they had been waxed.

The lawn mower and edger were in the driveway. He showed them to me. "Now, you take this mower and go up and down the lawn and don't miss any places. Dump the grass catcher here whenever it gets full. Now, when you've mowed the lawn in one direction and finished, take the mower and mow the lawn in the other direction, get it? First, you mow it north and south, then you mow it east and west. Do you understand?"

"Yes."

"And don't look so god-damned unhappy or I'll really give you something to be *unhappy* about! After you've finished mowing, then you take the edger. You trim the edges of the lawn with the little mower on the edger. Get *under* the hedge, get *every* blade of grass! Then . . . you take this circular blade on the edger and you *cut* along the edge of the lawn. It must be absolutely *straight* along the edge of the lawn! Understand?"

"Yes."

"Now when you're done with that, you take these . . ."

My father showed me some shears.

". . . and you get down on your knees and you go around cutting off any *hairs* that are still sticking up. Then you take the hose and you water the hedges and the flower beds. Then you turn on the sprinkler and you let it run fifteen minutes on each part of the lawn. You do all this on the front lawn and in the flower garden, and then you repeat it on the rear lawn and in the flower garden there. Are there any questions?"

"No."

"All right, now I want to tell you this. I am going to come out and check everything when you're finished, and when you're done I

DON'T WANT TO SEE ONE HAIR STICKING UP IN EITHER THE FRONT OR BACK LAWN! NOT ONE HAIR! IF THERE IS . . . !"

He turned, walked up the driveway, across his porch, opened the door, slammed it, and he was gone inside of his house. I took the mower, rolled it up the drive and began pushing it on its first run, north and south. I could hear the guys down the street playing football . . .

I finished mowing, edging and clipping the front lawn. I watered the flower beds, set the sprinkler going and began working my way toward the backyard. There was a stretch of lawn in the center of the driveway leading to the back. I got that too. I didn't know if I was unhappy. I felt too miserable to be unhappy. It was like everything in the world had turned to lawn and I was just pushing my way through it all. I kept pushing and working but then suddenly I gave up. It would take hours, all day, and the game would be over. The guys would go in to eat dinner, Saturday would be finished, and I'd still be mowing.

As I began mowing the back lawn I noticed my mother and my father standing on the back porch watching me. They just stood there silently, not moving. Once as I pushed the mower past I heard my mother say to my father, "Look, he doesn't sweat like you do when you mow the lawn. Look how *calm* he looks."

"CALM? HE'S NOT CALM, HE'S DEAD!"

When I came by again, I heard him:

"PUSH THAT THING FASTER! YOU MOVE LIKE A SNAIL!"

I pushed it faster. It was hard to do but it felt good. I pushed it faster and faster. I was almost running with the mower. The grass flew back so hard that much of it flew over the grass catcher. I knew that would anger him.

"YOU SON-OF-A-BITCH!" he screamed.

I saw him run off the back porch and into the garage. He came out with a two-by-four about a foot long. From the corner of my eye I saw him throw it. I saw it coming but made no attempt to avoid it. It hit me on the back of my right leg. The pain was terrible. The leg knotted up and I had to force myself to walk. I kept pushing the mower, trying not to limp. When I swung around to cut another section of the lawn the two-by-four was in the way. I picked it up, moved it aside and kept mowing. The pain was getting worse. Then my father was standing beside me.

"STOP!"

I stopped.

"I want you to go back and mow the lawn over again where you didn't catch the grass in the catcher! Do you *understand* me?"

"Yes."

My father walked back into the house. I saw him and my mother standing on the back porch watching me.

The end of the job was to sweep up all the grass that had fallen on the sidewalk, and then wash the sidewalk down. I was finally finished except for sprinkling each section of the lawn in the back yard for fifteen minutes. I dragged the hose back to set up the sprinkler when my father stepped out of the house.

"Before you start sprinkling I want to check this lawn for hairs."

My father walked to the center of the lawn, got down on his hands and knees and placed the side of his head low against the lawn looking for any blade of grass that might be sticking up. He kept looking, twisting his neck, peering around. I waited.

"AH HAH!"

He leaped up and ran toward the house.

"MAMA! MAMA!"

He ran into the house.

"What is it?"

"I found a *hair!*"

"You did?"

"Come, I'll show you!"

He came out of the house quickly with my mother following.

"Here! Here! I'll show you!"

He got down on his hands and knees.

"I can see it! I can see *two* of them!"

My mother got down with him. I wondered if they were crazy.

"See them?" he asked her. "*Two* hairs. See them?"

"Yes, Daddy, I see them . . ."

They both got up. My mother walked into the house. My father looked at me.

"Inside . . ."

I walked to the porch and inside the house. My father followed me.

"Into the bathroom."

My father closed the door.

"Take your pants down."

I heard him get down the razor strop. My right leg still ached. It didn't help, having felt the strop many times before. The whole world was out there indifferent to it all, but that didn't help. Millions of people were out there, dogs and cats and gophers, buildings, streets, but it didn't matter. There was only father and the razor strop and the bathroom and me. He used that strop to sharpen his razor, and early in the mornings I used to hate him with his face white with lather, standing before the mirror shaving himself. Then the first blow of the strop hit me. The sound of the strop was flat and loud, the sound itself was almost as bad as the pain. The strop landed again. It was as if my father was a machine, swinging that strop. There was the feeling of being in a tomb. The strop landed again and I thought, that is surely the last one. But it wasn't. It landed again. I didn't hate him. He was just unbelievable, I just wanted to get away from him. I couldn't cry. I was too sick to cry, too confused. The strop landed once again. Then he stopped. I stood and waited. I heard him hanging up the strop.

"Next time," he said, "I don't want to find any hairs."

I heard him walk out of the bathroom. He closed the bathroom door. The walls were beautiful, the bathtub was beautiful, the wash basin and the shower curtain were beautiful, and even the toilet was beautiful. My father was gone.

17

Of all the guys left in the neighborhood, Frank was the nicest. We got to be friends, we got to going around together, we didn't need the other guys much. They had more or less kicked Frank out of the group, anyway, so he became friends with me. He wasn't like David, who had walked home from school with me. Frank had a lot more going for him than David had. I even joined the Catholic church because Frank went there. My parents liked me going to church. The Sunday masses were very boring. And we had to go to Catechism classes. We had to study the Catechism book. It was just boring questions and answers.

One afternoon we were sitting on my front porch and I was reading the Catechism out loud to Frank. I read the line, "God has bodily eyes and sees all things."

"Bodily eyes?" Frank asked.

"Yes."

"You mean like this?" he asked.

He clenched his hands into fists and placed them over his eyes.

"He has milk bottles for eyes," Frank said, pushing his fists against his eyes and turning toward me. Then he began laughing. I began laughing too. We laughed a long time. Then Frank stopped.

"You think He heard us?"

"I guess so. If He can see everything He can probably hear everything too."

"I'm scared," said Frank. "He might kill us. Do you think He'll kill us?"

"I don't know."

"We better sit here and wait. Don't move. Sit still."

We sat on the steps and waited. We waited a long time.

"Maybe He isn't going to do it now," I said.

"He's going to take His time," said Frank.

We waited another hour, then we walked down to Frank's place. He was building a model airplane and I wanted to take a look at it . . .

The afternoon came when we decided to go to our first confession. We walked to the church. We knew one of the priests, the main man. We had met him in an ice cream parlor and he had spoken to us. We had even gone to his house once. He lived in a place next to the church with an old woman. We stayed quite a while and asked all sorts of questions about God. Like, how tall was He? And did He just sit in a chair all day? And did He go to the bathroom like everybody else? The priest never did answer our questions directly but still he seemed like a nice guy, he had a nice smile.

We walked to the church thinking about confession, thinking about what it would be like. As we got near the church a stray dog began walking along with us. He looked very thin and hungry. We stopped and petted him, scratched his back.

"It's too bad dogs can't go to heaven," said Frank.

"Why can't they?"

"You gotta be baptized to go to heaven."

"We ought to baptize him."

"Think we should?"

"He deserves a chance to go to heaven."

I picked him up and we walked into the church. We took him to the bowl of holy water and I held him there as Frank sprinkled the water on his forehead.

"I hereby baptize you," said Frank.

We took him outside and put him back on the sidewalk again.

"He even looks different," I said.

The dog lost interest and walked off down the sidewalk. We went back into the church, stopping first at the holy water, dipping our fingers into it and making the sign of the cross. We both kneeled at a pew near the confessional booth and waited. A fat woman came out from behind the curtain. She had body odor. I could smell her strong odor as she walked past. Her smell was mixed with the smell of the church, which smelled like piss. Every Sunday people came to mass and smelled that piss-smell and nobody said anything. I was going to tell the priest about it but I couldn't. Maybe it was the candles.

"I'm going in," said Frank.

Then he got up, walked behind the curtain and was gone. He was in there a long time. When he came out he was grinning.

"It was great, just great! You go in there now!"

I got up, pulled the curtain back and walked in. It was dark. I kneeled down. All I could see in front of me was a screen. Frank said God was back in there. I kneeled and tried to think of something bad that I had done, but I couldn't think of anything. I just knelt there and tried and tried to think of something but I couldn't. I didn't know what to do.

"*Go ahead*," said a voice. "*Say something!*"

The voice sounded angry. I didn't think there would be any voice. I thought God had plenty of time. I was frightened. I decided to lie.

"All right," I said. "I . . . kicked my father. I . . . cursed my mother . . . I stole money from my mother's purse. I spent it on candy bars. I let the air out of Chuck's football. I looked up a little girl's dress. I kicked my mother. I ate some of my snot. That's about all. Except today I baptized a dog."

"*You baptized a dog?*"

I was finished. A Mortal Sin. No use going on. I got up to leave. I didn't know if the voice recommended my saying some Hail Marys or if the voice didn't say anything at all. I pulled the curtain back and there was Frank waiting. We walked out of the church and were back on the street.

"I feel cleansed," said Frank, "don't you?"

"No."

I never went to confession again. It was worse than ten o'clock mass.

18

Frank liked airplanes. He lent me all his pulp magazines about World War I. The best was *Flying Aces*. The dog-fights were great, the Spads and the Fokkers mixing it. I read all the stories. I didn't like the way the Germans always lost but outside of that it was great.

I liked going over to Frank's place to borrow and return the magazines. His mother wore high heels and had great legs. She sat in a chair with her legs crossed and her skirt pulled high. And Frank's father sat in another chair. His mother and father were always drinking. His father had been a flyer in World War I and had crashed. He had a wire running down inside one of his arms instead of a bone. He got a pension. But he was all right. When we came in he always talked to us.

"How are you doing, boys? How's it going?"

Then we found out about the air show. It was going to be a big one. Frank got hold of a map and we decided to get there by hitch-hiking. I thought we'd probably never make it to the air show but Frank said we would. His father gave us the money.

We went down to the boulevard with our map and we got a ride right away. It was an old guy and his lips were very wet, he kept licking his lips with his tongue and he had on an old checkered shirt which he had buttoned to the throat. He wasn't wearing a necktie. He had strange eyebrows which curled down into his eyes.

"My name's Daniel," he said.

Frank said, "This is Henry. And I'm Frank."

74

Daniel drove along. Then he took out a Lucky Strike and lit it.

"You boys live at home?"

"Yes," said Frank.

"Yes," I said.

Daniel's cigarette was already wet from his mouth. He stopped the car at a signal.

"I was at the beach yesterday and they caught a couple of guys under the pier. The cops caught them and threw them in jail. One guy was sucking the other guy off. Now what business is that of the cops? It made me mad."

The signal changed and Daniel pulled away.

"Don't you guys think that was stupid? The cops stopping those guys from sucking-off?"

We didn't answer.

"Well," said Daniel, "don't you think a couple of guys have a right to a good blow job?"

"I guess so," said Frank.

"Yeah," I said.

"Where are you boys going?" asked Daniel.

"The air show," said Frank.

"Ah, the air show! I like air shows! I'll tell you what, you boys let me go with you and I'll drive you all the way there."

We didn't answer.

"Well, how about it?"

"All right," said Frank.

Frank's father had given us admission and transportation money, but we had decided to save the transportation money by hitch-hiking.

"Maybe you boys would rather go swimming," said Daniel.

"No," said Frank, "we want to see the air show."

"Swimming's more fun. We can race each other. I know a place where we can be alone. I'd never go under the pier."

"We want to go to the air show," said Frank.

"All right," said Daniel, "we'll go to the air show."

When we got to the air show parking lot we got out of the car and while Daniel was locking it Frank said, "RUN!"

We ran toward the admission gate and Daniel saw us running away.

"HEY, YOU LITTLE PERVERTS! COME BACK HERE! COME BACK!"

We kept running.

"Christ," said Frank, "that son-of-a-bitch is crazy!"

We were almost at the admission gate.

"I'LL GET YOU BOYS!"

We paid and ran inside. The show hadn't started yet but a large crowd was already there.

"Let's hide under the grandstand so he can't find us," said Frank.

The grandstand was built of temporary planks for the people to sit on. We went underneath. We saw two guys standing under the center of the grandstand and looking up. They were about 13 or 14 years old, about two or three years older than we were.

"What are they looking at?" I asked.

"Let's go see," said Frank.

We walked over. One of the guys saw us coming.

"Hey, you punks, get out of here!"

"What are you guys looking at?" Frank asked.

"I told you punks to get out of here!"

"Ah, hell, Marty, let 'em have a look!"

We walked over to where they were standing. We looked up.

"What is it?" I asked.

"Hell, can't you *see* it?" one of the big guys asked.

"See what?"

"It's a cunt."

"A cunt? Where?"

"Look, right there! See it?"

He pointed.

There was a woman sitting with her skirt bunched back underneath her. She didn't have any panties on, and looking up between the planks you could see her cunt.

"See it?"

"Yeah, I see it. It's a cunt," said Frank.

"All right, now you guys get out of here and keep your mouths shut."

"But we want to look at it a little longer," said Frank. "Just let us

76

look a little longer."

"All right, but not too long."

We stood there looking up at it.

"I can see it," I said.

"It's a cunt," said Frank.

"It's really a cunt," I said.

"Yeah," said one of the big guys, "that's what it is."

"I'll always remember this," I said.

"All right, you guys, it's time to go."

"What for?" asked Frank. "Why can't we keep looking?"

"Because," said one of the big guys, "I'm going to do something. Now get out of here!"

We walked off.

"I wonder what he's going to do?" I asked.

"I don't know," said Frank, "maybe he's going to throw a rock at it."

We got out from under the grandstand and looked around for Daniel. We didn't see him anywhere.

"Maybe he left," I said.

"A guy like that doesn't like airplanes," said Frank.

We climbed up into the grandstand and waited for the show to begin. I looked around at all the women.

"I wonder which one she was?" I asked.

"I guess you can't tell from the top," said Frank.

Then the air show began. There was a guy in a Fokker doing stunts. He was good, he looped and circled, stalled, pulled out of it, skimmed the ground, and did an Immelman. His best trick consisted of a hook on each wing. Two red handkerchiefs were fastened to poles about six feet above the ground. The Fokker flew down, dipped a wing, and picked a handkerchief off the pole with the hook on its wing. Then it came around, dipped the other wing, and got the other handkerchief.

Then there were some sky-writing acts which were dull and some balloon races which were silly, and then they had something good—a race around four pylons, close to the ground. The airplanes had to circle the pylons twelve times and the one that finished first got the prize. The pilot was automatically disqualified if he circled above the pylons. The racing planes sat on the ground warming up. They were all built differently. One had a long slim body with hardly any wings. Another was fat and round, it looked like a football. Another was almost all wings and no body. Each was different and each was grandly painted. The prize for the winner was $100. They sat there warming up, and you knew you were really going to see something exciting. The motors roared like they wanted to tear away from the airplanes and then the starter dropped the flag and they were off. There were six planes and there was hardly room for them as they went around the pylons. Some of the flyers took them low, others high, some in the middle. Some went faster and lost ground rounding the pylons; others went slower and made sharper turns. It was wonderful and it was terrible. Then one of them lost a wing. The plane bounced along the ground, the engine shooting flame and smoke. It flipped over on its back and the ambulance and the fire truck came running up. The other planes kept going. Then the engine just exploded in another plane, came loose, and the remainder of the plane dropped down like something lost. It hit the ground and everything came apart. But a strange thing happened. The pilot just slid back the cockpit cowling and climbed out and waited for the ambulance. He waved to the crowd and they applauded like mad. It was miraculous.

Suddenly the worst happened. Two planes tangled wings while circling the pylons. They both spun down and crashed and both caught on fire. The ambulance and fire engine ran up again. We saw them pull the two guys out and put them on stretchers. It was sad, those two brave good guys, both probably crippled for life or dead.

That left only two planes, number 5 and number 2, going for the grand prize. Number 5 was the slim plane almost without wings and it was much faster than number 2. Number 2 was the football, he didn't have much speed, but he made up a lot of ground on the turns. It didn't help much. The 5 kept lapping the 2.

"Plane number 5," said the announcer, "is now two laps ahead with two laps to go."

It looked like number 5 was going to get the grand prize. Then he ran into a pylon. Instead of making the turn he just ran into the pylon and knocked the whole thing down. He kept going, straight down the field, lower and lower, the engine at full throttle, and then he hit the ground. The wheels hit and the plane bounced high into the air, flipped over, skidded along the ground. The ambulance and fire engine had a long way to go.

Number 2 just kept circling the three pylons that were left and the one fallen pylon and then he landed. He had won the grand prize. He climbed out. He was a fat guy, just like his airplane. I had expected a handsome tough guy. He had been lucky. Hardly anybody applauded.

To close the show they had a parachute contest. There was a circle painted on the ground, a big bullseye, and the one who landed the closest won. It seemed dull to me. There wasn't much noise or action. The jumpers just bailed out and aimed for the circle.

"This isn't very good," I told Frank.

"Naw," he said.

They kept coming down near the circle. More jumpers bailed out of the planes overhead. Then the crowd started oohing and ahhhing.

"Look!" said Frank.

One chute had only partially opened. There wasn't much air in it. He was falling faster than the others. You could see him kicking his legs and working his arms, trying to untangle the parachute.

"Jesus Christ," said Frank.

The guy kept dropping, lower and lower, you could see him better and better. He kept yanking at the cords trying to untangle the chute but nothing worked. He hit the ground, bounced just a bit, then fell back and was still. The half-filled chute came down over him.

They cancelled the remainder of the jumps.

We walked out with the people, still watching out for Daniel.

"Let's not hitch-hike back," I said to Frank.

"All right," he said.

Walking out with the people, I didn't know which was more exciting, the air race, the parachute jump that failed, or the cunt.

19

The 5th grade was a little better. The other students seemed less hostile and I was growing larger physically. I still wasn't chosen for the homeroom teams but I was threatened less. David and his violin had gone away. The family had moved. I walked home alone. I was often trailed by one or two guys, of whom Juan was the worst, but they didn't start anything. Juan smoked cigarettes. He'd walk behind me smoking a cigarette and he always had a different buddy with him. He never followed me alone. It scared me. I wished they'd go away. Yet, in another way, I didn't care. I didn't like Juan. I didn't like anybody in that school. I think they knew that. I think that's why they disliked me. I didn't like the way they walked or looked or talked, but I didn't like my father or mother either. I still had the feeling of being surrounded by white empty space. There was always a slight nausea in my stomach. Juan was dark-skinned and he wore a brass chain instead of a belt. The girls were afraid of him, and the boys too. He and one of his buddies followed me home almost every day. I'd walk into the house and they'd stand outside. Juan would smoke his cigarette, looking tough, and his buddy would stand there. I'd watch them through the curtain. Finally, they would walk off.

Mrs. Fretag was our English teacher. The first day in class she asked us each our names.

"I want to get to know all of you," she said.

She smiled.

"Now, each of you has a father, I'm sure. I think it would be interesting if we found out what each of your fathers does for a living. We'll start with seat number one and we will go around the class. Now, Marie, what does your father do for a living?"

"He's a gardener."

"Ah, that's nice! Seat number two . . . Andrew, what does your father do?"

It was terrible. All the fathers in my immediate neighborhood had lost their jobs. My father had lost his job. Gene's father sat on his front porch all day. All the fathers were without jobs except Chuck's who worked in a meat plant. He drove a red car with the meat company's name on the side.

"My father is a fireman," said seat number two.

"Ah, that's interesting," said Mrs. Fretag. "Seat number three."

"My father is a lawyer."

"Seat number four."

"My father is a . . . policeman . . ."

What was I going to say? Maybe only the fathers in my neighborhood were without jobs. I'd heard of the stock market crash. It meant something bad. Maybe the stock market had only crashed in our neighborhood.

"Seat number eighteen."

"My father is a movie actor . . ."

"Nineteen . . ."

"My father is a concert violinist . . ."

"Twenty . . ."

"My father works in the circus . . ."

"Twenty-one . . ."

"My father is a bus driver . . ."

"Twenty-two . . ."

"My father sings in the opera . . ."

"Twenty-three . . ."

Twenty-three. That was me.

"My father is a dentist," I said.

Mrs. Fretag went right on through the class until she reached number thirty-three.

"My father doesn't have a job," said number thirty-three.

Shit, I thought, I wish I had thought of that.

One day Mrs. Fretag gave us an assignment.

"Our distinguished President, President Herbert Hoover, is going to visit Los Angeles this Saturday to speak. I want all of you to go hear our President. And I want you to write an essay about the experience and about what you think of President Hoover's speech."

Saturday? There was no way I could go. I had to mow the lawn. I had to get the hairs. (I could never get all the hairs.) Almost every Saturday I got a beating with the razor strop because my father found a hair. (I also got stropped during the week, once or twice, for other things I failed to do or didn't do right.) There was no way I could tell my father that I had to go see President Hoover.

So, I didn't go. That Sunday I took some paper and sat down to write about how I had seen the President. His open car, trailing flowing streamers, had entered the football stadium. One car, full of secret service agents went ahead and two cars followed close behind. The agents were brave men with guns to protect our President. The crowd rose as the President's car entered the arena. There had never been anything like it before. It was the President. It was him. He waved. We cheered. A band played. Seagulls circled overhead as if they too knew it was the President. And there were skywriting airplanes too. They wrote words in the sky like "Prosperity is just around the corner." The President stood up in his car, and just as he did the clouds parted and the light from the sun fell across his face. It was almost as if God knew too. Then the cars stopped and our great President, surrounded by secret service agents, walked to the speaker's platform. As he stood behind the microphone a bird flew down from the sky and landed on the speaker's platform near him. The President waved to the bird and laughed and we all laughed with him. Then he began to speak and the people listened. I couldn't quite hear the speech because I was sitting too near a popcorn machine which made a lot of noise popping the kernels, but I think I heard him say that the problems in Manchuria were not serious, and that at home everything was going to be all right, we shouldn't worry, all we had to do was to believe in America. There would be enough jobs for everybody. There would be enough dentists with enough teeth to pull, enough fires and enough firemen to put them out. Mills and factories would open again. Our friends in South America would pay their debts. Soon we would all sleep peacefully, our stomachs and our hearts full. God and our great country would surround us with love and protect us from evil, from the socialists, awaken us from our national nightmare, forever . . .

The President listened to the applause, waved, then went back to his car, got in, and was driven off followed by carloads of secret service agents as the sun began to sink, the afternoon turning into evening, red and gold and wonderful. We had seen and heard President Herbert Hoover.

I turned in my essay on Monday. On Tuesday Mrs. Fretag faced the class.

"I've read all your essays about our distinguished President's visit to Los Angeles. I was there. Some of you, I noticed, could not attend for one reason or another. For those of you who could not attend, I would like to read this essay by Henry Chinaski."

The class was terribly silent. I was the most unpopular member of the class by far. It was like a knife slicing through all their hearts.

"This is very creative," said Mrs. Fretag, and she began to read my essay. The words sounded good to me. Everybody was listening. My words filled the room, from blackboard to blackboard, they hit the ceiling and bounced off, they covered Mrs. Fretag's shoes and piled up on the floor. Some of the prettiest girls in the class began to sneak glances at me. All the tough guys were pissed. Their essays hadn't been worth shit. I drank in my words like a thirsty man. I even began to believe them. I saw Juan sitting there like I'd punched him in the face. I stretched out my legs and leaned back. All too soon it was over.

"Upon this grand note," said Mrs. Fretag, "I hereby dismiss the class . . ."

They got up and began packing out.

"Not you, Henry," said Mrs. Fretag.

I sat in my chair and Mrs. Fretag stood there looking at me. Then she said, "Henry, were you there?"

I sat there trying to think of an answer. I couldn't. I said, "No, I wasn't there."

She smiled. "That makes it all the more remarkable."

"Yes, ma'am . . ."

"You can leave, Henry."

I got up and walked out. I began my walk home. So, that's what they wanted: lies. Beautiful lies. That's what they needed. People were fools. It was going to be easy for me. I looked around. Juan and his buddy were not following me. Things were looking up.

20

There were times when Frank and I were friendly with Chuck, Eddie and Gene. But something would always happen (usually I caused it) and then I would be out, and Frank would be partly out because he was my friend. It was good hanging out with Frank. We hitch-hiked everywhere. One of our favorite places was this movie studio. We crawled under a fence surrounded by tall weeds to get in. We saw the huge wall and steps they used in the King Kong movie. We saw the fake streets and the fake buildings. The buildings were just fronts with nothing behind them. We walked all over that movie lot many times until the guard would chase us out. We hitch-hiked down to the beach to the Fun House. We would stay in the Fun House three or four hours. We memorized that place. It really wasn't that good. People shit and pissed in there and the place was littered with empty bottles. And there were rubbers in the crapper, hardened and wrinkled. Bums slept in the Fun House after it closed. There really wasn't anything funny about the Fun House. The House of Mirrors was good at first. We stayed in there until we had memorized how to walk through the maze of mirrors and then it wasn't any good any more. Frank and I never got into fights. We were curious about things. There was a movie featuring a Caesarean operation on the pier and we went in and saw it. It was bloody. Each time they cut into the woman blood squirted out, gushers of it, and then they pulled out the baby. We went fishing off the pier and when we caught something we would sell it to the old Jewish ladies who sat on the benches. I got some beatings from my father for running off with Frank but I figured I was going to get the beatings anyhow so I might as well have the fun.

But I continued to have trouble with the other kids in the neighborhood. My father didn't help. For example he bought me an Indian suit and a bow and arrow when all the other kids had cowboy outfits. It was the same then as in the schoolyard—I was ganged-up on. They'd circle me with their cowboy outfits and their guns, but when it got bad I'd just put an arrow into the bow, pull it back and wait. That always moved them off. I never wore that Indian suit unless my father made me put it on.

I kept falling out with Chuck, Eddie and Gene and then we'd get back together and then we'd fall out all over again.

One afternoon I was just standing around. I wasn't exactly in good or in bad with the gang, I was just waiting around for them to forget the last thing I had done that had made them angry. There wasn't anything else to do. Just white air and waiting. I got tired of standing around and decided to walk up the hill to Washington Boulevard, east to the movie house and then back down to West Adams Boulevard. Maybe I'd walk past the church. I started walking. Then I heard Eddie:

"Hey, Henry, come here!"

The guys were standing in a driveway between two houses. Eddie, Frank, Chuck and Gene. They were watching something. They were bent over a large bush watching something.

"Come here, Henry!"

"What is it?"

I walked up to where they were bending over.

"It's a spider getting ready to eat a fly!" said Eddie.

I looked. The spider had spun a web between the branches of a bush and a fly had gotten caught in there. The spider was very excited. The fly shook the whole web as it tried to pull free. It was buzzing wildly and helplessly as the spider wound the fly's wings and body in more and more spider web. The spider went around and around, webbing the fly completely as it buzzed. The spider was very big and ugly.

"It's going to close in now!" yelled Chuck. "It's going to sink its fangs!"

I pushed in between the guys, kicked out and knocked the spider and the fly out of the web with my foot.

"What the hell have you done?" asked Chuck.

"You son-of-a-bitch!" yelled Eddie. "You've *spoiled* it!"

I backed off. Even Frank stared at me strangely.

"Let's get his ass!" yelled Gene.

They were between me and the street. I ran down the driveway into the backyard of a strange house. They were after me. I ran through the backyard and behind the garage. There was a six-foot lattice fence covered with vines. I went straight up the fence and over the top. I ran through the next backyard and up the driveway and as I ran up the driveway I looked back and saw Chuck just reaching the top of the fence. Then he slipped and fell into the yard landing on his back. "Shit!" he said. I took a right and kept running. I ran for seven or eight blocks and then sat down on somebody's lawn and rested. There was nobody around. I wondered if Frank would forgive me. I wondered if the others would forgive me. I decided to stay out of sight for a week or so . . .

And so they forgot. Not much happened for a while. There were many days of nothing. Then Frank's father committed suicide. Nobody knew why. Frank told me he and his mother would have to move to a smaller place in another neighborhood. He said he would write. And he did. Only we didn't write. We drew cartoons. About cannibals. His cartoons were about troubles with cannibals and then I'd continue the cartoon story where his left off, about the troubles with the cannibals. My mother found one of Frank's cartoons and showed it to my father and our letter writing was over.

5th grade became 6th grade and I began to think about running away from home but I decided that if most of our fathers couldn't get jobs how in the hell could a guy under five feet tall get one? John Dillinger was everybody's hero, adults and kids alike. He took the money from the banks. And there was Pretty Boy Floyd and Ma Barker and Machine Gun Kelly.

People began going to vacant lots where weeds grew. They had learned that some of the weeds could be cooked and eaten. There were fist fights between men in the vacant lots and on street corners. Everybody was angry. The men smoked Bull Durham and didn't take any shit from anybody. They let the little round

Bull Durham tags hang out of their front shirt pockets and they could all roll a cigarette with one hand. When you saw a man with a Bull Durham tag dangling, that meant look out. People went around talking about 2nd and 3rd mortgages. My father came home one night with a broken arm and two black eyes. My mother had a low paying job somewhere. And each boy in the neighborhood had one pair of Sunday pants and one pair of daily pants. When shoes wore out there weren't any new ones. The department stores had soles and heels they sold for 15 or 20 cents along with the glue, and these were glued to the bottoms of the worn out shoes. Gene's parents had one rooster and some chickens in their backyard, and if some chicken didn't lay enough eggs they ate it.

As for me, it was the same—at school, and with Chuck, Gene and Eddie. Not only did the grownups get mean, the kids got mean, and even the animals got mean. It was like they took their cue from the people.

One day I was standing around, waiting as usual, not friendly with the gang, no longer really wanting to be, when Gene rushed up to me, "Hey, Henry, come on!"

"What is it?"

"COME ON!"

Gene started running and I ran after him. We ran down the driveway and into the Gibsons' backyard. The Gibsons had a large brick wall all around their backyard.

"LOOK! HE'S GOT THE CAT CORNERED! HE'S GOING TO KILL IT!"

There was a small white cat backed into a corner of the wall. It couldn't go up and it couldn't go in one direction or the other. Its back was arched and it was spitting, its claws ready. But it was very small and Chuck's bulldog, Barney, was growling and moving closer and closer. I got the feeling that the cat had been put there by the guys and then the bulldog had been brought in. I felt it strongly because of the way Chuck and Eddie and Gene were watching: they had a guilty look.

"You guys did this," I said.

"No," said Chuck, "it's the cat's fault. It came in here. Let it fight its way out."

"I hate you bastards," I said.

"Barney's going to kill that cat," said Gene.

"Barney will rip it to pieces," said Eddie. "He's afraid of the claws but when he moves in it will be all over."

Barney was a large brown bulldog with slobbering jaws. He was dumb and fat with senseless brown eyes. His growl was steady and he kept inching forward, the hairs standing up on his neck and along his back. I felt like kicking him in his stupid ass but I figured he would rip my leg off. He was entirely intent upon the kill. The white cat wasn't even fully grown. It hissed and waited, pressed against the wall, a beautiful creature, so clean.

The dog moved slowly forward. Why did the guys need this? This wasn't a matter of courage, it was just dirty play. Where were the grownups? Where were the authorities? They were always around accusing me. Now where were they?

I thought of rushing in, grabbing the cat and running, but I didn't have the nerve. I was afraid that the bulldog would attack me. The knowledge that I didn't have the courage to do what was necessary made me feel terrible. I began to feel physically sick. I was weak. I didn't want it to happen yet I couldn't think of any way to stop it.

"Chuck," I said, "let the cat go, please. Call your dog off."

Chuck didn't answer. He just kept watching.

Then he said, "Barney, go get him! *Get* that cat!"

Barney moved forward and suddenly the cat leaped. It was a furious blur of white and hissing, claws and teeth. Barney backed off and the cat retreated to the wall again.

"Go get him, Barney," Chuck said again.

"God damn you, shut up!" I told him.

"Don't talk to me that way," Chuck said.

Barney began to move in again.

"You guys set this up," I said.

I heard a slight sound behind us and looked around. I saw old Mr. Gibson watching from behind his bedroom window. He wanted the cat to get killed too, just like the guys. Why?

Old Mr. Gibson was our mailman with the false teeth. He had a wife who stayed in the house all the time. She only came out to empty the garbage. Mrs. Gibson always wore a net over her hair and she was always dressed in a nightgown, bathrobe and slippers.

Then as I watched, Mrs. Gibson, dressed as always came and

stood next to her husband, waiting for the kill. Old Mr. Gibson was one of the few men in the neighborhood with a job but he still needed to see the cat killed. Gibson was just like Chuck, Eddie and Gene.

There were too many of them.

The bulldog moved closer. I couldn't watch the kill. I felt a great shame at leaving the cat like that. There was always the chance that the cat might try to escape, but I knew that they would prevent it. That cat wasn't only facing the bulldog, it was facing Humanity.

I turned and walked away, out of the yard, up the driveway and to the sidewalk. I walked along the sidewalk toward where I lived and there in the front yard of his home, my father stood waiting.

"Where have you been?" he asked.

I didn't answer.

"Get inside," he said, "and stop looking so unhappy or I'll give you something that will *really* make you unhappy!"

21

Then I started attending Mt. Justin Jr. High. About half the guys from Delsey Grammar School went there, the biggest and toughest half. Another gang of giants came from other schools. Our 7th grade class was bigger than the 9th grade class. When we lined up for gym it was funny, most of us were bigger than the gym teachers. We would stand there for roll call, slouched, our guts hanging out, heads down, shoulders slumped.

"Jesus Christ," said Wagner, the gym teacher, "pull your shoulders back, stand straight!"

Nobody would change position. We were the way we were, and we didn't want to be anything else. We all came from Depression families and most of us were ill-fed, yet we had grown up to be huge and strong. Most of us, I think, got little love from our families, and we didn't ask for love or kindness from anybody. We were a joke but people were careful not to laugh in front of us. It was as if we had grown up too soon and we were bored with being children. We had no respect for our elders. We were like tigers with the mange. One of the Jewish fellows, Sam Feldman, had a black beard and had to shave every morning. By noon his chin was almost black. And he had a mass of black hair all over his chest and he smelled terrible under the arms. Another guy looked like Jack Dempsey. Another guy, Peter Mangalore, had a cock 10 inches long, soft. And when we got in the shower, I found out I had the biggest balls of anybody.

"*Hey! Look at that guy's balls, will ya?*"

"*Holy shit! Not much cock but look at those balls!*"

"Holy shit!"

I don't know what it was about us but we had something, and we felt it. You could see it in the way we walked and talked. We didn't talk much, we just *inferred,* and that's what got everybody mad, the way we took things for granted.

The 7th grade team would play touch football after school against the 8th and 9th graders. It was no match. We beat them easy, we knocked them down, we did it with style, almost without effort. In touch football most teams passed on every play, but our team worked in lots of runs. Then we could set up the blocking and our guys would go for the other guys and knock them down. It was just an excuse to be violent, we didn't give a damn about the runner. The other side was always glad when we called a pass play.

The girls stayed after school and watched us. Some of them were already going out with high school guys, they didn't want to mess with jr. high school punks, but they stayed to watch the 7th graders. We were known. The girls stayed after class and watched us and marveled. I wasn't on the team but I stood on the sidelines and sneaked smokes, feeling like a coach or something. We're all going to get fucked, we thought, watching the girls. But most of us only masturbated.

Masturbation. I remember how I learned about it. One morning Eddie scratched on my bedroom window.

"What is it?" I asked Eddie.

He held up a test tube and it had something white in the bottom of it.

"What's that?"

"Come," said Eddie, "it's my come."

"Yeah?"

"Yeah, all you do is spit on your hand and begin rubbing your cock, it feels good and pretty soon this white juice shoots out of the end of your cock. That stuff is called 'come.'"

"Yeah?"

"Yeah."

Eddie walked off with his test tube. I thought about it awhile and then I decided to try it. My cock got hard and it felt real good, it felt better and better, and I kept going and it felt like nothing I had ever felt before. Then juice spurted out of the head of my

92

cock. After that I did it every now and then. It got better if you imagined you were doing it with a girl while you whacked-off.

One day I was standing on the sidelines watching our team kick the shit out of some other team. I was sneaking a smoke and watching. There was a girl on either side of me. As our guys broke out of a huddle I saw the gym coach, Curly Wagner, walking toward me. I ditched the smoke and clapped my hands.

"Let's dump 'em on their butts, gang!"

Wagner walked up to me. He just stood there staring at me. I had developed an evil look on my face.

"I'm going to get *all* you guys!" Wagner said. "Especially you!"

I turned my head and glanced at him, casually, then turned my head away. Wagner stood there looking at me. Then he walked off.

I felt good about that. I liked being picked out as one of the bad guys. I liked to feel bad. Anybody could be a good guy, that didn't take guts. Dillinger had guts. Ma Barker was a great woman teaching those guys how to operate a submachine gun. I didn't want to be like my father. He only pretended to be bad. When you're bad you didn't pretend, it was just there. I liked being bad. Trying to be good made me sick.

The girl next to me said, "You don't have to take that from Wagner. Are you afraid of him?"

I turned and looked at her. I stared at her a long time, motionless.

"What's wrong with you?" she asked.

I looked away from her, spit on the ground, and walked off. I slowly walked the length of the field, exited through the rear gate and began walking home.

Wagner always wore a grey sweatshirt and grey sweatpants. He had a little pot belly. Something was continually bothering him. His only advantage was his age. He would try to bluff us but that was working less and less. There was always somebody pushing me who had no right to push. Wagner and my father. My father and Wagner. What did they want? Why was I in their way?

22

One day, just like in grammar school, like with David, a boy attached himself to me. He was small and thin and had almost no hair on top of his head. The guys called him Baldy. His real name was Eli LaCrosse. I liked his real name, but I didn't like him. He just glued himself to me. He was so pitiful that I couldn't tell him to get lost. He was like a mongrel dog, starved and kicked. Yet it didn't make me feel good going around with him. But since I knew that mongrel dog feeling, I let him hang around. He used a cuss word in almost every sentence, at least one cuss word, but it was all fake, he wasn't tough, he was scared. I wasn't scared but I was confused so maybe we were a good pair.

I walked him back to his place after school every day. He was living with his mother, his father and his grandfather. They had a little house across from a small park. I liked the area, it had great shade trees, and since some people had told me that I was ugly, I always preferred shade to the sun, darkness to light.

During our walks home Baldy had told me about his father. He had been a doctor, a successful surgeon, but he had lost his license because he was a drunk. One day I met Baldy's father. He was sitting in a chair under a tree, just sitting there.

"Dad," he said, "this is Henry."

"Hello, Henry."

It reminded me of when I had seen my grandfather for the first time, standing on the steps of his house. Only Baldy's father had black hair and a black beard, but his eyes were the same—brilliant and glowing, so strange. And here was Baldy, the son, and he didn't glow at all.

"Come on," Baldy said, "follow me."

We went down into a cellar, under the house. It was dark and damp and we stood awhile until our eyes grew used to the gloom. Then I could see a number of barrels.

"These barrels are full of different kinds of wine," Baldy said. "Each barrel has a spigot. Want to try some?"

"No."

"Go ahead, just try a god-damned sip."

"What for?"

"You think you're a god-damned man or what?"

"I'm tough," I said.

"Then take a fucking sample."

Here was little Baldy, daring me. No problem. I walked up to a barrel, ducked my head down.

"Turn the god-damned spigot! Open your god-damned mouth!"

"Are there any spiders around here?"

"Go on! Go on, god damn it!"

I put my mouth under the spigot and opened it. A smelly liquid trickled out and into my mouth. I spit it out.

"Don't be chicken! Swallow it, what the shit!"

I opened the spigot and I opened my mouth. The smelly liquid entered and I swallowed it. I turned off the spigot and stood there. I thought I was going to puke.

"Now, you drink some," I said to Baldy.

"Sure," he said, "I ain't fucking afraid!"

He got down under a barrel and took a good swallow. A little punk like that wasn't going to outdo me. I got under another barrel, opened it and took a swallow. I stood up. I was beginning to feel good.

"Hey, Baldy," I said, "I like this stuff."

"Well, shit, try some more."

I tried some more. It was tasting better. I was feeling better.

"This stuff belongs to your father, Baldy. I shouldn't drink it all."

"He doesn't care. He's stopped drinking."

Never had I felt so good. It was better than masturbating.

I went from barrel to barrel. It was magic. Why hadn't someone told me? With this, life was great, a man was perfect, nothing could touch him.

I stood up straight and looked at Baldy.

"Where's your mother? I'm going to fuck your mother!"

"I'll kill you, you bastard, you stay away from my mother!"

"You know I can whip you, Baldy."

"Yes."

"All right, I'll leave your mother alone."

"Let's go then, Henry."

"One more drink . . ."

I went to a barrel and took a long one. Then we went up the cellar stairway. When we were out, Baldy's father was still sitting in his chair.

"You boys been in the wine cellar, eh?"

"Yes," said Baldy.

"Starting a little early, aren't you?"

We didn't answer. We walked over to the boulevard and Baldy and I went into a store which sold chewing gum. We bought several packs of it and stuck it into our mouths. He was worried about his mother finding out. I wasn't worried about anything. We sat on a park bench and chewed the gum and I thought, well, now I have found something, I have found something that is going to help me, for a long long time to come. The park grass looked greener, the park benches looked better and the flowers were trying harder. Maybe that stuff wasn't good for surgeons but anybody who wanted to be a surgeon, there was something wrong with them in the first place.

23

At Mt. Justin, biology class was neat. We had Mr. Stanhope for our teacher. He was an old guy about 55 and we pretty much dominated him. Lilly Fischman was in the class and she was really developed. Her breasts were enormous and she had a marvelous behind which she wiggled while walking in her high-heeled shoes. She was great, she talked to all the guys and rubbed up against them while she talked.

Every day in biology class it was the same. We never learned any biology. Mr. Stanhope would talk for about ten minutes and then Lilly would say, "Oh, Mr. *Stanhope*, let's have a *show!*"

"No!"

"Oh, Mr. *Stanhope!*"

She would walk up to his desk, bend over him sweetly and whisper something.

"Oh, well, all right . . ." he'd say.

And then Lilly would begin singing and wiggling. She always opened up with "The Lullaby of Broadway" and then she went into her other numbers. She was great, she was hot, she was burning up, and we were too. She was like a grown woman, putting it to Stanhope, putting it to us. It was wonderful. Old Stanhope would sit there blubbering and slobbering. We'd laugh at Stanhope and cheer Lilly on. It lasted until one day the principal, Mr. Lacefield, came running in.

"What's going on here?"

Stanhope just sat there unable to speak.

"This class is dismissed!" Lacefield screamed.

As we filed out, Lacefield said, "And *you*, Miss Fischman, will report to my office!"

Of course, after that we never studied our homework, and that was all right until the day Mr. Stanhope gave us our first examination.

"Shit," said Peter Mangalore out loud, "what are we going to do?"

Peter was the guy with the 10-incher, soft.

"You'll never have to work for a living," said the guy who looked like Jack Dempsey. "This is our problem."

"Maybe we ought to burn the school down," said Red Kirkpatrick.

"Shit," said a guy from the back of the room, "every time I get an 'F' my father pulls out one of my fingernails."

We all looked at our examination sheets. I thought about *my* father. Then I thought about Lilly Fischman. Lilly Fischman, I thought, you are a whore, an evil woman, wiggling your body in front of us and singing like that, you will send us all to hell.

Stanhope was watching us.

"Why isn't anybody writing? Why isn't anybody answering the questions? Does everybody have a pencil?"

"Yeah, yeah, we all got pencils," one of the guys said.

Lilly sat up in front, right by Mr. Stanhope's desk. We saw her open her biology textbook and look up the answer to the first question. That was it. We all opened up our textbooks. Stanhope just sat there and watched us. He didn't know what to do. He began to sputter. He sat there a good five minutes, then he jumped up. He ran back and forth up and down the center aisle of the room.

"What are you people doing? Close those textbooks! Close those textbooks!"

As he ran by, the students would close their books only to open them again when he had run past.

Baldy was in the seat next to mine, laughing. "He's an *asshole!* Oh, what an old *asshole!*"

I felt a little sorry for Stanhope but it was either him or me. Stanhope stood behind his desk and screamed, "*All textbooks must be closed or I will flunk the entire class!*"

Then Lilly Fischman stood up. She pulled her skirt up and yanked at one of her silk stockings. She adjusted the garter, we saw white flesh. Then she pulled at and adjusted the other stocking. Such a sight we had never seen, nor had Stanhope ever seen anything like it. Lilly sat down and we all finished the exam with our textbooks open. Stanhope sat behind his desk, utterly defeated.

Another guy we jerked around was Pop Farnsworth. It began the first day in Machine Shop. He said, "Here we learn by doing. We will begin right now. You will each take an engine apart and put it back together, until it is in working order, during the semester. There are charts on the wall and I will answer your questions. You will also be shown movies about how an engine works. But right now please begin to dismantle your engines. The tools are on your workshelf."

"Hey, Pop, how about the movies first?" some guy asked.

"I said, 'Begin your project!'"

I don't know where they got all those engines. They were greasy and black and rusted. They looked really dismal.

"Fuck," said some guy, "this one is a hunk of clogged shit."

We stood over our engines. Most of the guys reached for monkey wrenches. Red Kirkpatrick took a screwdriver and scraped it slowly along the top of his engine carefully creating a black ribbon of grease two feet long.

"Come on, Pop, how about a movie? We just got out of gym, our asses are dragging! Wagner had us doing the hop, skip and jump like a bunch of frogs!"

"Begin your assignment as requested!"

We started in. It was senseless. It was worse than Music Appreciation. Some clanking of tools could be heard and some heavy breathing.

"FUCK!" hollered Harry Henderson, "I'VE JUST SKINNED MY WHOLE GOD-DAMNED KNUCKLE! THIS IS NOTHING BUT FUCKING WHITE SLAVERY!"

He wrapped a handkerchief tenderly around his right hand and watched the blood soak through. "*Shit*," he said.

The rest of us kept trying. "I'd rather stick my head up an elephant's cunt," said Red Kirkpatrick.

Jack Dempsey threw his wrench to the floor. "I quit," he said, "do anything you want to me, I quit. Kill me. Cut my balls off. I quit."

He walked over and leaned against a wall. He folded his arms and looked down at his shoes.

The situation seemed truly terrible. There weren't any girls. When you looked out the back door of the shop you could see the open schoolyard, all that sunlight and empty space out there where there was nothing to do. And here we were bent over stupid engines that weren't even attached to cars, they were useless. Just stupid steel. It was dumb and it was hard. We needed mercy. Our lives were dumb enough. Something had to save us. We'd heard Pop was a soft touch but it didn't seem true. He was a giant son-of-a-bitch with a beer gut, dressed in his greasy outfit, and with hair hanging down in his eyes and grease on his chin.

Arnie Whitechapel threw down his wrench and walked up to Mr. Farnsworth. Arnie had a big grin on his face. "Hey, Pop, what the fuck?"

"Get back to your engine, Whitechapel!"

"Ah, come on, Pop, what the shit!"

Arnie was a couple of years older than the rest of us. He had spent a few years in some boys' correctional school. But even though he was older than we were, he was smaller. He had very black hair slicked back with vaseline. He would stand in front of the mirror in the men's crapper squeezing his pimples. He talked dirty to the girls and carried Sheik rubbers in his pockets.

"I got a good one for you, Pop!"

"Yeah? Get back to your engine, Whitechapel."

"It's a good one, Pop."

We stood there and watched as Arnie began to tell Pop a dirty joke. Their heads were close together. Then the joke was over. Pop began laughing. That big body was doubled over, he was holding his gut. "Holy shit! Oh my god, holy shit!" he laughed. Then he stopped. "O.K., Arnie, back to your machine!"

"No, wait, Pop, I got another one!"

"Yeah?"

"Yeah, listen . . ."

100

We all left our machines and walked over. We circled them, listening as Arnie told the next joke. When it was over Pop doubled up. "Holy shit, oh lord, holy shit!"

"Then there's another one, Pop. This guy is driving his car in the desert. He notices this guy jumping along the road. He's naked and his hands and feet are tied with rope. The guy stops his car and asks the guy, 'Hey, buddy, what's the matter?' And the guy tells him, 'Well, I was driving along and I saw this bastard hitch-hiking so I stopped and the son-of-a-bitch pulls a gun on me, takes my clothes away and then ties me up. Then the dirty son-of-a-bitch reams me in the ass!' 'Oh yeah?' says the guy getting out of his car. 'Yeah, that's what that dirty son-of-a-bitch did!' says the man. 'Well,' says the guy unzipping his fly, 'I guess this just isn't your lucky day!'"

Pop began laughing, he doubled over. "Oh, no! Oh, NO! OH . . . HOLY . . . SHIT, CHRIST . . . HOLY SHIT . . . !"

He finally stopped.

"God damn," he said quietly, "oh my lord . . ."

"How about a movie, Pop?"

"Oh well, all right."

Somebody closed the back door and Pop pulled out a dirty white screen. He started the projector. It was a lousy movie but it beat working on those engines. The gas was ignited by the spark plugs and the explosion hit the cylinder head and the head was thrust down and that turned the crankshaft and the valves opened and closed and the cylinder heads kept going up and down and the crankshaft turned some more. Not very interesting, but it was cool in there and you could lean back in your chair and think about what you wanted to think about. You didn't have to bust your knuckles on dumb steel.

We never did get those engines taken apart let alone put back together again and I don't know how many times we saw that same movie. Whitechapel's jokes kept coming and we all laughed our heads off even though most of the jokes were pretty terrible, except to Pop Farnsworth who kept doubling over and laughing, "Holy shit! Oh, no! Oh, no, no, no!"

He was an O.K. guy. We all liked him.

24

Our English teacher, Miss Gredis, was the absolute best. She was
a blonde with a long sharp nose. Her nose wasn't much good but
you didn't notice it when you looked at the rest of her. She wore
tight dresses and low v-necks, black high-heeled shoes and silk
stockings. She was snake-like with long beautiful legs. She only
sat behind her desk when she took roll call. She kept one desk
vacant at the front of the room and after roll call she would come
down and sit on that desk top, facing us. Miss Gredis sat perched
there with her legs crossed and her skirt pulled high. Never had
we seen such ankles, such legs, such thighs. Well, there was Lilly
Fischman, but Lilly was a girl-woman while Miss Gredis was in
full bloom. And we got to gaze upon her for a full hour each day.
There wasn't a boy in that class who wasn't sad when the bell rang
ending the English period. We'd talk about her.

"Do you think she wants to be fucked?"

"No, I think she's just teasing us. She knows she's driving us
crazy, that's all she needs, that's all she wants."

"I know where she lives. I'm going over there some night."

"You wouldn't have the balls!"

"Yeah? Yeah? I'll fuck the shit out of her! She's asking for it!"

"A guy I know in the 8th grade said he went over there one
night."

"Yeah? What happened?"

"She came to the door in a nightgown, her tits were practically
hanging out. The guy said he had forgotten the next day's
homework and wondered what it was. She asked him in."

102

"No shit?"

"Yeah. Nothing happened. She made him some tea, told him about the homework and he left."

"If I had of gotten in, *that* would have been *it!*"

"Yeah? What would you have done?"

"First I would have corn-holed her, then I would have eaten her pussy, then I would fuck her between the tits and then I would force her to give me a blow job."

"No kidding, dreamer boy. You ever been laid?"

"Fuck yes, I've been laid. Several times."

"How was it?"

"Lousy."

"Couldn't come, huh?"

"I came all over the place, I thought I'd never stop."

"Came all over the palm of your hand, huh?"

"Ha, ha, ha, ha!"

"Ah, ha, ha, ha, ha, ha!"

"Ha, ha!"

"All over your hand, huh?"

"Fuck you guys!"

"I don't think any of us has been laid," said one of the guys. There was silence.

"That's shit. I was laid when I was seven years old."

"That's nothing. I was laid when I was four."

"Sure, Red. Lay it on good!"

"I got this little girl under the house."

"You got a hard?"

"Sure."

"You came?"

"I think so. Something squirted out."

"Sure. You pissed in her cunt, Red."

"Balls!"

"What was her name?"

"Betty Ann."

"Fuck," said the guy who claimed to have gotten laid when he was seven. "Mine was named Betty Ann too."

"That whore," said Red.

One fine Spring day we were sitting in English class and Miss Gredis was sitting on the front desk facing us. She had her skirt pulled especially high, it was terrifying, beautiful, wondrous and dirty. Such legs, such thighs, we were very close to the magic. It was unbelievable. Baldy sat in the seat across the aisle from me. He reached over and began poking me on the leg with his finger: *"She's breaking all the records!"* he whispered. *"Look! Look!"*

"My God," I said, "shut up or she'll pull her skirt down!"

Baldy pulled his hand back and I waited. We hadn't spooked Miss Gredis. Her skirt remained as high as ever. It was truly a day to remember. There wasn't a boy in class without a hard-on and Miss Gredis went on talking. I'm sure that none of the boys heard a word she was saying. The girls, though, turned and glanced at each other as if to say, this bitch is going too far. Miss Gredis couldn't go too far. It was almost as if there weren't even a cunt up there but something much better. Those legs. The sun came through the window and poured in on those legs and thighs, the sun played on that warm silk pulled so tightly. The skirt was so *high*, pulled back, we all prayed for a glimpse of panty, a glimpse of *something*, Jesus Christ, it was like the world ending and beginning and ending again, it was everything real and unreal, the sun, the thighs, and the silk, so smooth, so warm, so alluring. The whole room throbbed. Eyesight blurred and returned and Miss Gredis went on sitting there as if nothing was happening and she kept talking as if everything was normal. That's what made it so good and so terrible: the fact that she pretended that it wasn't happening. I looked down at my desk top for a moment and saw the grain in the wood heightened as if each pattern was a pool of whirling liquid. Then I quickly looked back at the legs and thighs, angered with myself that I had looked away for a moment, and perhaps missed something.

Then the sound began: *"Thump, thump, thump, thump . . ."*

Richard Waite. He sat in a seat in the back. He had huge ears and thick lips, the lips were swollen and monstrous and he had a very large head. His eyes were almost without color, they didn't reflect interest or intelligence. He had large feet and his mouth always hung open. When he spoke the words came out one by one, halting, with long pauses in between. He wasn't even a sissy. Nobody ever spoke to him. Nobody knew what he was doing there in our school. He gave the impression that something important was missing from his makeup. He wore clean clothing, but his shirt was always out in the back, one or two buttons were gone on his shirt or on his pants. Richard Waite. He lived somewhere and he came to school every day.

"Thump, thump, thump, thump, thump . . ."

Richard Waite was jerking-off, a salute to Miss Gredis' thighs and legs. He had finally weakened. Perhaps he didn't understand society's ways. Now we all heard him. Miss Gredis heard him. The girls heard him. We all knew what he was doing. He was so fucking dumb he didn't even have sense enough to keep it quiet. And he was becoming more and more excited. The thumps grew louder. His closed fist was hitting the underside of his desk top.

"THUMP, THUMP THUMP . . ."

We looked at Miss Gredis. What would she do? She hesitated. She glanced about the class. She smiled, as composed as ever, and then she continued speaking:
"I believe that the English language is the most expressive and contagious form of communication. To begin with, we should be thankful that we have this unique gift of a great language. And if we abuse it we are only abusing ourselves. So let us listen, heed, acknowledge our heritage, and yet explore and take risks with language . . ."

"THUMP, THUMP, THUMP . . ."

"We must forget England and their use of our common tongue. Even though English usage is fine, our own American language contains many deep wells of unexplored resources. These resources, as yet, remain untapped. Given the proper moment and the proper writers, there will one day be a literary explosion . . ."

"THUMP, THUMP, THUMP . . ."

Yes, Richard Waite was one of the few we never talked to. Actually, we were afraid of him. He wasn't somebody you could beat the shit out of, that would never make anybody feel better. You just wanted to get as far away from him as possible, you didn't want to look at him, you didn't want to look at those big lips, that big unfolding mouth like the mouth of a bruised frog. You shunned him because you couldn't defeat Richard Waite.

We waited and waited while Miss Gredis talked on about English versus American culture. We waited, while Richard Waite went on and on. Richard's fist banged against the underside of his desk top and the little girls glanced at each other and the guys were thinking, why is this asshole in this class with us? He's going to spoil everything. One asshole and Miss Gredis will pull her skirt down forever.

"THUMP, THUMP, THUMP . . ."

And then it stopped. Richard sat there. He was finished. We sneaked glances at him. He looked the same. Was his sperm laying in his lap or was it in his hand?

The bell rang. English class was over.

After that, there was more of the same. Richard Waite thumped it often while we listened to Miss Gredis sitting on that front desk with her legs crossed high. We boys accepted the situation. After a while we even were amused. The girls accepted it but they didn't like it, especially Lilly Fischman who was almost forgotten.

106

Besides Richard Waite, there was another problem for me in that class: Harry Walden. Harry Walden was pretty, the girls thought, and he had long golden curls and wore strange, delicate clothing. He looked like an 18th century fop, lots of strange colors, dark green, dark blue, I don't know where the hell his parents found his clothes. And he always sat very still and listened attentively. Like he understood everything. The girls said, "He's a genius." He didn't look like anything to me. What I couldn't understand was that the tough guys didn't mess with him. It bothered me. How could he get off so easy?

I found him one day in the hall. I stopped him.

"You don't look like shit to me," I said. "How come everybody thinks you're hot shit?"

Walden glanced over to his right and when I turned my head to look in that direction, he slid around me as if I were something from the sewer and then a moment later he was in his seat in the class.

Almost every day it was Miss Gredis showing it all and Richard thumping away and this guy Walden sitting there saying nothing and acting like he believed he was a genius. I got sick of it.

I asked some of the other guys, "Listen, do you really think Harry Walden is a genius? He just sits around in his pretty clothes and doesn't say anything. What does that prove? We could all do that."

They didn't answer me. I couldn't understand their feelings about this fucking guy. And it got worse. Word got out that Harry Walden was going to see Miss Gredis every night, that he was her favorite pupil, and that they were making love. It made me sick. I could just imagine him getting out of his delicate green and blue outfit, folding it across a chair, then climbing out of his orange satin shorts and sliding under the sheets where Miss Gredis cuddled his curly golden head on her shoulder and fondled it and other things as well.

It was whispered about by the girls who always seemed to know everything. And even though the girls didn't particularly like Miss Gredis, they thought the situation was all right, that it was reasonable because Harry Walden was such a delicate genius and needed all the sympathy he could get.

I caught Harry Walden in the hall one more time.

"I'll kick your ass, you son-of-a-bitch, you don't fool me!"

Harry Walden looked at me. Then he looked over my shoulder and pointed and said, "What's that over there?"

I looked around. When I looked back he was gone. He was sitting in the class safely surrounded by all the girls who thought he was a genius and who loved him.

There was more and more whispering about Harry Walden going over to Miss Gredis' house at night and some days Harry wouldn't even be in class. Those were the best days for me because I only had to deal with the thumping and not the golden curls and the adoration for that kind of stuff by all the little girls with their skirts and sweaters and starched gingham dresses. When Harry wasn't there the little girls would whisper, "He's just too *sensitive* . . ."

And Red Kirkpatrick would say, "She's fucking him to death."

One afternoon I walked into class and Harry Walden's seat was empty. I figured he was just fucking-off as usual. Then the word drifted from desk to desk. I was always the last to know anything. It finally got to me: Harry Walden had committed suicide. The night before. Miss Gredis didn't know yet. I looked over at his seat. He'd never sit there again. All those colorful clothes shot to hell. Miss Gredis finished roll call. She came and sat on the front desk, crossed her legs high. She had on a lighter shade of silk hose than ever before. Her skirt was hiked way back to her thighs.

"Our American culture," she said, "is destined for greatness. The English language, now so limited and structured, will be reinvented and improved upon. Our writers will use what I like to think of, in my mind, as *Americanese* . . ."

Miss Gredis' stockings were almost skin-colored. It was as if she were not wearing stockings at all, it was as if she were naked there in front of us, but since she wasn't and only appeared to be, that made it better than ever.

"More and more we will discover our own truths and our own way of speaking, and this new voice will be uncluttered by old histories, old mores, old dead and useless dreams . . ."

"*Thump, thump, thump . . .*"

25

Curly Wagner picked out Morris Moscowitz. It was after school and eight or ten of us guys had heard about it and we walked out behind the gym to watch. Wagner laid down the rules, "We fight until somebody hollers quit."

"O.K. with me," said Morris. Morris was a tall thin guy, he was a little bit dumb and he never said much or bothered anybody.

Wagner looked over at me. "And after I finish with this guy, I'm taking you on!"

"*Me,* coach?"

"Yeah, you, Chinaski."

I sneered at him.

"I'm going to get some god-damned respect from you guys if I have to whip all of you one by one!"

Wagner was cocky. He was always working out on the parallel bars or tumbling on the mat or taking laps around the track. He swaggered when he walked but he still had his pot belly. He liked to stand and stare at a guy for a long time like he was shit. I didn't know what was bothering him. We worried him. I believe he thought we were fucking all the girls like crazy and he didn't like to think about that.

They squared off. Wagner had some good moves. He bobbed, he weaved, he shuffled his feet, he moved in and out, and he made little hissing sounds. He was impressive. He caught Moscowitz with three straight left jabs. Moscowitz just stood there with his hands at his sides. He didn't know anything about boxing. Then Wagner cracked Moscowitz with a right to the jaw. "Shit!" said

Morris and he threw a roundhouse right which Wagner ducked. Wagner countered with a right and left to Moscowitz' face. Morris had a bloody nose. "Shit!" he said and then he started swinging. And landing. You could hear the shots, they cracked against Wagner's head. Wagner tried to counter but his punches just didn't have the force and the fury of Moscowitz'.

"Holy shit! Get him, Morrie!"

Moscowitz was a puncher. He dug a left to that pot belly. Wagner gasped and dropped. He fell to both knees. His face was cut and bleeding. His chin was on his chest and he looked sick.

"I quit," Wagner said.

We left him there behind the building and we followed Morris Moscowitz out of there. He was our new hero.

"Shit, Morrie, you ought to turn pro!"

"Naw, I'm only thirteen years old."

We walked over behind the machine shop and stood around the steps. Somebody lit up some cigarettes and we passed them around.

"What has that man got against us?" asked Morrie.

"Hell, Morrie, don't you know? He's jealous. He thinks we're fucking all the chicks!"

"Why, I've never even kissed a girl."

"No shit, Morrie?"

"No shit."

"You ought to try dry-fucking, Morrie, it's great!"

Then we saw Wagner walking past. He was working on his face with his handkerchief.

"Hey, coach," yelled one of the guys, "how about a rematch?"

He stood and looked at us. "You boys put out those cigarettes!"

"Ah, no, coach, we like to smoke!"

"Come on over here, coach, and make us put out our cigarettes!"

"Yeah, come on, coach!"

Wagner stood looking at us. "I'm not done with you yet! I'll get every one of you, one way or the other!"

"How ya gonna do that, coach? Your talents seem limited."

"Yeah, coach, how ya gonna do it?"

He walked off the field to his car. I felt a little sorry for him. When a guy was that nasty he should be able to back it up.

"I guess he doesn't think there'll be a virgin on the grounds by the time we graduate," said one of the guys.

"I think," said another guy, "that somebody jacked-off into his ear and he has come for brains."

We left after that. It had been a fairly good day.

26

My mother went to her low-paying job each morning and my father, who didn't have a job, left each morning too. Although most of the neighbors were unemployed he didn't want them to think he was jobless. So he got into his car each morning at the same time and drove off as if he were going to work. Then in the evening he would return at exactly the same time. It was good for me because I had the place to myself. They locked the house but I knew how to get in. I would unhook the screen door with a piece of cardboard. They locked the porch door with a key from the inside. I slid a newspaper under the door and poked the key out. Then I pulled the newspaper from under the door and the key came with it. I would unlock the door and go in. When I left I would hook the screen door, lock the back porch door from the inside, leaving the key in. Then I would leave through the front door, putting the latch on lock.

I liked being alone. One day I was playing one of my games. There was a clock on the mantle with a second hand and I held contests to see how long I could hold my breath. Each time I did it I exceeded my own record. I went through much agony but I was proud each time I added some seconds to my record. This day I added a full five seonds and I was standing getting my breath back when I walked to the front window. It was a large window covered by red drapes. There was a crack between the drapes and I looked out. Jesus Christ! Our window was directly across from the front porch of the Andersons' house. Mrs. Anderson was sitting on the steps, and I could look right up her dress. She was about 23 and had marvelously shaped legs. I could see almost all the way up her dress. Then I remember my father's army binoculars. They were on the top shelf of his closet. I ran and got them, ran back, crouched down and adjusted them to Mrs. Anderson's legs. It took me right up there! And it was different from looking at Miss Gredis' legs: you didn't have to pretend you weren't looking. You could concentrate. And I did. I was right there. I was red hot. Jesus Christ, what legs, what flanks! And each time she moved, it was unbearable and unbelievable.

I got down on my knees and I held the binoculars with one hand and pulled my cock out with the other. I spit in my palm and began. For a moment I thought I saw a flash of panties. I was about to come. I stopped. I kept looking with the binocs and then I started rubbing again. When I was about to come I stopped again. Then I waited and began rubbing again. This time I knew I wouldn't be able to stop. She was right there. I was looking right up her! It was like fucking. I came. I spurted all over the hardwood floor in front of the window. It was white and thick. I got up and went to the bathroom and got some toilet paper, came back and wiped it up. I took it back to the toilet and flushed it away.

Mrs. Anderson came and sat on those steps almost every day and each time she did I got the binocs and whacked-off.

If Mr. Anderson ever finds out about this, I thought, he'll kill me . . .

My parents went to the movies every Wednesday night. The theatre had drawings for money and they wanted to win some money. It was on a Wednesday night that I discovered something. The Pirozzis lived in the house south of ours. Our driveway ran along the north side of their house and there was a window which looked into their front room. The window was veiled by a thin curtain. There was a wall which became an arch over the front of our driveway and there were bushes all about. When I got between that wall and the window, in among all those bushes, nobody could see me from the street, especially at night.

I crawled in there. It was great, better than I expected. Mrs. Pirozzi was sitting on the couch reading a newspaper. Her legs were crossed, and in an easy chair across the room, Mr. Pirozzi was reading a newspaper. Mrs. Pirozzi was not as young as Miss Gredis or Mrs. Anderson, but she had good legs and she had on high heels and almost every time she turned a page of her newspaper, she'd cross her legs and her skirt would climb higher and I would see more.

If my parents come home from the movie and catch me here, I thought, then my life is over. But it's worth it. It's worth the risk.

I stayed very quiet behind the window and stared at Mrs. Pirozzi's legs. They had a large collie, Jeff, who was asleep in front of the door. I had looked at Miss Gredis' legs that day in English class, then I had whacked-off to Mrs. Anderson's legs, and now there was *more*. Why didn't Mr. Pirozzi look at Mrs. Pirozzi's legs? He just kept reading his newspaper. It was obvious that Mrs. Pirozzi was trying to tease him because her skirt kept climbing higher and higher. Then she turned a page and crossed her legs very fast and her skirt *flipped* back exposing her pure white thighs. She was just like *buttermilk! Unbelievable!* She was best of *all!*

Then from the corner of my eye I saw Mr. Pirozzi's legs move. He stood up very quickly and moved toward the front door. I started running, crashing through the bushes. I heard him open his front door. I was down the driveway and into our backyard and behind the garage. I stood a moment, listening. Then I climbed the back fence, over the vines and on over into the next backyard. I ran through that yard and up the driveway and I began dog-trotting south down the street like a guy practicing for track. There was nobody behind me but I kept trotting.

If he knows it was me, if he tells my father, I'm dead.

But maybe he just let the dog out to take a shit?

I trotted down to West Adams Boulevard and sat on a streetcar bench. I sat there five minutes or so, then I walked back home. When I got there, my parents weren't back yet. I went inside, undressed, turned out the lights and waited for morning . . .

Another Wednesday night Baldy and I were taking our usual short cut between two apartment houses. We were on our way to his father's wine cellar when Baldy stopped at a window. The shade was almost down but not quite. Baldy stopped, bent, and peeked inside. He waved me over.

"What is it?" I whispered.

"Look!"

There was a man and a woman in bed, naked. There was just a bedsheet partly over them. The man was trying to kiss the woman and she was pushing him away.

"God damn it, let me have it, Marie!"

"No!"

"But I'm hot, *please!*"

"Take your god-damned hands off me!"

"But, Marie, I love you!"

"You and your fucking love . . ."

"Marie, *please.*"

"Will you shut up?"

The man turned toward the wall. The woman picked up a magazine, bunched a pillow behind her head, and began reading it.

Baldy and I walked away from the window.

"Jesus," said Baldy, "that made me sick!"

"I thought we were going to see something," I said.

When we got to the wine cellar Baldy's old man had put a big padlock on the cellar door.

We tried that window again and again but we never actually saw anything happen. It was always the same.

"Marie, it's been a long time. We're *living* together, you know. We're *married!*"

"Big fucking *deal!*"

"Just this *once*, Marie, and I won't bother you again, I won't bother you for a long time, I promise!"

"Shut up! You make me sick!"

Baldy and I walked away.

"Shit," I said.

"Shit," he said.

"I don't think he's got a cock," I said.

"He might as well not have," said Baldy.

We stopped going back there.

27

Wagner wasn't done with us. I was standing in the yard during gym class when he walked up to me.

"What are you doing, Chinaski?"

"Nothing."

"Nothing?"

I didn't answer.

"How come you're not in any of the games?"

"Shit. That's kid stuff."

"I'm putting you on garbage detail until further notice."

"What for? What's the charge?"

"Loitering. 50 demerits."

The kids had to work off their demerits on garbage detail. If you had more than ten demerits and didn't work them off, you couldn't graduate. I didn't care whether I graduated or not. That was their problem. I could just stay around getting older and older and bigger and bigger. I'd get all the girls.

"50 demerits?" I asked. "Is that all you're going to give me? How about a hundred?"

"O.K., one hundred. You got 'em."

Wagner swaggered off. Peter Mangalore had 500 demerits. Now I was in second place, and gaining . . .

The first garbage detail was during the last thirty minutes of lunch. The next day I was carrying a garbage can with Peter Mangalore. It was simple. We each had a stick with a sharp nail on the end of it. We picked up papers with the stick and stuck them into the can. The girls watched us as we walked by. They knew we were *bad*. Peter looked bored and I looked like I didn't give a damn. The girls knew we were *bad*.

"You know Lilly Fischman?" Pete asked as we walked along.

"Oh, yes, yes."

"Well, she's not a virgin."

"How do you know?"

"She told me."

"Who got her?"

"Her father."

"Hmmm . . . Well you can't blame him."

"Lilly's heard I've got a big cock."

"Yeah, it's all over school."

"Well, Lilly wants it. She claims she can handle it."

"You'll rip her to pieces."

"Yeah, I will. Anyhow, she wants it."

We put the garbage can down and stared at some girls who were sitting on a bench. Pete walked toward the bench. I stood there. He walked up to one of the girls and whispered something in her ear. She started giggling. Pete walked back to the garbage can. We picked it up and walked away.

"So," said Pete, "this afternoon at 4 p.m. I'm going to rip Lilly to pieces."

"Yeah?"

"You know that broken-down car at the back of the school that Pop Farnsworth took the engine out of?"

"Yeah."

"Well, before they haul that son-of-a-bitch away, that's going to be my bedroom. I'm going to take her in the back seat."

"Some guys really live."

"I'm getting a hard just thinking about it," said Pete.

"I am too and I'm not even the guy who's going to do it."

"There's one problem though," said Pete.

"You can't come?"

"No, it's not that. I need a look-out. I need somebody to tell me the coast is clear."

"Yeah? Well, look, I can do that."

"Would you?" asked Pete.

118

"Sure. But we should have one more guy so we can watch in both directions."

"All right. Who you got in mind?"

"Baldy."

"Baldy? Shit, he's not much."

"No, but he's trustworthy."

"All right. So I'll see you guys at four."

"We'll be there."

At four p.m. we met Pete and Lilly at the car.

"Hi!" said Lilly. She looked hot. Pete was smoking a cigarette. He looked bored.

"Hello, Lilly," I said.

"Hi, Lilly baby," said Baldy.

There were some guys playing a game of touch football in the other field but that only made it better, a kind of camouflage. Lilly was wiggling around, breathing heavily, her breasts were moving up and down.

"Well," said Pete, throwing his cigarette away, "let's make friends, Lilly."

He opened the back door, bowed, and Lilly climbed in. Pete got in after her and took his shoes off, then his pants and his shorts. Lilly looked down and saw Pete's meat hanging.

"Oh my," she said, "I don't know . . ."

"Come on, baby," said Pete, "nobody lives forever."

"Well, all right, I guess . . ."

Pete looked out the window. "Hey, are you guys watching to see if the coast is clear?"

"Yeah, Pete," I said, "we're watching."

"We're looking," said Baldy.

Pete pulled Lilly's skirt all the way up. There was white flesh above her knee socks and you could see her panties. Glorious.

Pete grabbed Lilly and kissed her. Then he pulled away.

"You whore!" he said.

"Talk to me nice, Pete!"

"You bitch-whore!" he said and slapped her across the face, hard.

She began sobbing. "Don't, Pete, don't . . ."

"Shut up, cunt!"

Pete began pulling at Lilly's panties. He was having a terrible time. Her panties were tight around her big ass. Pete gave a violent tug, they ripped and he pulled the panties down around her legs and off over her shoes. He threw them on the floorboard. Then he began playing with her cunt. He played with her cunt and played with her cunt and kissed her again and again. Then he leaned back against the car seat. He only had half a hard.

Lilly looked down at him.

"What are you, a queer?"

"No, it's not that, Lilly. It's just that I don't think these guys are watching to see if the coast is clear. They're watching *us*. I don't want to get caught in here."

"The coast is clear, Pete," I said. "We're watching!"

"We're watching!" said Baldy.

"I don't believe them," said Pete. "All they're watching is your cunt, Lilly."

"You're *chicken!* All that meat and it's only at half-mast!"

"I'm scared of getting caught, Lilly."

"I know what to do," she said.

Lilly bent over and ran her tongue along Pete's cock. She lapped her tongue around the monstrous head. Then she had it in her mouth.

"Lilly . . . Christ," said Pete, "I love you . . ."

"Lilly, Lilly, Lilly . . . oh, oh, oooh ooooh . . ."

"*Henry!*" Baldy screamed. "*LOOK!*"

I looked. It was Wagner running toward us from across the field and also coming behind him were the guys who had been playing touch football, plus some of the people who had been watching the football game, boys and girls both.

"*Pete!*" I yelled, "It's Wagner coming with 50 people!"

"*Shit!*" moaned Pete.

"Oh, shit," said Lilly.

Baldy and I took off. We ran out the gate and halfway up the block. We looked back through the fence. Pete and Lilly never had a chance. Wagner ran up and ripped open the car door hoping for a good look. Then the car was surrounded and we couldn't see any more . . .

120

After that, we never saw Pete or Lilly again. We had no idea what happened to them. Baldy and I each got 1,000 demerits which put me in the lead over Magalore with 1,100. There was no way I could work them off. I was in Mt. Justin for life. Of course, they informed our parents.

"Let's go," said my father, and I walked into the bathroom.

He got the strop down.

"Take down your pants and shorts," he said.

I didn't do it. He reached in front of me, yanked my belt open, unbuttoned me and yanked my pants down. He pulled down my shorts. The strop landed. It was the same, the same explosive sound, the same pain.

"You're going to kill your mother!" he screamed.

He hit me again. But the tears weren't coming. My eyes were strangely dry. I thought about killing him. That there must be a way to kill him. In a couple of years I could beat him to death. But I wanted him now. He wasn't much of anything. I must have been adopted. He hit me again. The pain was still there but the fear of it was gone. The strop landed again. The room no longer blurred. I could see everything clearly. My father seemed to sense the difference in me and he began to lash me harder, again and again, but the more he beat me the less I felt. It was almost as if he was the one who was helpless. Something had occurred, something had changed. My father stopped, puffing, and I heard him hanging up the strop. He walked to the door. I turned.

"Hey," I said.

My father turned and looked at me.

"Give me a couple more," I told him, "if it makes you feel any better."

"Don't you *dare* talk to me that way!" he said.

I looked at him. I saw folds of flesh under his chin and around his neck. I saw sad wrinkles and crevices. His face was tired pink putty. He was in his undershirt, and his belly sagged, wrinkling his undershirt. The eyes were no longer fierce. His eyes looked away and couldn't meet mine. Something had happened. The bath towels knew it, the shower curtain knew it, the mirror knew it, the bathtub and the toilet knew it. My father turned and walked out the door. He knew it. It was my last beating. From him.

121

28

Jr. high went by quickly enough. About the 8th grade, going into the 9th, I broke out with acne. Many of the guys had it but not like mine. Mine was really terrible. I was the worst case in town. I had pimples and boils all over my face, back, neck, and some on my chest. It happened just as I was beginning to be accepted as a tough guy and a leader. I was still tough but it wasn't the same. I had to withdraw. I watched people from afar, it was like a stage play. Only they were on stage and I was an audience of one. I'd always had trouble with the girls but with acne it was impossible. The girls were further away than ever. Some of them were truly beautiful—their dresses, their hair, their eyes, the way they stood around. Just to walk down the street during an afternoon with one, you know, talking about everything and anything, I think that would have made me feel very good.

Also, there was still something about me that continually got me into trouble. Most teachers didn't trust or like me, especially the lady teachers. I never said anything out of the way but they claimed it was my "attitude." It was something about the way I sat slouched in my seat and my "voice tone." I was usually accused of "sneering" although I wasn't conscious of it. I was often made to stand outside in the hall during class or I was sent to the principal's office. The principal always did the same thing. He had a phone booth in his office. He made me stand in the phone booth with the door closed. I spent many hours in that phone booth. The only reading material in there was the *Ladies Home Journal*. It was deliberate torture. I read the *Ladies Home Journal* anyhow. I got to read each new issue. I hoped that maybe I could learn something about women.

I must have had 5,000 demerits by graduation time but it didn't seem to matter. They wanted to get rid of me. I was standing outside in the line that was filing into the auditorium one by one. We each had on our cheap little cap and gown that had been passed down again and again to the next graduating group. We could hear each person's name as they walked across the stage. They were making one big god-damned deal out of graduating from jr. high. The band played our school song:

> *Oh, Mt. Justin, Oh, Mt. Justin*
> *We will be true,*
> *Our hearts are singing wildly*
> *All our skies are blue . . .*

We stood in line, each of us waiting to march across the stage. In the audience were our parents and friends.
"I'm about to puke," said one of the guys.
"We only go from crap to more crap," said another.
The girls seemed to be more serious about it. That's why I didn't really trust them. They seemed to be part of the wrong things. They and the school seemed to have the same song.
"This stuff brings me down," said one of the guys. "I wish I had a smoke."
"Here you are . . ."
Another of the guys handed him a cigarette. We passed it around between four or five of us. I took a hit and exhaled through my nostrils. Then I saw Curly Wagner walking in.
"Ditch it!" I said. "Here comes vomit-head!"
Wagner walked right up to me. He was dressed in his grey gym suit, including sweatshirt, just as he had been the first time I saw him and all the other times afterward. He stood in front of me.
"Listen," he said, "you think you're getting away from me because you're getting out of here, but you're not! I'm going to follow you the rest of your life. I'm going to follow you to the ends of the earth and I'm going to get you!"

I just glanced at him without comment and he walked off. Wagner's little graduation speech only made me that much bigger with the guys. They thought I must have done some big god-damned thing to rile him. But it wasn't true. Wagner was just simple-crazy.

We got nearer and nearer to the doorway of the auditorium. Not only could we hear each name being announced, and the applause, but we could see the audience.

Then it was my turn.

"Henry Chinaski," the principal said over the microphone. And I walked forward. There was no applause. Then one kindly soul in the audience gave two or three claps.

There were rows of seats set up on the stage for the graduating class. We sat there and waited. The principal gave his speech about opportunity and success in America. Then it was all over. The band struck up the Mt. Justin school song. The students and their parents and friends rose and mingled together. I walked around, looking. My parents weren't there. I made sure. I walked around and gave it a good look-see.

It was just as well. A tough guy didn't need that. I took off my ancient cap and gown and handed it to the guy at the end of the aisle—the janitor. He folded the pieces up for the next time.

I walked outside. The first one out. But where could I go? I had eleven cents in my pocket. I walked back to where I lived.

29

That summer, July 1934, they gunned down John Dillinger outside the movie house in Chicago. He never had a chance. The Lady in Red had fingered him. More than a year earlier the banks had collapsed. Prohibition was repealed and my father drank Eastside beer again. But the worst thing was Dillinger getting it. A lot of people admired Dillinger and it made everybody feel terrible. Roosevelt was President. He gave Fireside Chats over the radio and everybody listened. He could really talk. And he began to enact programs to put people to work. But things were still very bad. And my boils got worse, they were unbelievably large.

That September I was scheduled to go to Woodhaven High but my father insisted I go to Chelsey High.

"Look," I told him, "Chelsey is out of this district. It's too far away."

"You'll do as I tell you. You'll register at Chelsey High."

I knew why he wanted me to go to Chelsey. The rich kids went there. My father was crazy. He still thought about being rich. When Baldy found out I was going to Chelsey he decided to go there too. I couldn't get rid of him or my boils.

The first day we rode our bikes to Chelsey and parked them. It was a terrible feeling. Most of those kids, at least all the older ones, had their own automobiles, many of them new convertibles, and they weren't black or dark blue like most cars, they were bright yellow, green, orange and red. The guys sat in them outside of the school and the girls gathered around and went for rides. Everybody was nicely dressed, the guys and the girls, they had pullover sweaters, wrist watches and the latest in shoes. They seemed very adult and poised and superior. And there I was in my homemade shirt, my one ragged pair of pants, my rundown shoes, and I was covered with boils. The guys with the cars didn't worry about acne. They were very handsome, they were tall and clean with bright teeth and they didn't wash their hair with hand soap. They seemed to know something I didn't know. I was at the bottom again.

Since all the guys had cars Baldy and I were ashamed of our bicycles. We left them home and walked to school and back, two-and-one-half miles each way. We carried brown bag lunches. But most of the other students didn't even eat in the school cafeteria. They drove to malt shops with the girls, played the juke boxes and laughed. They were on their way to U.S.C.

I was ashamed of my boils. At Chelsey you had a choice between gym and R.O.T.C. I took R.O.T.C. because then I didn't have to wear a gym suit and nobody could see the boils on my body. But I hated the uniform. The shirt was made of wool and it irritated my boils. The uniform was worn from Monday to Thursday. On Friday we were allowed to wear regular clothes.

We studied the Manual of Arms. It was about warfare and shit like that. We had to pass exams. We marched around the field. We practiced the Manual of Arms. Handling the rifle during various drills was bad for me. I had boils on my shoulders. Sometimes when I slammed the rifle against my shoulder a boil would break and leak through my shirt. The blood would come through but because the shirt was thick and made of wool the spot wasn't obvious and didn't look like blood.

I told my mother what was happening. She lined the shoulders of my shirts with white patches of cloth, but it only helped a little.

Once an officer came through on inspection. He grabbed the rifle out of my hands and held it up, peering through the barrel, for dust in the bore. He slammed the rifle back at me, then looked at a blood spot on my right shoulder.

"Chinaski!" he snapped, "your rifle is leaking oil!"

"Yes, sir."

126

I got through the term but the boils got worse and worse. They were as large as walnuts and covered my face. I was very ashamed. Sometimes at home I would stand before the bathroom mirror and break one of the boils. Yellow pus would spurt and splatter on the mirror. And little white hard pits. In a horrible way it was fascinating that all that stuff was in there. But I knew how hard it was for other people to look at me.

The school must have advised my father. At the end of that term I was withdrawn from school. I went to bed and my parents covered me with ointments. There was a brown salve that stank. My father preferred that one for me. It burned. He insisted that I keep it on longer, much longer than the instructions advised. One night he insisted that I leave it on for hours. I began screaming. I ran to the tub, filled it with water and washed the salve off, with difficulty. I was burned, on my face, my back and chest. That night I sat on the edge of the bed. I couldn't lay down.

My father came into the room.

"I thought I told you to leave that stuff on!"

"Look what happened," I told him.

My mother came into the room.

"The son-of-a-bitch doesn't *want* to get well," my father told her. "Why did I have to have a son like this?"

My mother lost her job. My father kept leaving in his car every morning as if he were going to work. "I'm an engineer," he told people. He had always wanted to be an engineer.

It was arranged for me to go to the L.A. County General Hospital. I was given a long white card. I took the white card and got on the #7 streetcar. The fare was seven cents (or four tokens for a quarter). I dropped in my token and walked to the back of the streetcar. I had an 8:30 a.m. appointment.

A few blocks later a young boy and a woman got on the streetcar. The woman was fat and the boy was about four years old. They sat in the seat behind me. I looked out the window. We rolled along. I liked that #7 streetcar. It went really fast and rocked back and forth as the sun shone outside.

"Mommy," I heard the young boy say, "What's *wrong* with that man's face?"

The woman didn't answer.

The boy asked her the same question again.

She didn't answer.

Then the boy screamed it out, *"Mommy! What's wrong with that man's face?"*

"Shut up! I don't know what's wrong with his face!"

I went to Admissions at the hospital and they instructed me to report to the fourth floor. There the nurse at the desk took my name and told me to be seated. We sat in two long rows of green metal chairs facing one another. Mexicans, whites and blacks. There were no Orientals. There was nothing to read. Some of the patients had day-old newspapers. The people were of all ages, thin and fat, short and tall, old and young. Nobody talked. Everybody seemed very tired. Orderlies walked back and forth, sometimes you saw a nurse, but never a doctor. An hour went by, two hours. Nobody's name was called. I got up to look for a water fountain. I looked in the little rooms where people were to be examined. There wasn't anybody in any of the rooms, neither doctors or patients.

I went to the desk. The nurse was staring down into a big fat book with names written in it. The phone rang. She answered it.

"Dr. Menen isn't here yet." She hung up.

"Pardon me," I said.

"Yes?" the nurse asked.

"The doctors aren't here yet. Can I come back later?"

"No."

"But there's nobody here."

"The doctors are on call."

"But I have an 8:30 appointment."

"Everybody here has an 8:30 appointment."

There were 45 or 50 people waiting.

"Since I'm on the waiting list, suppose I come back in a couple of hours, maybe there will be some doctors here then."

"If you leave now, you will automatically lose your appointment. You will have to return tomorrow if you still wish treatment."

I walked back and sat in a chair. The others didn't protest.

There was very little movement. Sometimes two or three nurses would walk by laughing. Once they pushed a man past in a wheelchair. Both of his legs were heavily bandaged and his ear on the side of his head toward me had been sliced off. There was a black hole divided into little sections, and it looked like a spider had gone in there and made a spider web. Hours passed. Noon came and went. Another hour. Two hours. We sat and waited. Then somebody said, "There's a doctor!"

The doctor walked into one of the examination rooms and closed the door. We all watched. Nothing. A nurse went in. We heard her laughing. Then she walked out. Five minutes. Ten minutes. The doctor walked out with a clipboard in his hand.

"Martinez?" the doctor asked. "José Martinez?"

An old thin Mexican man stood up and began walking toward the doctor.

"Martinez? Martinez, old boy, how are you?"

"Sick, doctor . . . I think I die . . ."

"Well, now . . . Step in here . . ."

Martinez was in there a long time. I picked up a discarded newspaper and tried to read it. But we were all thinking about Martinez. If Martinez ever got out of there, someone would be next.

Then Martinez screamed. "AHHHHH! AHHHHH! STOP! STOP! AHHHH! MERCY! GOD! PLEASE STOP!"

"Now, now, that doesn't hurt . . ." said the doctor.

Martinez screamed again. A nurse ran into the examination room. There was silence. All we could see was the black shadow of the half-open doorway. Then an orderly ran into the examination room. Martinez made a gurgling sound. He was taken out of there on a rolling stretcher. The nurse and the orderly pushed him down the hall and through some swinging doors. Martinez was under a sheet but he wasn't dead because the sheet wasn't pulled over his face.

The doctor stayed in the examination room for another ten minutes. Then he came out with the clipboard.

"Jefferson Williams?" he asked.

There was no answer.

"Is Jefferson Williams here?"

There was no response.

"Mary Blackthorne?"
There was no answer.
"Harry Lewis?"
"Yes, doctor?"
"Step forward, please . . ."

It was very slow. The doctor saw five more patients. Then he left the examination room, stopped at the desk, lit a cigarette and talked to the nurse for fifteen minutes. He looked like a very intelligent man. He had a twitch on the right side of his face, which kept jumping, and he had red hair with streaks of grey. He wore glasses and kept taking them off and putting them back on. Another nurse came in and gave him a cup of coffee. He took a sip, then holding the coffee in one hand he pushed the swinging doors open with the other and was gone.

The office nurse came out from behind the desk with our long white cards and she called our names. As we answered, she handed each of us our card back. "This ward is closed for the day. Please return tomorrow if you wish. Your appointment time is stamped on your card."

I looked down at my card. It was stamped 8:30 a.m.

30

I got lucky the next day. They called my name. It was a different doctor. I stripped down. He turned a hot white light on me and looked me over. I was sitting on the edge of the examination table.

"Hmmm, hmmmm," he said, "uh huh . . ."

I sat there.

"How long have you had this?"

"A couple of years. It keeps getting worse and worse."

"Ah hah."

He kept looking.

"Now, you just stretch out there on your stomach. I'll be right back."

Some moments passed and suddenly there were many people in the room. They were all doctors. At least they looked and talked like doctors. Where had they come from? I had thought there were hardly any doctors at L.A. County General Hospital.

"Acne vulgaris. The worst case I've seen in all my years of practice!"

"Fantastic!"

"Incredible!"

"Look at the face!"

"The neck!"

"I just finished examining a young girl with acne vulgaris. Her back was covered. She cried. She told me, 'How will I ever get a man? My back will be scarred forever. I want to kill myself!' And now look at *this* fellow! If she could see him, she'd know that she really had nothing to complain about!"

You dumb fuck, I thought, don't you realize that I can hear what you're saying?

How did a man get to be a doctor? Did they take anybody?

"Is he asleep?"

"Why?"

"He seems very calm."

"No, I don't think he's asleep. Are you asleep, my boy?"

"Yes."

They kept moving the hot white light about on various parts of my body.

"Turn over."

I turned over.

"Look, there's a lesion inside of his mouth!"

"Well, how will we treat it?"

"The electric needle, I think . . ."

"Yes, of course, the electric needle."

"Yes, the needle."

It was decided.

31

The next day I sat in the hall in my green tin chair, waiting to be called. Across from me sat a man who had something wrong with his nose. It was very red and very raw and very fat and long and it was growing upon itself. You could see where section had grown upon section. Something had irritated the man's nose and it had just started growing. I looked at the nose and then tried not to look. I didn't want the man to see me looking, I knew how he felt. But the man seemed very comfortable. He was fat and sat there almost asleep.

They called him first: "Mr. Sleeth?"
He moved forward a bit in his chair.
"Sleeth? Richard Sleeth?"
"Uh? Yes, I'm here . . ."
He stood up and moved toward the doctor.
"How are you today, Mr. Sleeth?"
"Fine . . . I'm all right . . ."
He followed the doctor into the examination room.

I got my call an hour later. I followed the doctor through some swinging doors and into another room. It was larger than the examination room. I was told to disrobe and to sit on a table. The doctor looked at me.
"You really have a case there, haven't you?"
"Yeah."
He poked at a boil on my back.

"That hurt?"

"Yeah."

"Well," he said, "we're going to try to get some drainage."

I heard him turn on the machinery. It made a whirring sound. I could smell oil getting hot.

"Ready?" he asked.

"Yeah."

He pushed the electric needle into my back. I was being drilled. The pain was immense. It filled the room. I felt the blood run down my back. Then he pulled the needle out.

"Now we're going to get another one," said the doctor.

He jammed the needle into me. Then he pulled it out and jammed it into a third boil. Two other men had walked in and were standing there watching. They were probably doctors. The needle went into me again.

"I never saw anybody go under the needle like that," said one of the men.

"He gives no sign at all," said the other man.

"Why don't you guys go out and pinch some nurse's ass?" I asked them.

"Look, son, you can't talk to us like that!"

The needle dug into me. I didn't answer.

"The boy is evidently very bitter . . ."

"Yes, of course, that's it."

The men walked out.

"Those are fine professional men," said my doctor. "It's not good of you to abuse them."

"Just go ahead and drill," I told him.

He did. The needle got very hot but he went on and on. He drilled my entire back, then he got my chest. Then I stretched out and he drilled my neck and my face.

A nurse came in and she got her instructions. "Now, Miss Ackerman, I want these . . . pustules . . . thoroughly drained. And when you get to the blood, keep squeezing. I want thorough drainage."

"Yes, Dr. Grundy."

"And afterwards, the ultra-violet ray machine. Two minutes on each side to begin with . . ."

"Yes, Dr. Grundy."

134

I followed Miss Ackerman into another room. She told me to lay down on the table. She got a tissue and started on the first boil.

"Does this hurt?"

"It's all right."

"You poor boy . . ."

"Don't worry. I'm just sorry you have to do this."

"You poor boy . . ."

Miss Ackerman was the first person to give me any sympathy. It felt strange. She was a chubby little nurse in her early thirties.

"Are you going to school?" she asked.

"No, they had to take me out."

Miss Ackerman kept squeezing as she talked.

"What do you do all day?"

"I just stay in bed."

"That's awful."

"No, it's nice. I like it."

"Does this hurt?"

"Go ahead. It's all right."

"What's so nice about laying in bed all day?"

"I don't have to see anybody."

"You like that?"

"Oh, yes."

"What do you do all day?"

"Some of the day I listen to the radio."

"What do you listen to?"

"Music. And people talking."

"Do you think of girls?"

"Sure. But that's out."

"You don't want to think that way."

"I make charts of airplanes going overhead. They come over at the same time each day. I have them timed. Say that I know that one of them is going to pass over at 11:15 a.m. Around 11:10, I start listening for the sound of the motor. I try to hear the first sound. Sometimes I imagine I hear it and sometimes I'm not sure and then I begin to hear it, 'way off, for sure. And the sound gets stronger. Then at 11:15 a.m. it passes overhead and the sound is as loud as it's going to get."

"You do that every day?"

"Not when I'm here."

"Turn over," said Miss Ackerman.

I did. Then in the ward next to us a man started screaming. We were next to the disturbed ward. He was really loud.

"What are they doing to him?" I asked Miss Ackerman.

"He's in the shower."

"And it makes him scream like that?"

"Yes."

"I'm worse off than he is."

"No, you're not."

I liked Miss Ackerman. I sneaked a look at her. Her face was round, she wasn't very pretty but she wore her nurse's cap in a perky manner and she had large dark brown eyes. It was the eyes. As she balled up some tissue to throw into the dispenser I watched her walk. Well, she was no Miss Gredis, and I had seen many other women with better figures, but there was something warm about her. She wasn't constantly thinking about being a woman.

"As soon as I finish your face," she said, "I will put you under the ultra-violet ray machine. Your next appointment will be the day after tomorrow at 8:30 a.m."

We didn't talk any more after that.

Then she was finished. I put on goggles and Miss Ackerman turned on the ultra-violet ray machine.

There was a ticking sound. It was peaceful. It might have been the automatic timer, or the metal reflector on the lamp heating up. It was comforting and relaxing, but when I began to think about it, I decided that everything that they were doing for me was useless. I figured that at best the needle would leave scars on me for the remainder of my life. That was bad enough but it wasn't what I really minded. What I minded was that they didn't know how to deal with me. I sensed this in their discussions and in their manner. They were hesitant, uneasy, yet also somehow disinterested and bored. Finally it didn't matter what they did. They just had to do something—anything—because to do nothing would be unprofessional.

They experimented on the poor and if that worked they used the treatment on the rich. And if it didn't work, there would still be more poor left over to experiment upon.

The machine signaled its warning that two minutes were up. Miss Ackerman came in, told me to turn over, re-set the machine, then left. She was the kindest person I had met in eight years.

32

The drilling and squeezing continued for weeks but there was little result. When one boil vanished another would appear. I often stood in front of the mirror alone, wondering how ugly a person could get. I would look at my face in disbelief, then turn to examine all the boils on my back. I was horrified. No wonder people stared, no wonder they said unkind things. It was not simply a case of teen-age acne. These were inflamed, relentless, large, swollen boils filled with pus. I felt singled out, as if I had been *selected* to be this way. My parents never spoke to me about my condition. They were still on relief. My mother left each morning to look for work and my father drove off as if he were working. On Saturdays people on relief got free foodstuffs from the markets, mostly canned goods, almost always cans of hash for some reason. We ate a great deal of hash. And bologna sandwiches. And potatoes. My mother learned to make potato pancakes. Each Saturday when my parents went for their free food they didn't go to the nearest market because they were afraid some of the neighbors might see them and then know that they were on the dole. So they walked two miles down Washington Boulevard, to a store a couple of blocks past Crenshaw. It was a long walk. They walked the two miles back, sweating, carrying their shopping bags full of canned hash and potatoes and bologna and carrots. My father didn't drive because he wanted to save gas. He needed the gas to drive to and from his invisible job. The other fathers weren't like that. They just sat quietly on their front porches or played horseshoes in the vacant lot.

The doctor gave me a white substance to apply to my face. It hardened and caked on the boils, giving me a plaster-like look. The substance didn't seem to help. I was home alone one afternoon, applying this substance to my face and body. I was standing in my shorts trying to reach the infected areas of my back with my hand when I heard voices. It was Baldy and his friend Jimmy Hatcher. Jimmy Hatcher was a good looking fellow and he was a wise-ass.

"Henry!" I heard Baldy calling. I heard him talking to Jimmy. Then he walked up on the porch and beat on the door. "Hey, Hank, it's Baldy! Open up!"

You damn fool, I thought, don't you understand that I don't want to see anybody?

"Hank! Hank! It's Baldy and Jim!"

He beat on the front door.

I heard him talking to Jim. "Listen, I saw him! I saw him walking around in there!"

"He doesn't answer."

"We better go in. He might be in trouble."

You fool, I thought, I befriended you. I befriended you when nobody else could stand you. Now, look at this!

I couldn't believe it. I ran into the hall and hid in a closet, leaving the door slightly open. I was sure they wouldn't come into the house. But they did. I had left the back door open. I heard them walking around in the house.

"He's got to be here," said Baldy. "I saw something moving in here . . ."

Jesus Christ, I thought, can't I move around in here? I live in this house.

I was crouched in the dark closet. I knew I couldn't let them find me in there.

I swung the closet door open and leaped out. I saw them both standing in the front room. I ran in there.

"GET OUT OF HERE, YOU SONS-OF-BITCHES!"

They looked at me.

"GET OUT OF HERE! YOU'VE GOT NO RIGHT TO BE IN HERE! GET OUT OF HERE BEFORE I KILL YOU!"

They started running toward the back porch.

"GO ON! GO ON, OR I'LL KILL YOU!"

138

I heard them run up the driveway and out onto the sidewalk. I didn't want to watch them. I went into my bedroom and stretched out on the bed. Why did they want to see me? What could they do? There was nothing to be done. There was nothing to talk about.

A couple of days later my mother didn't leave to go job hunting, and it wasn't my day to go to the L.A. County General Hospital. So we were in the house together. I didn't like it. I liked the place to myself. I heard her moving about the house and I stayed in my bedroom. The boils were worse than ever. I checked my airplane chart. The 1:20 p.m. flight was due. I began listening. He was late. It was 1:20 and he was still approaching. As he passed over I timed him as being three minutes late. Then I heard the doorbell ring. I heard my mother open the door.

"Emily, how are you?"

"Hello, Katy, how are you?"

It was my grandmother, now very old. I heard them talking but I couldn't make out what they were saying. I was thankful for that. They talked for five or ten minutes and then I heard them walking down the hall to my bedroom.

"I will bury all of you," I heard my grandmother say. "Where is the boy?"

The door opened and my grandmother and mother stood there.

"Hello, Henry," my grandmother said.

"Your grandmother is here to help you," my mother said.

My grandmother had a large purse. She set it down on the dresser and pulled a huge silver crucifix out of it.

"Your grandmother is here to help you, Henry . . ."

Grandmother had more warts on her than ever before and she was fatter. She looked invincible, she looked as if she would never die. She had gotten so old that it was almost senseless for her to die.

"Henry," said my mother, "turn over on your stomach."

I turned over and my grandmother leaned over me. From the corner of my eye I saw her dangling the huge crucifix over me. I had decided against religion a couple of years back. If it were true, it made fools out of people, or it drew fools. And if it weren't true, the fools were all the more foolish.

But it was my grandmother and my mother. I decided to let them have their way. The crucifix swung back and forth above my back, over my boils, over me.

"God," prayed my grandmother, "purge the devil from this poor boy's body! Just look at all those sores! They make me sick, God! *Look* at them! It's the devil, God, dwelling in this boy's body. Purge the devil from his body, Lord!"

"Purge the devil from his body, Lord!" said my mother.

What I need is a good doctor, I thought. What is wrong with these women? Why don't they leave me alone?

"God," said my grandmother, "why do you allow the devil to dwell inside this body's body? Don't you see how the devil is enjoying this? Look at these sores, O Lord, I am about to vomit just looking at them! They are red and big and full!"

"Purge the devil from my boy's body!" screamed my mother.

"May God save us from this evil!" screamed my grandmother.

She took the crucifix and poked it into the center of my back, dug it in. The blood spurted out, I could feel it, at first warm, then suddenly cold. I turned over and sat up in the bed.

"What the fuck are you doing?"

"I am making a hole for the devil to be pushed out by God!" said my grandmother.

"All right," I said, "I want you both to get out of here, and fast! Do you understand me?"

"He is still possessed!" said my grandmother.

"GET THE FUCKING HELL OUT OF HERE!" I screamed.

They left, shocked and disappointed, closing the door behind them.

I went into the bathroom, wadded up some toilet paper and tried to stop the bleeding. I pulled the toilet paper away and looked at it. It was soaked. I got a new batch of toilet paper and held it to my back awhile. Then I got the iodine. I made passes at my back, trying to reach the wound with the iodine. It was difficult. I finally gave up. Who ever heard of an infected back, anyhow? You either lived or died. The back was something the assholes had never figured out how to amputate.

140

I walked back into the bedroom and got into bed and pulled the covers to my throat. I looked up at the ceiling as I talked to myself.

All right, God, say that You are really there. You have put me in this fix. You want to test me. Suppose I test You? Suppose I say that You are not there? You've given me a supreme test with my parents and with these boils. I think that I have passed Your test. I am tougher than You. If You will come down here right now, I will spit into Your face, if You have a face. And do You shit? The priest never answered that question. He told us not to doubt. Doubt what? I think that You have been picking on me too much so I am asking You to come down here so I can put You to the test!

I waited. Nothing. I waited for God. I waited and waited. I believe I slept.

I never slept on my back. But when I awakened I was on my back and it surprised me. My legs were bent at the knees in front of me, making a mountain-like effect with the blankets. And as I looked at the blanket-mountain before me I saw two eyes staring at me. Only the eyes were dark, black, blank . . . looking at me from underneath a hood, a black hood with a sharp tall peak, like a ku-klux-klansman. They kept staring at me, dark blank eyes, and there was nothing I could do about it. I was truly terrified. I thought, it's God but God isn't supposed to look like that.

I couldn't stare it down. I couldn't move. It just stayed there looking at me over the mound of my knees and the blanket. I wanted to get away. I wanted *it* to leave. It was powerful and black and threatening.

It seemed to remain there for hours, just staring at me.

Then it was gone . . .

I stayed in bed thinking about it.

I couldn't believe that it had been God. Dressed like that. That would be a cheap trick.

It had been an illusion, of course.

I thought about it for ten or fifteen minutes, then I got up and went to get the little brown box my grandmother had given me many years ago. Inside of it were tiny rolls of paper with quotations from the Bible. Each tiny roll was held in a cubicle of its own. One was supposed to ask a question and the little roll of paper one pulled out was supposed to answer that question. I had tried it before and found it useless. Now I tried it again. I asked the brown box, "What did that mean? What did those eyes mean?"

I pulled out a paper and unrolled it. It was a tiny stiff white piece of paper. I unrolled and read it.

GOD HAS FORSAKEN YOU.

I rolled the paper up and stuck it back into its cubicle in the brown box. I didn't believe it. I went back to bed and thought about it. It was too simple, too direct. I didn't believe it. I considered masturbating to bring me back to reality. I still didn't believe it. I got back up and started unrolling all the little papers inside the brown box. I was looking for the one that said, GOD HAS FORSAKEN YOU. I unrolled them all. None of them said that. I read them all and none of them said that. I rolled them up and put them carefully back into their cubicles in the little brown box.

Meanwhile, the boils got worse. I kept getting onto streetcar #7 and going to L.A. County General Hospital and I began to fall in love with Miss Ackerman, my nurse of the squeezings. She would never know how each stab of pain caused courage to well up in me. Despite the horror of the blood and the pus, she was always humane and kind. My love-feeling for her wasn't sexual. I just wished that she would enfold me in her starched whiteness and that together we could vanish forever from the world. But she never did that. She was too practical. She would only remind me of my next appointment.

142

33

The ultra-violet ray machine clicked off. I had been treated on both sides. I took off the goggles and began to dress. Miss Ackerman walked in.

"Not yet," she said, "keep your clothes off."

What is she going to do to me, I thought?

"Sit up on the edge of the table."

I sat there and she began rubbing salve over my face. It was a thick buttery substance.

"The doctors have decided on a new approach. We're going to bandage your face to effect drainage."

"Miss Ackerman, what ever happened to that man with the big nose? The nose that kept growing?"

"Mr. Sleeth?"

"The man with the big nose."

"That was Mr. Sleeth."

"I don't see him anymore. Did he get cured?"

"He's dead."

"You mean he died from that big nose?"

"Suicide." Miss Ackerman continued to apply the salve.

Then I heard a man scream from the next ward, "*Joe, where are you? Joe, you said you'd come back! Joe, where are you?*"

The voice was loud and so sad, so agonized.

"He's done that every afternoon this week," said Miss Ackerman, "and Joe's not going to come get him."

"Can't they help him?"

"I don't know. They all quiet down, finally. Now take your

finger and hold this pad while I bandage you. There. Yes. That's it. Now let go. Fine."

"*Joe! Joe, you said you'd come back! Where are you, Joe?*"

"Now, hold your finger on this pad. There. Hold it there. I'm going to wrap you up good! There. Now I'll secure the dressings."

Then she was finished.

"O.K., put on your clothes. See you the day after tomorrow. Goodbye, Henry."

"Goodbye, Miss Ackerman."

I got dressed, left the room and walked down the hall. There was a mirror on a cigarette machine in the lobby. I looked into the mirror. It was great. My whole head was bandaged. I was all white. Nothing could be seen but my eyes, my mouth and my ears, and some tufts of hair sticking up at the top of my head. I was *hidden*. It was wonderful. I stood and lit a cigarette and glanced about the lobby. Some in-patients were sitting about reading magazines and newspapers. I felt very exceptional and a bit evil. Nobody had any idea of what had happened to me. Car crash. A fight to the death. A murder. Fire. Nobody knew.

I walked out of the lobby and out of the building and I stood on the sidewalk. I could still hear him. "*Joe! Joe! Where are you, Joe!*"

Joe wasn't coming. It didn't pay to trust another human being. Humans didn't have it, whatever it took.

On the streetcar ride back I sat in the back smoking cigarettes out of my bandaged head. People stared but I didn't care. There was more fear than horror in their eyes now. I hoped I could stay this way forever.

I rode to the end of the line and got off. The afternoon was going into evening and I stood on the corner of Washington Boulevard and Westview Avenue watching the people. Those few who had jobs were coming home from work. My father would soon be driving home from his fake job. I didn't have a job, I didn't go to school. I didn't do anything. I was bandaged, I was standing on the corner smoking a cigarette. I was a tough man, I was a dangerous man. I knew things. Sleeth had suicided. I wasn't going to suicide. I'd rather kill some of them. I'd take four or five of them with me. I'd show them what it meant to play around with me.

A woman walked down the street toward me. She had fine legs. First I stared right into her eyes and then I looked down at her

144

legs, and as she passed I watched her ass, I drank her ass in. I memorized her ass and the seams of her silk stockings.

I never could have done that without my bandages.

34

The next day in bed I got tired of waiting for the airplanes and I found a large yellow notebook that had been meant for high school work. It was empty. I found a pen. I went to bed with the notebook and the pen. I made some drawings. I drew women in high-heeled shoes with their legs crossed and their skirts pulled back.

Then I began writing. It was about a German aviator in World War I. Baron Von Himmlen. He flew a red Fokker. And he was not popular with his fellow fliers. He didn't talk to them. He drank alone and he flew alone. He didn't bother with women, although they all loved him. He was above that. He was too busy. He was busy shooting Allied planes out of the sky. Already he had shot down 110 and the war wasn't over. His red Fokker, which he referred to as the "October Bird of Death," was known everywhere. Even the enemy ground troops knew him as he often flew low over them, taking their gunfire and laughing, dropping bottles of champagne to them suspended from little parachutes. Baron Von Himmlen was never attacked by less than five Allied planes at a time. He was an ugly man with scars on his face, but he was beautiful if you looked long enough—it was in the eyes, his style, his courage, his fierce aloneness.

I wrote pages and pages about the Baron's dog fights, how he would knock down three or four planes, fly back, almost nothing left of his red Fokker. He'd bounce down, leap out of the plane while it was still rolling and head for the bar where he'd grab a bottle and sit at a table alone, pouring shots and slamming them down. Nobody drank like the Baron. The others just stood at the bar and watched him. One time one of the other fliers said, "What is it, Himmlen? You think you're too good for us?" It was Willie Schmidt, the biggest, strongest guy in the outfit. The Baron downed his drink, set down his glass, stood up and slowly started walking toward Willie who was standing at the bar. The other fliers backed off.

"Jesus, what are you going to *do?*" asked Willie as the Baron advanced.

The Baron kept moving slowly toward Willie, not answering.

"Jesus, Baron, I was just *kidding!* Mother's honor! Listen to me, Baron . . . Baron . . . the enemy is *elsewhere!* Baron!"

The Baron let go with his right. You couldn't see it. It smashed into Willie's face propelling him over the top of the bar, flipping him over completely! He crashed into the bar mirror like a cannonball and the bottles tumbled down. The Baron pulled a cigar out and lit it, then walked back to his table, sat down and poured another drink. They didn't bother the Baron after that. Behind the bar they picked Willie up. His face was a mass of blood.

The Baron shot plane after plane out of the sky. Nobody seemed to understand him and nobody knew how he had become so skillful with the red Fokker and in his other strange ways. Like fighting. Or the graceful way he walked. He went on and on. His luck was sometimes bad. One day flying back after downing three Allied planes, limping in low over enemy lines, he was hit by shrapnel. It blew off his right hand at the wrist. He managed to bring the red Fokker in. From that time on he flew with an iron hand in place of his original right hand. It didn't affect his flying. And the fellows at the bar were more careful than ever when they talked to him.

Many more things happened to the Baron after that. Twice he crashed in no-man's-land and each time he crawled back to his squadron, half-dead, through barbed wire and flares and enemy fire. Many times he was given up for dead by his comrades. Once he was gone for eight days and the other flyers were sitting in the bar, talking about what an exceptional man he had been. When they looked up, there was the Baron standing in the doorway, eight-day beard, uniform torn and muddy, eyes red and bleary, iron hand glinting in the bar light. He stood there and he said, "There better be some god-damned whiskey in this place or I'm tearing it apart!"

The Baron went on doing magic things. Half the notebook was filled with Baron Von Himmlen. It made me feel good to write about the Baron. A man needed somebody. There wasn't anybody around, so you had to make up somebody, make him up to be like a man *should* be. It wasn't make-believe or cheating. The other way was make-believe and cheating: living your life without a man like him around.

35

The bandages were helpful. L.A. County Hospital had finally come up with something. The boils drained. They didn't vanish but they flattened a bit. Yet some new ones would appear and rise up again. They drilled me and wrapped me again.

My sessions with the drill were endless. Thirty-two, thirty-six, thirty-eight times. There was no fear of the drill anymore. There never had been. Only an anger. But the anger was gone. There wasn't even resignation on my part, only disgust, a disgust that this had happened to me, and a disgust with the doctors who couldn't do anything about it. They were helpless and I was helpless, the only difference being that I was the victim. They could go home to their lives and forget while I was stuck with the same face.

But there were changes in my life. My father found a job. He passed an examination at the L.A. County Museum and got a job as a guard. My father was good at exams. He loved math and history. He passed the exam and finally had a place to go each morning. There had been three vacancies for guards and he had gotten one of them.

L.A. County General Hospital somehow found out and Miss Ackerman told me one day, "Henry, this is your last treatment. I'm going to miss you."

"Aw come on," I said, "stop your kidding. You're going to miss me like I'm going to miss that electric needle!"

But she was very strange that day. Those big eyes were watery. I heard her blow her nose.

I heard one of the nurses ask her, "Why, Janice, what's wrong with you?"

"Nothing. I'm all right."

Poor Miss Ackerman. I was 15 years old and in love with her and I was covered with boils and there was nothing that either of us could do.

"All right," she said, "this is going to be your last ultra-violet ray treatment. Lay on your stomach."

"I know your first name now," I told her. "Janice. That's a pretty name. It's just like you."

"Oh, shut up," she said.

I saw her once again when the first buzzer sounded. I turned over, Janice re-set the machine and left the room. I never saw her again.

My father didn't believe in doctors who were not free. "They make you piss in a tube, take your money, and drive home to their wives in Beverly Hills," he said.

But once he did send me to one. To a doctor with bad breath and a head as round as a basketball, only with two little eyes where a basketball had none. I didn't like my father and the doctor wasn't any better. He said, no fried foods, and to drink carrot juice. That was it.

I would re-enter high school the next term, said my father.

"I'm busting my ass to keep people from stealing. Some nigger broke the glass on a case and stole some rare coins yesterday. I caught the bastard. We rolled down the stairway together. I held him until the others came. I risk my life every day. Why should you sit around on your ass, moping? I want you to be an engineer. How the hell you gonna be an engineer when I find notebooks full of women with their skirts pulled up to their ass? Is *that* all you can draw? Why don't you draw flowers or mountains or the ocean? You're going back to school!"

I drank carrot juice and waited to re-enroll. I had only missed one term. The boils weren't cured but they weren't as bad as they had been.

"You know what carrot juice costs me? I have to work the first hour every day just for your god-damned carrot juice!"

I discovered the La Cienega Public Library. I got a library card. The library was near the old church down on West Adams. It was a very small library and there was just one librarian in it. She was class. About 38 but with pure white hair pulled tightly into a bun behind her neck. Her nose was sharp and she had deep green eyes behind rimless glasses. I felt that she knew everything.

I walked around the library looking for books. I pulled them off the shelves, one by one. But they all tricks. They were very dull. There were pages and pages of words that didn't say anything. Or if they did say something they took too long to say it and by the time they said it you already were too tired to have it matter at all. I tried book after book. Surely, out of all those books, there was *one*.

Each day I walked down to the library at Adams and La Brea and there was my librarian, stern and infallible and silent. I kept pulling the books off the shelves. The first real book I found was by a fellow named Upton Sinclair. His sentences were simple and he spoke with anger. He wrote with anger. He wrote about the hog pens of Chicago. He came right out and said things plainly. Then I found another author. His name was Sinclair Lewis. And the book was called *Main Street*. He peeled back the layers of hypocrisy that covered people. Only he seemed to lack passion.

I went back for more. I read each book in a single evening.

I was walking around one day sneaking glances at my librarian when I came upon a book with the title *Bow Down To Wood and Stone*. Now, that was good, because that was what we were all doing. At last, some *fire!* I opened the book. It was by Josephine Lawrence. A woman. That was all right. Anybody could find knowledge. I opened the pages. But they were like many of the other books: milky, obscure, tiresome. I replaced the book. And while my hand was there I reached for a book nearby. It was by another Lawrence. I opened the book at random and began reading. It was about a man at a piano. How false it seemed at first. But I kept reading. The man at the piano was troubled. His mind was saying things. Dark and curious things. The lines on the page

151

were pulled tight, like a man screaming, but not "Joe, where are you?" More like *Joe, where is anything?* This Lawrence of the tight and bloody line. I had never been told about him. Why the secret? Why wasn't he advertised?

I read a book a day. I read all the D. H. Lawrence in the library. My librarian began to look at me strangely as I checked out the books.

"How are you today?" she would ask.

That always sounded so good. I felt as if I had already gone to bed with her. I read all the books by D. H. And they led to others. To H. D., the poetess. And Huxley, the youngest of the Huxleys, Lawrence's friend. It all came rushing at me. One book led to the next. Dos Passos came along. Not too good, really, but good enough. His trilogy, about the U.S.A., took longer than a day to read. Dreiser didn't work for me. Sherwood Anderson did. And then along came Hemingway. What a thrill! He knew how to lay down a line. It was a joy. Words weren't dull, words were things that could make your mind hum. If you read them and let yourself feel the magic, you could live without pain, with hope, no matter what happened to you.

But back at home . . .

"LIGHTS OUT!" my father would scream.

I was reading the Russians now, reading Turgenev and Gorky. My father's rule was that all lights were to be out by 8 p.m. He wanted to sleep so that he could be fresh and effective on the job the next day. His conversation at home was always about "the job." He talked to my mother about his "job" from the moment he entered the door in the evenings until they slept. He was determined to rise in the ranks.

"All right, that's enough of those god-damned books! Lights out!"

To me, these men who had come into my life from nowhere were my only chance. They were the only voices that spoke to me.

"All right," I would say.

Then I took the reading lamp, crawled under the blanket, pulled the pillow under there, and read each new book, propping it against the pillow, under the quilt. It got very hot, the lamp got hot, and I had trouble breathing. I would lift the quilt for air.

"What's that? Do I see a light? Henry, are your lights out?"

I would quickly lower the quilt again and wait until I heard my father snoring.

Turgenev was a very serious fellow but he could make me laugh because a truth first encountered can be very funny. When someone else's truth is the same as your truth, and he seems to be saying it just for you, that's great.

I read my books at night, like that, under the quilt with the overheated reading lamp. Reading all those good lines while suffocating. It was magic.

And my father had found a job, and that was magic for him . . .

36

Back at Chelsey High it was the same. One group of seniors had graduated but they were replaced by another group of seniors with sports cars and expensive clothes. I was never confronted by them. They left me alone, they ignored me. They were busy with the girls. They never spoke to the poor guys in or out of class.

About a week into my second semester I talked to my father over dinner.

"Look," I said, "it's hard at school. You're giving me 50 cents a week allowance. Can't you make it a dollar?"

"A dollar?"

"Yes."

He put a forkful of sliced pickled beets into his mouth and chewed. Then he looked at me from under his curled-up eyebrows.

"If I gave you a dollar a week that would mean 52 dollars a year, that would mean I would have to work over a *week* on my job just so you could have an allowance."

I didn't answer. But I thought, my god, if you think like that, item by item, then you can't buy anything: bread, watermelon, newspapers, flour, milk or shaving cream. I didn't say any more because when you hate, you don't beg . . .

Those rich guys like to dart their cars in and out, swiftly, sliding up, burning rubber, their cars glistening in the sunlight as the girls gathered around. Classes were a joke, they were all going somewhere to college, classes were just a routine laugh, they got good grades, you seldom saw them with books, you just saw them burning more rubber, gunning from the curb with their cars full of squealing and laughing girls. I watched them with my 50 cents in my pocket. I didn't even know how to drive a car.

Meanwhile the poor and the lost and the idiots continued to flock around me. I had a place I liked to eat under the football grandstand. I had my brown bag lunch with my two bologna sandwiches. They came around, "Hey, Hank, can I eat with you?"

"Get the fuck out of here! I'm not going to tell you twice!"

Enough of this kind had attached themselves to me already. I didn't much care for any of them: Baldy, Jimmy Hatcher, and a thin gangling Jewish kid, Abe Mortenson. Mortenson was a straight-A student but one of the biggest idiots in school. He had something radically wrong with him. Saliva kept forming in his mouth but instead of spitting on the ground to get rid of it he spit into his hands. I don't know why he did it and I didn't ask. I didn't like to ask. I just watched him and I was disgusted. I went home with him once and I found out how he got straight A's. His mother made him stick his nose into a book right away and she made him keep it there. She made him read all of his school books over and over, page after page. "He must pass his exams," she told me. It never occurred to her that maybe the books were wrong. Or that maybe it didn't matter. I didn't ask her.

It was like grammar school all over again. Gathered around me were the weak instead of the strong, the ugly instead of the beautiful, the losers instead of the winners. It looked like it was my destiny to travel in their company through life. That didn't bother me so much as the fact that I seemed irresistible to these dull idiot fellows. I was like a turd that drew flies instead of like a flower that butterflies and bees desired. I wanted to live alone, I felt best being alone, cleaner, yet I was not clever enough to rid myself of them. Maybe they were *my* masters: fathers in another form. In any event, it was hard to have them hanging around while I was eating my bologna sandwiches.

37

But there were some good moments. My sometime friend from the neighborhood, Gene, who was a year older than I, had a buddy, Harry Gibson, who had had one professional fight (he'd lost). I was over at Gene's one afternoon smoking cigarettes with him when Harry Gibson showed up with two pairs of boxing gloves. Gene and I were smoking with his two older brothers, Larry and Dan.

Harry Gibson was cocky. "Anybody want to try me?" he asked. Nobody said anything. Gene's oldest brother, Larry, was about 22. He was the biggest, but he was kind of timid and subnormal. He had a *huge* head, he was short and stocky, really well-built, but everything frightened him. So we all looked at Dan who was the next oldest, since Larry said, "No, no I don't want to fight." Dan was a musical genius, he had almost won a scholarship but not quite. Anyhow, since Larry had passed up Harry's challenge, Dan put the gloves on with Harry Gibson.

Harry Gibson was a son-of-a-bitch on shining wheels. Even the sun glinted off his gloves in a certain way. He moved with precision, aplomb and grace. He pranced and danced around Dan. Dan held up his gloves and waited. Gibson's first punch streaked in. It cracked like a rifle shot. There were some chickens in a pen in the yard and two of them jumped into the air at the sound. Dan spilled backwards. He was stretched out on the grass, both of his arms spread out like some cheap Christ.

Larry looked at him and said, "I'm going into the house." He walked quickly to the screen door, opened it and was gone.

We walked over to Dan. Gibson stood over him with a little grin on his face. Gene bent down, lifted Dan's head up a bit. "Dan? You all right?"

Dan shook his head and slowly sat up.

"Jesus Christ, the guy's carrying a lethal weapon. Get these gloves off me!"

Gene unlaced one glove and I got the other. Dan stood up and walked toward the back door like an old man. "I'm gonna lay down . . ." He went inside.

Harry Gibson picked up the gloves and looked at Gene. "How about it, Gene?"

Gene spit in the grass. "What the hell you trying to do, knock off the whole family?"

"I know you're the best fighter, Gene, but I'll go easy on you anyhow."

Gene nodded and I laced on his gloves for him. I was a good glove man.

They squared off. Gibson circled around Gene, getting ready. He circled to the right, then he circled to the left. He bobbed and he weaved. Then he stepped in, gave Gene a hard left jab. It landed right between Gene's eyes. Gene backpedaled and Gibson followed. When he got Gene up against the chicken pen he steadied him with a soft left to the forehead and then cracked a hard right to Gene's left temple. Gene slid along the chicken wire until he hit the fence, then he slid along the fence, covering up. He wasn't attempting to fight back. Dan came out of the house with a piece of ice wrapped in a rag. He sat on the porch steps and held the rag to his forehead. Gene retreated along the fence. Harry got him in the corner between the fence and the garage. He looped a left to Gene's gut and when Gene bent over he straightened him with a right uppercut. I didn't like it. Gibson wasn't going easy on Gene like he'd promised. I got excited.

"Hit that fucker back, Gene! He's yellow! Hit him!"

Gibson lowered his gloves, looked at me and walked over. "What did you say, punk?"

"I was rooting my man on," I said.

Dan was over getting the gloves off Gene.

"Did I hear something about being 'yellow'?"

"You said you were going to go easy on him. You didn't. You're hitting him with every shot you've got."

"You callin' me a liar?"

"I'm saying you don't keep your word."

"Come on over and put the gloves on this punk!"

Gene and Dan came over and began putting the gloves on me. "Take it easy on this guy, Hank," Gene said. "Remember he's all tired out from fighting us."

Gene and I had fought barefisted one memorable day from 9 a.m. to 6 p.m. Gene had done pretty good. I had small hands and if you have small hands you've either got to be able to hit hard as hell or else be some kind of a boxer. I was only a little of each. The next day my entire upper body was purple with bruises and I had two fat lips and a couple of loose front teeth. Now I had to fight the guy who had just whipped the guy who had whipped me.

Gibson circled to the left, then the right, then he moved in on me. I didn't see the left jab at all. I don't know where it caught me but I went down from the left jab. It hadn't hurt but I was down. I got up. If the left could do that what would the right do? I had to figure something out.

Harry Gibson began to circle to the left, my left. Instead of circling to my right like he expected, I circled to my left. He looked surprised and as we came together I looped a wild left which caught him high and hard on the head. It felt great. If you can hit a guy once, you can hit him twice.

Then we were facing each other and he came straight at me. Gibson got me with the jab but as it hit me I ducked my head down and to one side as quickly as I could. His right swung around over the top, missing. I moved into him and clinched, giving him a rabbit punch. We broke and I felt like a pro.

"You can take him, Hank!" yelled Gene.

"Go get him, Hank!" yelled Dan.

158

I rushed Gibson and tried a right lead. I missed and his left cross flashed on my jaw. I saw green and yellow and red lights, then he dug a right to my belly. It felt like it went through to my backbone. I grabbed him and clinched. But I wasn't frightened, for a change, and that felt good.

"I'll kill you, you fucker!" I told him.

Then it was just head-to-head, no more boxing. His punches came fast and hard. He was more accurate, had more power, yet I was landing some hard shots too and it made me feel good. The more he hit me the less I felt it. I had my gut sucked in, I liked the action. Then Gene and Dan were between us. They pulled us apart.

"What's wrong?" I asked. "Don't stop this thing! I can take his ass!"

"Cut the shit, Hank," said Gene. "Look at yourself."

I looked down. The front of my shirt was dark with blood and there were splotches of pus. The punches had broken open three or four boils. That hadn't happened in my fight with Gene.

"That's nothing," I said. "That's just bad luck. He hasn't hurt me. Give me a chance and I'll cut him down."

"No, Hank, you'll get an infection or something," said Gene.

"All right, shit," I said, "cut the gloves off me!"

Gene unlaced me. When he got the gloves off I noticed that my hands were trembling, and also my arms to a lesser extent. I put my hands in my pockets. Dan took Harry's gloves off.

Harry looked at me. "You're pretty good, kid."

"Thanks. Well, I'll see you guys . . ."

I walked off. As I walked away I took my hands out of my pockets. Then up the driveway, just at the sidewalk, I stopped, pulled out a cigarette and stuck it into my mouth. When I tried to strike a match my hands were trembling so much I couldn't do it. I gave them a wave, a real nonchalant wave, and walked away.

Back at the house I looked at myself in the mirror. Pretty damn good. I was coming along.

I took off my shirt and threw it under the bed. I'd have to find a way to clean the blood off. I didn't have many shirts and they'd notice a missing one right away. But for me, it had finally been a successful day, and I hadn't had too many of those.

38

Abe Mortenson was bad enough to be around but he was just a fool. You can forgive a fool because he only runs in one direction and doesn't deceive anybody. It's the deceivers who make you feel bad. Jimmy Hatcher had straight black hair, fair skin, he wasn't as big as I was but he kept his shoulders back, dressed better than most of us, and he had a way of getting along with anybody he felt like getting along with. His mother was a bar maid and his father had committed suicide. Jimmy had a nice smile, perfect teeth, and the girls liked him even though he didn't have the money the rich guys had. I would always see him talking to some girl. I don't know what he said to them. I didn't know what any of the guys said to any of them. The girls were impossibly out of reach for me and so I pretended that they didn't exist.

But Hatcher was another matter. I knew he wasn't a fairy but he kept hanging around.

"Listen, Jimmy, why do you follow me around? I don't like anything about you."

"Ah, come on, Hank, we're friends."

"Yeah?"

"Yes."

He even got up once in English class and read an essay called "The Value of Friendship," and while he was reading it he kept glancing at me. It was a stupid essay, soft and standard, but the class applauded when he finished, and I thought, well, that's what people think and what can you do about it? I wrote a counter-essay called, "The Value of No Friendship At All." The teacher didn't let me read it to the class. She gave me a "D."

Jimmy and Baldy and I walked home together from high school each day. (Abe Mortenson lived in the other direction so that saved us from having to walk with him.) One day we were walking along and Jimmy said, "Hey, let's go to my girlfriend's house. I want you to meet her."

"Ah, balls, fuck that," I said.

"No, no," said Jimmy, "she's a nice girl. I want you to meet her. I've finger-fucked her."

I'd seen his girl, Ann Weatherton, she was really beautiful, long brown hair and large brown eyes, quiet, and with a good figure. I'd never spoken to her but I knew she was Jimmy's girl. The rich guys had tried to hit on her but she ignored them. She looked like she was first-rate.

"I've got the key to her house," said Jimmy. "We'll go there and wait for her. She's got a late class."

"Sounds dull to me," I said.

"Ah, come on, Hank," said Baldy, "you're just going to go home and whack-off anyhow."

"That's not always without its own merits," I said.

Jimmy opened the front door with his key and we walked in. A nice clean little house. A small black and white bulldog ran up to Jimmy, wagging its stub tail.

"This is Bones," said Jimmy. "Bones loves me. Watch this!"

Jimmy spit in the palm of his right hand and grabbed Bones' penis and began rubbing it.

"Hey, what the fuck you doing?" asked Baldy.

"They keep Bones on a leash in the yard. He never gets any. He needs *release!*" Jimmy worked away.

Bones' penis got disgustingly red, a thin, long string of dripping inanity. Bones began making whimpering sounds. Jimmy looked up as he worked away. "Hey, you wanna know what our song is? I mean, Ann's song and my song? It's 'When the Deep Purple Falls Over Sleepy Garden Walls.'"

Then Bones was making it. The sperm spurted out and on the carpet. Jimmy stood up and with the sole of his shoe rubbed the come down into the nap of the carpet.

"I'm gonna fuck Ann one of these days. It's getting close. She says she loves me. And I love her too, I love her god-damned cunt."

"You prick," I told Jimmy, "you make me sick."

"I know you don't mean that, Hank," he said.

Jimmy walked into the kitchen. "She's got a nice family. She lives here with her father, mother and brother. Her brother knows I am going to fuck her. He's right. But there's nothing he can do about it because I can beat the shit out of him. He's nothing. Hey, watch this!"

Jimmy opened the refrigerator door and pulled out a bottle of milk. At our place we still had an icebox. The Weathertons were obviously a well-off family. Jimmy pulled out his cock and then peeled the cardboard cap off the bottle and put his cock in there.

"Just a little, you know. They'll never taste it but they'll be drinking my piss . . ."

He pulled his cock out, capped the bottle, shook it, and then placed it back in the refrigerator.

"Now," he said, "here's some jello. They are going to eat jello for dessert tonight. They are also going to eat . . ." He took the bowl of jello out and held it and then we heard a key in the front door and the front door opening. Jimmy quickly put the jello back into the refrigerator and closed the door.

Then Ann walked in. Into the kitchen.

"Ann," said Jimmy, "I want you to meet my good friends, Hank and Baldy."

"Hi!"

"Hi!"

"Hi!"

"*This* one's Baldy. The other guy is Hank."

"Hi."

"Hi."

"Hi."

"I've seen you guys around campus."

"Oh yeah," I said, "we're around there. And we've seen you too."

162

"Yeah," said Baldy.

Jimmy looked at Ann. "You all right, baby?"

"Yes, Jimmy, I've been thinking about you."

She moved toward him and they embraced, then they were kissing. They were standing right in front of us as they were kissing. Jimmy was facing us. We could see his right eye. It winked.

"Well," I said, "we've got to get going."

"Yeah," said Baldy.

We walked out of the kitchen, through the front room and out of there. We walked down the sidewalk toward Baldy's place.

"That guy's really got it made," said Baldy.

"Yeah," I said.

39

One Sunday Jimmy talked me into going to the beach with him. He wanted to go swimming. I didn't want to be seen wearing swimming trunks because my back was covered with boils and scars. Outside of that, I had a good body. But nobody would notice *that*. I had a good chest and great legs but nobody would see that.

There was nothing to do and I didn't have any money and the guys didn't play in the streets on Sunday. I decided that the beach belonged to everybody. I had a right. My scars and boils weren't against the law.

So we got on our bikes and started out. It was fifteen miles. That didn't bother me. I had the legs.

I breezed with Jimmy all the way to Culver City. Then I gradually began to pedal faster. Jimmy pumped, trying to keep up. I could see him getting winded. I pulled out a cigarette and lit it, held out the pack to him. "Want one, Jim?"

"No . . . thanks . . ."

"This beats shooting birds with a beebee gun," I told him. "We ought to do this more often!"

I began pumping harder. I still had plenty of reserve strength.

"This really gets it," I told him. "This beats whacking-off!"

"Hey, slow up a little!"

I looked back at him. "There's nothing like a good friend to go biking with. Come on, friend!"

Then I gave it all I had and pulled away. The wind was blowing in my face. It felt good.

"Hey, wait! WAIT, GOD DAMN IT!" yelled Jimmy.

I started laughing and really opened up. Soon Jim was half-a-block back, a block, two blocks. Nobody knew how good I was, nobody knew what I could do. I was some kind of miracle. The sun tossed yellow everywhere and I cut through it, a crazy knife on wheels. My father was a beggar in the streets of India but all the women in the world loved me . . .

I was traveling at full speed as I reached the signal. I shot through inside the row of waiting cars. Now even the cars were back there behind me. But not for long. A guy and his girl in a green coupe pulled up and drove alongside me.

"Hey, kid!"

"Yeah?" I looked at him. He was a big guy in his twenties with hairy arms and a tattoo.

"Where the fuck do you think you're going?" he asked me.

He was trying to show off in front of his girl. She was a looker, her long blond hair blowing in the wind.

"Up *yours*, buddy!" I told him.

"*What?*"

"I said, 'Up *yours!*'"

I gave him the finger.

He kept driving along beside me.

"You gonna take shit off that kid, Nick?" I heard his girl ask him.

He kept driving along beside me.

"Hey, kid," he said, "I didn't quite hear what you said. Would you mind saying that again?"

"Yeah, say that again," said the looker, her long blond hair blowing in the wind.

That pissed me. She pissed me.

I looked at him. "All right, you want trouble? *Park it.* I'm trouble."

He zoomed ahead of me about half a block, parked, and swung the door open. As he got out I swung wide around him almost into the path of a Chevy who gave me the horn. As I swung around into a side street I could hear the big guy laughing.

After the guy was gone I wheeled back onto Washington Boulevard, went a few blocks, got off the bike and waited for Jim on a bus stop bench. I could see him coming along. When he pulled up I pretended that I was asleep.

"Come on, Hank! Don't give me that shit!"

"Oh, hello, Jim. You here?"

I tried to get Jim to pick a spot on the beach where there weren't too many people. I felt normal standing there in my shirt but when I undressed I was exposed. I hated the other bathers for their unmarred bodies. I hated all the god-damned people who were sunbathing or in the water or eating or sleeping or talking or throwing beachballs. I hated their behinds and their faces and their elbows and their hair and their eyes and their bellybuttons and their bathing suits.

I stretched out on the sand thinking, I should have punched that fat son-of-a-bitch. What the hell did he know?

Jim stretched out beside me.

"What the hell," he said, "let's go swimming."

"Not yet," I said.

The water was full of people. What was the fascination of the beach? Why did people like the beach? Didn't they have anything better to do? What chicken-brained fuckers they were.

"Just think," said Jim, "women go into the water and they piss in there."

"Yeah, and you swallow it."

There would never be a way for me to live comfortably with people. Maybe I'd become a monk. I'd pretend to believe in God and live in a cubicle, play an organ and stay drunk on wine. Nobody would fuck with me. I could go into a cell for months of meditation where I wouldn't have to look at anybody and they could just send in the wine. The trouble was, the black robes were pure wool. They were worse than R.O.T.C. uniforms. I couldn't wear them. I'd have to think of something else.

"Oh, oh," said Jim.

"What is it?"

"There are some girls down there looking at us."

"So what?"

"They're talking and laughing. They might come down here."

"Yeah?"

"Yeah. And if they start coming over I'll warn you. When I do, turn on your back."

166

My chest had only a few boils and scars.

"Don't forget," said Jim, "when I warn you, turn over on your back."

"I heard you."

I had my head down in my arms. I knew that Jim was looking at the girls and smiling. He had a way with them.

"Simple cunts," he said, "they're really stupid."

Why did I come here? I thought. Why is it always only a matter of choosing between something bad and something worse?

"Oh, oh, Hank, here they come!"

I looked up. There were five of them. I rolled over on my back. They walked up giggling and stood there. One of them said, "Hey, these guys are cute!"

"You girls live around here?" Jim asked.

"Oh yeah," one of them said, "we nest with the seagulls!"

They giggled.

"Well," said Jim, "we're eagles. I'm not sure we'd know what to do with five seagulls."

"How do birds do it anyhow?" one of them asked.

"Damned if I know," Jim said, "maybe we can find out."

"Why don't you guys come over to our blanket?" one of them asked.

"Sure," Jim said.

Three of the girls had spoken. The other two had just stood there pulling their bathing suits down over what they didn't want seen.

"Count me out," I said.

"What's wrong with your friend?" asked one of the girls who had been covering her ass.

Jim said, "He's strange."

"What's wrong with him?" asked the last girl.

"He's just strange," said Jim.

He got up and walked off with the girls. I closed my eyes and listened to the waves. Thousands of fish out there, eating each other. Endless mouths and assholes swallowing and shitting. The whole earth was nothing but mouths and assholes swallowing and shitting, and fucking.

I rolled over and watched Jim with the five girls. He was standing up, sticking his chest out and showing off his balls. He didn't have my barrel chest and big legs. He was slim and neat, with that black hair and that little nasty mouth with perfect teeth, and his little round ears and his long neck. I didn't have a neck. Not much of one, anyway. My head seemed to sit on my shoulders. But I was strong, and mean. Not good enough, the ladies liked dandies. If it wasn't for the boils and scars, though, I'd be down there now showing them a thing or two. I'd flash my balls for them, bringing their dead air-headed minds to attention. Me, with my 50-cents-a-week life.

Then I saw the girls leap up and follow Jim into the water. I heard them giggling and screaming like mindless . . . what? No, they were nice. They weren't like grown-ups and parents. They laughed. Things were funny. They weren't afraid to care. There was no sense to life, to the structure of things. D. H. Lawrence had known that. You needed love, but not the kind of love most people used and were used up by. Old D. H. had known something. His buddy Huxley was just an intellectual fidget, but what a marvelous one. Better than G. B. Shaw with that hard keel of a mind always scraping bottom, his labored wit finally only a task, a burden on himself, preventing him from really feeling anything, his brilliant speech finally a bore, scraping the mind and the sensibilities. It was good to read them all though. It made you realize that thoughts and words could be fascinating, if finally useless.

Jim was splashing water on the girls. He was the Water God and they loved him. He was the possibility and the promise. He was great. He knew how to do it. I had read many books but he had read a book that I had never read. He was an artist with his little pair of bathing trunks and his balls and his wicked little look and his round ears. He was the best. I couldn't challenge him any more than I could have challenged that big son-of-a-bitch in the green coupe with the looker whose hair flowed in the wind. They both had got what they deserved. I was just a 50-cent turd floating around in the green ocean of life.

I watched them come out of the water, glistening, smooth-skinned and young, undefeated. I wanted them to want me. But never out of pity. Yet, despite their smooth untouched bodies and minds they still were missing something because they were as yet basically untested. When adversity finally arrived in their lives it might come too late or too hard. I was ready. Maybe.

168

I watched Jim toweling off, using one of their towels. As I watched, somebody's child, a boy of about four came along, picked up a handful of sand and threw it in my face. Then he just stood there, glowering, his sandy stupid little mouth puckered in some kind of victory. He was a daring darling little shit. I wiggled my finger for him to come closer, come, come. He stood there.

"Little boy," I said, "come here. I have a bag of candy-covered shit for you to eat."

The fucker looked, turned and ran off. He had a stupid ass. Two little pear-shaped buttocks wobbling, almost disjointed. But, another enemy gone.

Then Jim, the lady killer, was back. He stood there over me. Glowering also.

"They're gone," he said.

I looked down to where the five girls had been and sure enough they were gone.

"Where did they go?" I asked.

"Who gives a fuck? I've got the phone numbers of the two best ones."

"Best ones for what?"

"For *fucking*, you jerk!"

I stood up.

"I think I'll deck you, jerk!"

His face looked good in the sea wind. I could already see him, knocked down, squirming on the sand, kicking up his white-bottomed feet.

Jim backed off.

"Take it easy, Hank. Look, you can have their phone numbers!"

"Keep them. I don't have your god-damned dumb ears!"

"O.K., O.K., we're friends, remember?"

We walked up the beach to the strand where we had our bicycles locked behind someone's beach house. And as we walked along we both knew whose day it had been, and knocking somebody on their ass could not have changed that, although it might have helped, but not enough. All the way home, on our bikes, I didn't try to show him up as I had earlier. I needed something more. Maybe I needed that blonde in the green coupe with her long hair blowing in the wind.

40

R.O.T.C. (Reserve Officer Training Corps) was for the misfits. Like I said, it was either that or gym. I would have taken gym but I didn't want people to see the boils on my back. There was something wrong with everybody enrolled in R.O.T.C. It almost entirely consisted of guys who didn't like sports or guys whose parents forced them to take R.O.T.C. because they thought it was patriotic. The parents of rich kids tended to be more patriotic because they had more to lose if the country went under. The poor parents were far less patriotic, and then often professed their patriotism only because it was expected or because it was the way they had been raised. Subconsciously they knew it wouldn't be any better or worse for *them* if the Russians or the Germans or the Chinese or the Japanese ran the country, especially if they had dark skin. Things might even improve. Anyhow, since many of the parents of Chelsey High were rich, we had one of the biggest R.O.T.C.'s in the city.

So we marched around in the sun and learned to dig latrines, cure snake-bite, tend the wounded, tie tourniquets, bayonet the enemy; we learned about hand grenades, infiltration, deployment of troops, maneuvers, retreats, advances, mental and physical discipline; we got on the firing range, bang bang, and we got our marksmen's medals. We had actual field maneuvers, we went out into the woods and waged a mock war. We crawled on our bellies toward each other with our rifles. We were very serious. Even I was serious. There was something about it that got your blood going. It was stupid and we all knew it was stupid, most of us, but something clicked in our brains and we really wanted to get involved in it. We had an old retired Army man, Col. Sussex. He was getting senile and drooled, little trickles of saliva running out of the corners of his mouth and down, around and under his chin. He never said anything. He just stood around in his uniform covered with medals and drew his pay from the high school. During our mock maneuvers he carried around a clipboard and kept score. He stood on a high hill and made marks on the clipboard—probably. But he never told us who won. Each side claimed victory. It made for bad feelings.

Lt. Herman Beechcroft was best. His father owned a bakery and a hotel catering service, whatever that was. Anyhow, he was best. He always gave the same speech before a maneuver.

"Remember, you must *hate* the enemy! They want to rape your mother and sisters! Do you want those monsters to rape your mother and sisters?"

Lt. Beechcroft had almost no chin at all. His face dropped away suddenly and where the jaw bone should have been there was only a little button. We weren't sure if it was a deformity or not. But his eyes were magnificent in their fury, large blue blazing symbols of war and victory.

"*Whitlinger!*"

"Yes, sir!"

"Would you want those guys raping your mother?"

"My mother's dead, sir."

"Oh, sorry . . . *Drake!*"

"Yes, sir!"

"Would you want those guys raping your mother?"

"*No, sir!*"

"Good. Remember, this is *war!* We accept mercy but we do not give mercy. You must hate the enemy. *Kill him!* A dead man can't defeat you. Defeat is a disease! Victory writes history! NOW LET'S GO GET THOSE COCKSUCKERS!"

We deployed our line, sent out the advance scouts and began crawling through the brush. I could see Col. Sussex on his hill with his clipboard. It was the Blues vs. the Greens. We each had a piece of colored rag tied around our upper right arm. We were the Blues. Crawling through those bushes was pure hell. It was hot. There were bugs, dust, rocks, thorns. I didn't know where I was.

171

Our squad leader, Kozak, had vanished somewhere. There was no communication. We were fucked. Our mothers were going to get raped. I kept crawling forward, bruising and scratching myself, feeling lost and scared, but really feeling more the fool. All this vacant land and empty sky, hills, streams, acres and acres. Who owned it all? Probably the father of one of the rich guys. We weren't going to capture anything. The whole place was on loan to the high school. NO SMOKING. I crawled forward. We had no air cover, no tanks, nothing. We were just a bunch of fairies out on a half-assed maneuver without food, without women, without reason. I stood up, walked over and sat down with my back against a tree, put my rifle down and waited.

Everybody was lost and it didn't matter. I pulled my arm band off and waited for a Red Cross Ambulance or something. War was probably hell but the in-between parts were boring.

Then the bushes cracked open and a guy leaped out and saw me. He had on a Green arm band. A rapist. He pointed his rifle at me. I had no arm band on, it was down in the grass. He wanted to take a prisoner. I knew him. He was Harry Missions. His father owned a lumber company. I sat there against the tree.

"Blue or Green?" he hollered at me.

"I'm Mata Hari."

"A spy! I take spies!"

"Come on, cut the shit, Harry. This is a game for children. Don't bother me with your fetid melodrama."

The bushes cracked open again and there was Lt. Beechcroft. Missions and Beechcroft faced each other.

"I hereby take you prisoner!" screamed Beechcroft at Missions.

"I hereby take you prisoner!" screamed Missions at Beechcroft.

They both were really nervous and angry, I could feel it.

Beechcroft drew his sabre. "Surrender or I'll run you through!"

Missions grabbed his gun by the barrel. "Come over here and I'll knock your god-damned head off!"

Then the bushes cracked open everywhere. The screaming had attracted both the Blues and the Greens. I sat against the tree while they mixed it up. There was dust and scuffling and now and then the evil sound of rifle stock against skull. "Oh, Jesus! Oh, my God!" Some bodies were down. Rifles were lost. There were fist fights and headlocks. I saw two guys with Green arm bands locked

172

in a death-grip. Then Col. Sussex appeared. He blew frantically on his whistle. Spit sprayed everywhere. Then he ran over with his swagger stick and began beating the troops with it. He was good. It cut like a whip and sliced like a razor.

"Oh shit! I QUIT!"

"No, *stop!* Jesus! Mercy!"

"Mother!"

The troops separated and stood looking at each other. Col. Sussex picked up his clipboard. His uniform was unwrinkled. His medals were still in place. His cap sat at the correct angle. He flipped his swagger stick, caught it, and walked off. We followed.

We climbed into the old army trucks with their ripped canvas sides and tops that had brought us. The engines started and we drove off. We faced each other on the long wooden benches. We had come out, all the Blues in one of the trucks, all the Greens in the other. Now we were mixed together, sitting there, most of us looking down at our scuffed and dusty shoes, being jiggled this way and that, to the left, to the right, up and down, as the truck tires hit the ruts in the old roads. We were tired and we were defeated and we were frustrated. The war was over.

41

R.O.T.C. kept me away from sports while the other guys practiced every day. They made the school teams, won their letters and got the girls. My days were spent mostly marching around in the sun. All you ever saw were the backs of some guy's ears and his buttocks. I quickly became disenchanted with military proceedings. The others shined their shoes brightly and seemed to go through maneuvers with relish. I couldn't see any sense in it. They were just getting shaped up in order to get their balls blown off later. On the other hand, I couldn't see myself crouched down in a football helmet, shoulder pads laced on, decked out in Blue and White, #69, trying to block some mean son-of-a-bitch from across town, trying to move out some brute with tacos on his breath so that the son of the district attorney could slant off left tackle for six yards. The problem was you had to keep choosing between one evil or another, and no matter what you chose, they sliced a little bit more off you, until there was nothing left. At the age of 25 most people were finished. A whole god-damned nation of assholes driving automobiles, eating, having babies, doing everything in the worst way possible, like voting for the presidential candidate who reminded them most of themselves.

I had no interests. I had no interest in anything. I had no idea how I was going to escape. At least the others had some taste for life. They seemed to understand something that I didn't understand. Maybe I was lacking. It was possible. I often felt inferior. I just wanted to get away from them. But there was no place to go. Suicide? Jesus Christ, just more work. I felt like sleeping for five years but they wouldn't let me.

So there I was, at Chelsey High, still in the R.O.T.C., still with my boils. That always reminded me of how fucked up I was.

It was a grand day. One man from each squad who had won the Manual of Arms competition within his squad stepped into a long line where the final competition was to be held. Somehow I had won the competition in my squad. I had no idea how. I was no hot shot.

It was Saturday. Many mothers and fathers were in the stands. Somebody blew a bugle. A sword flashed. Commands rang out. Right shoulder arms! Left shoulder arms! Rifles hit shoulders, rifle butts hit the ground, rifle stocks slammed into shoulders again. Little girls sat in the stands in their blue and green and yellow and orange and pink and white dresses. It was hot, it was boring, it was insanity.

"Chinaski, you are competing for the honor of our squadron!"

"Yes, Corporal Monty."

All those little girls in the stands each waiting for her lover, for her winner, for her corporate executive. It was sad. A flock of pigeons, frightened by a piece of paper blown in the wind, flapped noisily away. I yearned to be drunk on beer. I wanted to be anywhere but here.

As each man made an error he dropped out of line. Soon there were six, then five, then three. I was still there. I had no desire to win. I knew that I wouldn't win. I'd soon be out of it. I wanted to be out of there. I was tired and bored. And covered with boils. I didn't give cream-shit for what they were chasing. But I couldn't make an obvious error. Corporal Monty would be hurt.

Then there were just two of us. Me and Andrew Post. Post was a darling. His father was a great criminal lawyer. He was in the stands with his wife, Andrew's mother. Post was sweating but determined. We both knew that he would win. I could feel the energy and all the energy was his.

175

It's all right, I thought, he needs it, they need it. It's the way it works. It's the way it's meant to work.

We went on and on, repeating various Manual of Arms maneuvers. From the corner of my eye I saw the goal posts on the field and I thought, maybe if I had tried harder I could have become a great football player.

"ORDER!" shouted the Commander and I ripped my bolt home. There had been only one click. There had been no click to my left. Andrew Post had frozen. A little moan rose from the grandstands.

"ARMS!" the Commander finished and I completed the maneuver. Post did too but his bolt was open . . .

The actual ceremony for the winner came some days later. Luckily for me there were other awards to be given. I stood and waited with the others as Col. Sussex came down the line. My boils were worse than ever and as always when I was wearing that itchy brown wool uniform the sun was up and hot and making me conscious of every wool fiber in that son-of-a-bitching shirt. I wasn't much of a soldier and everybody knew it. I had won on a fluke because I hadn't cared enough to be nervous. I felt badly for Col. Sussex because I knew what he was thinking and maybe he knew what I was thinking: that his peculiar type of devotion and courage didn't seem exceptional to me.

Then he was standing right in front of me. I stood at attention but managed to sneak a peek at him. He had his saliva in good order. Maybe when he was pissed-off it dried up. In spite of the heat there was a good west wind blowing. Col. Sussex pinned the medal on me. Then he reached out and shook my hand.

"Congratulations," he said. Then he smiled at me. And moved on.

Why the old fuck. Maybe he wasn't so bad after all . . .

Walking home I had the medal in my pocket. Who was Col. Sussex? Just some guy who had to shit like the rest of us. Everybody had to conform, find a mold to fit into. Doctor, lawyer, soldier—it didn't matter what it was. Once in the mold you had to

176

push forward. Sussex was as helpless as the next man. Either you managed to do something or you starved in the streets.

I was alone, walking. On my side of the street just before reaching the first boulevard on the long walk home there was a small neglected store. I stopped and looked in the window. Various objects were on display with their soiled price tags. I saw some candle holders. There was an electric toaster. A table lamp. The glass of the window was dirty inside and out. Through the rather dusty brown smear I saw two toy dogs grinning. A miniature piano. These things were for sale. They didn't look very appealing. There weren't any customers in the store and I couldn't see a clerk either. It was a place I had passed many times before but had never stopped to examine.

I looked in and I liked it. There was nothing happening there. It was a place to rest, to sleep. Everything in there was dead. I could see myself happily employed as a clerk there so long as no customers entered the door.

I turned away from the window and walked along some more. Just before reaching the boulevard I stepped into the street and saw an enormous storm drain almost at my feet. It was like a great black mouth leading down to the bowels of the earth. I reached into my pocket and took the medal and tossed it toward the black opening. It went right in. It disappeared into the darkness.

Then I stepped onto the sidewalk and walked back home. When I got there my parents were busy with various cleaning chores. It was a Saturday. Now I had to mow and clip the lawn, water it and the flowers.

I changed into my working clothes, went out, and with my father watching me from beneath his dark and evil eyebrows, I opened the garage doors and carefully pulled the mower out backwards, the mower blades not turning then, but waiting.

42

"You ought to try to be like Abe Mortenson," said my mother, "he gets straight A's. Why can't you ever get any A's?"

"Henry is dead on his ass," said my father. "Sometimes I can't believe he's my son."

"Don't you *want* to be happy, Henry?" asked my mother. "You never smile. Smile and be happy."

"Stop feeling sorry for yourself," said my father. "Be a man!"

"Smile, Henry!"

"What's going to become of you? How the hell you going to make it? You don't have any get up and go!"

"Why don't you go see Abe? Talk to him, learn to be like him," said my mother . . .

I knocked on the door of the Mortensons' apartment. The door opened. It was Abe's mother.

"You can't see Abe. He's busy studying."

"I know, Mrs. Mortenson. I just want to see him a minute."

"All right. His room is right down there."

I walked on down. He had his own desk. He was sitting with a book open on top of two other books. I knew the book by the color of the cover: Civics. Civics, for Christ sake, on a Sunday.

Abe looked up and saw me. He spit on his hands and then turned back to the book. "Hi," he said, looking down at the page.

"I bet you've read that same page ten times over, sucker."

"I've got to memorize everything."

"It's just crap."

"I've got to pass my tests."

"You ever thought of fucking a girl?"

"What?" he spit on his hands.

"You ever looked up a girl's dress and wanted to see more? Ever thought about her snatch?"

"That's not important."

"It's important to her."

"I've got to study."

"We're having a pick-up game of baseball. Some of the guys from school."

"On Sunday?"

"What's wrong with Sunday? People do a lot of things on Sunday."

"But baseball?"

"The pros play on Sunday."

"But they get paid."

"Are you getting paid for reading that same page over and over? Come on, get some air in your lungs, it might clear your head."

"All right. But just for a little while."

He got up and I followed him up the hall and into the front room. We walked toward the door.

"Abe, where are you going?"

"I'll just be gone a little while."

"All right. But hurry back. You've got to study."

"I know . . ."

"All right, Henry, you make sure he gets back."

"I'll take care of him, Mrs. Mortenson."

There was Baldy and Jimmy Hatcher and some other guys from school and a few guys from the neighborhood. We only had seven guys on each side which left a couple of defensive holes, but I liked that. I played center field. I had gotten good, I was catching up. I covered most of the outfield. I was fast. I liked to play in close to grab the short ones. But what I liked best was running back to grab those high hard ones hit over my head. That's what Jigger Statz did with the Los Angeles Angels. He only hit about .280 but the hits he took away from the other team made him as valuable as a .500 hitter.

Every Sunday a dozen or more girls from the neighborhood would come and watch us. I ignored them. They really screamed when something exciting happened. We played hardball and we each had our own glove, even Mortenson. He had the best one. It had hardly been used.

I trotted out to center and the game began. We had Abe at second base. I slammed my fist into my mitt and hollered in at Mortenson, "Hey, Abe, you ever jacked-off into a raw egg? You don't have to die to go to heaven!"

I heard the girls laughing.

The first guy struck out. He wasn't much. I struck out a lot too but I was the hardest hitter of them all. I could really put the wood to it: out of the lot and into the street. I always crouched low over the plate. I looked like a wound-up spring standing there.

Each moment of the game was exciting to me. All the games I had missed mowing that lawn, all those early school days of being chosen next-to-last were over. I had blossomed. I had something and I knew I had it and it felt good.

"Hey, Abe!" I yelled in. "With all that spit you don't need a raw egg!"

The next guy connected hard with one but it was high, very high and I ran back to make an over-the-shoulder catch. I sprinted back, feeling great, knowing that I would create the miracle once again.

Shit. The ball sailed into a tall tree at the back of the lot. Then I saw the ball bouncing down through the branches. I stationed myself and waited. No good, it was going left. I ran left. Then it bounced back to the right. I ran right. It hit a branch, lingered there, then slithered through some leaves and dropped into my glove.

The girls screamed.

I fired the ball into our pitcher on one bounce then trotted back into shallow center. The next guy struck out. Our pitcher, Harvey Nixon, had a good fireball.

We changed sides and I was first up. I had never seen the guy on the mound. He wasn't from Chelsey. I wondered where he was from. He was big all over, big head, big mouth, big ears, big body. His hair fell down over his eyes and he looked like a fool. His hair was brown and his eyes were green and those green eyes stared at me through that hair as if he hated me. It looked like his left arm was longer than his right. His left arm was his pitching arm. I'd never faced a lefty, not in hardball. But they could all be had. Turn them upside down and they were all alike.

"Kitten" Floss, they called him. Some kitten. 190 pounds.

"Come on, Butch, hit one out!" one of the girls pleaded.

They called me "Butch" because I played a good game and ignored them.

The Kitten looked at me from between his big ears. I spit on the plate, dug in and waved my bat.

The Kitten nodded like he was getting a signal from the catcher. He was just showboating. Then he looked around the infield. More showboating. It was for the benefit of the girls. He couldn't keep his pecker-mind off of snatch-thoughts.

He took his wind-up. I watched that ball in his left hand. My eyes never left that ball. I had learned the secret. You concentrated on the ball and followed it all the way in until it reached the plate and then you murdered it with the wood.

I watched the ball leave his fingers through a blaze of sun. It was a murderous humming blur, but it could be had. It was below my knees and far out of the strike zone. His catcher had to dive to get it.

"Ball one," mumbled the old neighborhood fart who umpired our games. He was a night watchman in a department store and he liked to talk to the girls. "I got two daughters at home just like you girls. Real cute. They wear tight dresses too." He liked to crouch over the plate and show them his big buttocks. That's all he had, that and one gold tooth.

The catcher threw the ball back to Kitten Floss.

"Hey, Pussy!" I yelled out to him.

"You talkin' to me?"

"I'm talking to you, short-arm. You gotta come closer than that or I'll have to call a cab."

"The next one is all yours," he told me.

"Good," I said. I dug in.

He went through his routine again, nodding like he was getting a sign, checking the infield. Those green eyes stared at me through that dirty brown hair. I watched him wind-up. I saw the ball leave his fingers, a dark fleck against the sky in the sun and then suddenly it was zooming toward my skull. I dropped in my tracks, feeling it brush the hair of my head.

"Strike one," mumbled the old fart.

"What?" I yelled. The catcher was still holding the ball. He was as surprised at the call as I was. I took the ball from him and showed it to the umpire.

"What's this?" I asked him.

"It's a baseball."

"Fine. Remember what it looks like."

I took the ball and walked out to the mound. The green eyes didn't flinch under the dirty hair. But the mouth opened up just a bit, like a frog sucking air.

I walked up to Kitten.

"I don't swing with my head. The next time you do that I am going to jam this thing right up through your shorts and past where you forget to wipe."

I handed him the ball and walked back to the plate. I dug in and waved my bat.

"One and one," said the old fart.

Floss kicked dirt around on the mound. He stared off into left field. There was nothing out there except a starving dog scratching his ear. Floss looked in for a sign. He was thinking of the girls, trying to look good. The old fart crouched low, spreading his dumb buttocks, also trying to look good. I was probably one of the few with his mind on the business at hand.

The time came, Kitten Floss went into his wind-up. That left hand windmill could panic you if you let it. You had to be patient and wait for the ball. Finally they had to let it go. Then it was yours to destroy and the harder they threw it in the harder you could hit it out of there.

I saw the ball leave his fingers as one of the girls screamed. Floss hadn't lost his zip. The ball looked like a bee-bee, only it got larger and it was headed right for my skull again. All I knew was that I was trying to find the dirt as fast as I could. I got a mouthful.

"SEERIKE TWO!" I heard the old fart yell. He couldn't even pronounce the word. Get a man who works for nothing and you get a man who just likes to hang around.

I got up and brushed the dirt off. It was even down in my shorts. My mother was going to ask me, "Henry, how did you ever get your shorts so dirty? Now don't make that face. Smile, and be happy!"

I walked to the mound. I stood right there. Nobody said anything. I just looked at Kitten. I had the bat in my hand. I took the bat by the end and pressed it against his nose. He slapped it away. I turned and walked back toward the plate. Halfway there I stopped. I turned and stared at him again. Then I walked to the plate.

I dug in and waved my bat. This one was going to be mine. The Kitten peered in for the non-existent sign. He looked a long time, then shook his head, no. He kept staring through that dirty hair with those green eyes.

I waved my bat more powerfully.

"*Hit it out, Butch!*" screamed one of the girls.

"*Butch! Butch! Butch!*" screamed another girl.

Then the Kitten turned his back on us and just stared out into center field.

"Time," I said and stepped out of the box. There was a very cute girl in an orange dress. Her hair was blond and it hung straight down, like a yellow waterfall, beautiful, and I caught her eye for a moment and she said, "Butch, please do it."

"Shut up," I said and stepped back into the box.

The pitch came. I saw it all the way. It was my pitch. Unfortunately, I was looking for the duster. I wanted the duster so I could go out to the mound and kill or be killed. The ball sailed right over the center of the plate. By the time I adjusted the best I could do was swing weakly over the top of it as it went by.

The bastard had suckered me all the way.

He got me on three straight strikes next time. I swear he must have been at least 23 years old. Probably a semi-pro.

One of our guys finally did get a single off him.

But I was good in the field. I made some catches. I moved out there. I knew that the more I saw of the Kitten's fireball the more I was apt to solve it. He wasn't trying to knock out my brains anymore. He didn't have to. He was just smoking them down the middle. I hoped it was only a matter of time before I golfed one out of there.

But things got worse and worse. I didn't like it. The girls didn't either. Not only was green eyes great on the mound, he was great at the plate. The first two times up he hit a homer and a double. The third time up he swung under a pitch and looped a high blooper between Abe at second base and me in center field. I came charging in, the girls screaming, but Abe kept looking up and back over his shoulder, his mouth drooping down, looking up, looking like a fool really, that wet mouth open. I came charging in screaming, "It's mine!" It was really his but somehow I couldn't bear to let him make the catch. The guy was nothing but an idiot book-reader and I didn't really like him so I came charging in very hard as the ball dropped. We crashed into one another, the ball popped out of his glove and into the air as he fell to the ground, and I caught the ball off his glove.

I stood there over him as he lay on the ground.

"Get up, you dumb bastard," I told him.

Abe stayed on the ground. He was crying. He was holding his left arm.

"I think my arm is broken," he said.

"Get up, chickenshit."

Abe finally got up and walked off the field, crying and holding his arm.

I looked around. "All right," I said, "let's play ball!"

But everybody was walking away, even the girls. The game was evidently over. I hung around awhile and then I started walking home . . .

Just before dinner the phone rang. My mother answered it. Her voice became very excited. She hung up and I heard her talking to my father.

Then she came into my bedroom.

"Please come to the front room," she said.

I walked in and sat on the couch. They each had a chair. It was always that way. Chairs meant you belonged. The couch was for visitors.

184

"Mrs. Mortenson just phoned. They've taken x-rays. You broke her son's arm."

"It was an accident," I said.

"She says she is going to sue us. She'll get a Jewish lawyer. They'll take everything we have."

"We don't have very much."

My mother was one of those silent criers. As she cried the tears came faster and faster. Her cheeks were starting to glisten in the evening twilight.

She wiped her eyes. They were a dull light brown.

"Why did you break that boy's arm?"

"It was a pop-up. We both went for it."

"What is this 'pop-up'?"

"Whoever gets it, gets it."

"So you got the 'pop-up'?"

"Yes."

"But how can this 'pop-up' help us? The Jewish lawyer will still have the broken arm on his side."

I got up and walked back to my bedroom to wait for dinner. My father hadn't said anything. He was confused. He was worried about losing what little he had but at the same time he was very proud of a son who could break somebody's arm.

43

Jimmy Hatcher worked part time in a grocery store. While none of us could get jobs he could always get one. He had his little movie star face and his mother had a great body. With his face and her body he didn't have trouble finding employment.

"Why don't you come up to the apartment after dinner to-night?" he asked me one day.

"What for?"

"I steal all the beer I want. I take it out the back. We can drink the beer."

"Where you got it?"

"In the refrigerator."

"Show me."

We were about a block away from his place. We walked over. In the hallway Jimmy said, "Wait a minute, I've got to check the mail." He took out his key and opened the lock box. It was empty. He locked it again.

"My key opens this woman's box. Watch."

Jimmy opened the box and pulled out a letter and opened it. He read the letter to me. "Dear Betty: I know that this check is late and that you've been waiting for it. I lost my job. I have found another one, but it put me behind. Here's the check, finally. I hope that everything is all right with you. Love, Don."

Jimmy took the check and looked at it. He tore it up and he tore the letter up and he put the pieces in his coat pocket. Then he locked the mailbox.

"Come on."

We went into his apartment and into the kitchen and he opened the refrigerator. It was packed with cans of beer.

"Does your mother know?"

"Sure. She drinks it."

He closed the refrigerator.

"Jim, did your father really blow his brains out because of your mother?"

"Yeah. He was on the telephone. He told her he had a gun. He said, 'If you don't come back to me I'm going to kill myself. Will you come back to me?' And my mother said, 'No.' There was a shot and that was that."

"What did your mother do?"

"She hung up."

"All right, I'll see you tonight."

I told my parents that I was going over to Jimmy's to do some homework with him. My kind of homework, I thought to myself.

"Jimmy's a nice boy," my mother said.

My father didn't say anything.

Jimmy got the beer out and we began. I really liked it. Jimmy's mother worked at a bar until 2 a.m. We had the place to ourselves.

"Your mother really has a body, Jim. How come some women have great bodies and most of the others look like they're deformed? Why can't all women have great bodies?"

"God, I don't know. Maybe if women were all the same we'd get bored with them."

"Drink some more. You drink too slow."

"O.K."

"Maybe after a few beers I'll beat the shit out of you."

"We're friends, Hank."

"I don't have any friends. Drink up!"

"All right. What's the hurry?"

"You've got to slam them down to get the effect."

We opened some more cans of beer.

"If I was a woman I'd go around with my skirt hiked up giving all the men hard-ons," Jimmy said.

"You make me sick."

"My mother knew a guy who drank her piss."

"What?"

"Yeah. They'd drink all night and then he'd lay down in the bathtub and she'd piss in his mouth. Then he'd give her twenty-five dollars."

"She told you that?"

"Since my father died she confides in me. It's like I've taken his place."

"You mean . . . ?"

"Oh, no. She just confides."

"Like the guy in the tub?"

"Yeah, like him."

"Tell me some more stuff."

"No."

"Come on, drink up. Does anybody eat your mother's shit?"

"Don't talk that way."

I finished the can of beer in my hand and threw it across the room.

"I like this joint. I might move in here."

I walked to the refrigerator and brought back a new six-pack.

"I'm one tough son-of-a-bitch," I said. "You're lucky I let you hang around me."

"We're friends, Hank."

I jammed a can of beer under his nose.

"Here, drink this!"

I went to the bathroom to piss. It was a very ladylike bathroom, brightly colored towels, deep pink floormats. Even the toilet seat was pink. She sat her big white ass on there and her name was Clare. I looked at my virgin cock.

"I'm a man," I said. "I can whip anybody's ass."

"I need the bathroom, Hank . . ." Jim was at the door.

He went into the bathroom. I heard him puking.

"Ah, shit . . ." I said and opened a new can of beer.

After a few minutes, Jim came out and sat in a chair. He looked very pale. I stuck a can of beer under his nose.

"Drink up! Be a man! You were man enough to steal it, now be man enough to drink it!"

"Just let me rest a while."

"Drink it!"

I sat down on the couch. Getting drunk was good. I decided that I would always like getting drunk. It took away the obvious and maybe if you could get away from the obvious often enough, you wouldn't become obvious yourself.

I looked over at Jimmy.

"Drink up, punk."

I threw my empty beer can across the room.

"Tell me some more about your mother, Jimmy boy. What did she say about the man who drank her piss in the bathtub?"

"She said, 'There's a sucker born every minute.'"

"Jim."

"Uh?"

"Drink up. Be a man!"

He lifted his beer can. Then he ran to the bathroom and I heard him puking again. He came out after a while and sat in his chair. He didn't look well. "I've got to lay down," he said.

"Jimmy," I said, "I'm going to wait around until your mother comes home."

Jimmy got up from his chair and started walking toward the bedroom.

"When she comes home I'm going to fuck her, Jimmy."

He didn't hear me. He just walked into the bedroom.

I went into the kitchen and came back with more beer.

I sat and drank the beer and waited for Clare. Where *was* that whore? I couldn't allow this kind of thing. I ran a tight ship.

I got up and walked into the bedroom. Jim was face down on the bed, all his clothes on, his shoes on. I walked back out.

Well, it was obvious that boy had no belly for booze. Clare needed a man. I sat down and opened another can of beer. I took a good hit. I found a pack of cigarettes on the coffee table and lit one.

I don't know how many more beers I drank waiting for Clare but finally I heard the key in the door and it opened. There was Clare of the body and the bright blond hair. That body stood on those high heels and it swayed just a little. No artist could have imagined it better. Even the walls stared at her, the lampshades, the chairs, the rug. Magic. Standing there . . .

"Who the hell are you? What is this?"

"Clare, we've met. I'm Hank. Jimmy's friend."

"Get out of here!"

I laughed. "I'm movin' in, baby, it's you and me!"

"Where's Jimmy?"

She ran into the bedroom, then came back out.

"You little prick! What's going on here?"

I picked up a cigarette, lit it. I grinned.

"You're beautiful when you're angry . . ."

"You're nothing but a god-damned little kid drunk on beer. Go home."

"Sit down, baby. Have a beer."

Clare sat down. I was very surprised when she did that.

"You go to Chelsey, don't you?" she asked.

"Yeah. Jim and I are buddies."

"You're Hank."

"Yes."

"He's told me about you."

I handed Clare a can of beer. My hand shook. "Here, have a drink, baby."

She opened the beer and took a sip.

I looked at Clare, lifted my beer and had a hit. She was plenty of woman, a Mae West type, wore the same kind of tight-fitting gown—big hips, big legs. And breasts. Startling breasts.

Clare crossed her wondrous legs, a bit of skirt falling back. Her legs were full and golden and the stockings fit like skin.

"I've met your mother," she said.

I drained my can of beer and put it down by my feet. I opened a new one, took a sip, then looked at her, not knowing whether to look at her breasts or at her legs or into her tired face.

"I'm sorry that I got your son drunk. But I've got to tell you something."

She turned her head, lighting a cigarette as she did so, then faced me again.

"Yes?"

"Clare, I love you."

She didn't laugh. She just gave me a little smile, the corners of her mouth turning up a little.

"Poor boy. You're nothing but a little chicken just out of the egg."

It was true but it angered me. Maybe because it was true. The dream and the beer wanted it to be something else. I took another drink and looked at her and said, "Cut the shit. Lift your skirt. Show me some leg. Show me some flank."

"You're just a boy."

Then I said it. I don't know where the words came from, but I said it, "I could tear you in half, baby, if you gave me the chance."

"Yeah?"

"Yeah."

"All right. Let's see."

Then she did it. Just like that. She uncrossed her legs and pulled her skirt back.

She didn't have on panties.

I saw her huge white upper flanks, rivers of flesh. There was a large protruding wart on the inside of her left thigh. And there was a jungle of tangled hair between her legs, but it was not bright yellow like the hair on her head, it was brown and shot with grey, old like some sick bush dying, lifeless and sad.

I stood up.

"I've got to go, Mrs. Hatcher."

"Christ, I thought you wanted to *party!*"

"Not with your son in the other room, Mrs. Hatcher."

"Don't worry about him, Hank. He's passed out."

"No, Mrs. Hatcher, I've *really* got to go."

"All right, get out of here you god-damned little piss-ant!"

I closed the door behind me and walked down the hall of the apartment building and out into the street.

To think, somebody had suicided for that.

The night suddenly looked good. I walked along toward my parents' house.

44

I could see the road ahead of me. I was poor and I was going to stay poor. But I didn't particularly want money. I didn't know what I wanted. Yes, I did. I wanted someplace to hide out, someplace where one didn't have to do anything. The thought of being something didn't only appall me, it sickened me. The thought of being a lawyer or a councilman or an engineer, anything like that, seemed impossible to me. To get married, to have children, to get trapped in the family structure. To go someplace to work every day and to return. It was impossible. To do things, simple things, to be part of family picnics, Christmas, the 4th of July, Labor Day, Mother's Day . . . was a man born just to endure those things and then die? I would rather be a dishwasher, return alone to a tiny room and drink myself to sleep.

My father had a master plan. He told me, "My son, each man during his lifetime should buy a house. Finally he dies and leaves that house to his son. Then his son gets his own house and dies, leaves both houses to *his* son. That's two houses. That son gets his own house, that's three houses . . ."

The family structure. Victory over adversity through the family. He believed in it. Take the family, mix with God and Country, add the ten-hour day and you had what was needed.

I looked at my father, at his hands, his face, his eyebrows, and I knew that this man had nothing to do with me. He was a stranger. My mother was non-existent. I was cursed. Looking at my father I saw nothing but indecent dullness. Worse, he was even more afraid to fail than most others. Centuries of peasant blood and peasant training. The Chinaski bloodline had been thinned by a series of peasant-servants who had surrendered their real lives for fractional and illusionary gains. Not a man in the line who said, "I don't want a house, I want a *thousand* houses, *now!*"

He had sent me to that rich high school hoping that the ruler's attitude would rub off on me as I watched the rich boys screech up in their cream-colored coupes and pick up the girls in bright dresses. Instead I learned that the poor usually stay poor. That the young rich smell the stink of the poor and learn to find it a bit amusing. They had to laugh, otherwise it would be too terrifying. They'd learned that, through the centuries. I would never forgive the girls for getting into those cream-colored coupes with the laughing boys. They couldn't help it, of course, yet you always think, maybe . . . But no, there weren't any maybes. Wealth meant victory and victory was the only reality.

What woman chooses to live with a dishwasher?

Throughout high school I tried not to think too much about how things might eventually turn out for me. It seemed better to delay thinking . . .

Finally it was the day of the Senior Prom. It was held in the girls' gym with live music, a real band. I don't know why but I walked over that night, the two-and-one-half miles from my parents' place. I stood outside in the dark and I looked in there, through the wire-covered window, and I was astonished. All the girls looked very grown-up, stately, lovely, they were in long dresses, and they all looked beautiful. I almost didn't recognize them. And the boys in their tuxes, they looked great, they danced so straight, each of them holding a girl in his arms, their faces pressed against the girl's hair. They all danced beautifully and the music was loud and clear and good, powerful.

Then I caught a glimpse of my reflection staring in at them— boils and scars on my face, my ragged shirt. I was like some jungle animal drawn to the light and looking in. Why had I come? I felt sick. But I kept watching. The dance ended. There was a pause. Couples spoke easily to each other. It was natural and civilized.

Where had they learned to converse and to dance? I couldn't converse or dance. Everybody knew something I didn't know. The girls looked so good, the boys so handsome. I would be too terrified to even look at one of those girls, let alone be close to one. To look into her eyes or dance with her would be beyond me.

And yet I knew that what I saw wasn't as simple and good as it appeared. There was a price to be paid for it all, a general falsity, that could be easily believed, and could be the first step down a dead-end street. The band began to play again and the boys and girls began to dance again and the lights revolved overhead throwing shades of gold, then red, then blue, then green, then gold again on the couples. As I watched them I said to myself, someday my dance will begin. When that day comes I will have something that they don't have.

But then it got to be too much for me. I hated them. I hated their beauty, their untroubled youth, and as I watched them dance through the magic colored pools of light, holding each other, feeling so good, little unscathed children, temporarily in luck, I hated them because they had something I had not yet had, and I said to myself, I said to myself again, *someday I will be as happy as any of you, you will see.*

They kept dancing, and I repeated it to them.

Then there was a sound behind me.

"Hey! What are you doing?"

It was an old man with a flashlight. He had a head like a frog's head.

"I'm watching the dance."

He held the flashlight right up under his nose. His eyes were round and large, they gleamed like a cat's eyes in the moonlight. But his mouth was shriveled, collapsed, and his head was round. It had a peculiar senseless roundness that reminded me of a pumpkin trying to play pundit.

"Get your ass out of here!"

He ran the flashlight up and down all over me.

"Who are you?" I asked.

"I'm the night custodian. Get your ass out of here before I call the cops!"

"What for? This is the Senior Prom and I'm a senior."

He flashed his light into my face. The band was playing "Deep Purple."

194

"Bullshit!" he said. "You're at least 22 years old!"

"I'm in the yearbook, Class of 1939, graduating class, Henry Chinaski."

"Why aren't you in there dancing?"

"Forget it. I'm going home."

"*Do that.*"

I walked off. I kept walking. His flashlight leaped on the path, the light following me. I walked off campus. It was a nice warm night, almost hot. I thought I saw some fireflies but I wasn't sure.

45

Graduation Day. We filed in with our caps and gowns to "Pomp and Circumstance." I suppose that in our three years we must have learned something. Our ability to spell had probably improved and we had grown in size. I was still a virgin. "Hey, Henry, you busted your cherry yet?" "No way," I'd say.

Jimmy Hatcher sat next to me. The principal was giving his address and really scraping the bottom of the old shit barrel. "America is the great land of Opportunity and any man or woman with a desire to do so will succeed . . ."

"Dishwasher," I said.

"Dog catcher," said Jimmy.

"Burglar," I said.

"Garbage collector," said Jimmy.

"Madhouse attendant," I said.

"America is brave, America was built by the brave . . . Ours is a just society."

"Just so much for the few," said Jimmy.

". . . a fair society and all those who search for that dream at the end of the rainbow will find . . ."

"A hairy crawling turd," I suggested.

". . . and I can say, without hesitation, that this particular Class of Summer 1939, less than a decade removed from the beginning of our terrible national Depression, this class of Summer '39 is more ripe with courage, talent and love than *any* class it has been my pleasure to witness!"

196

The mothers, fathers, relatives applauded wildly; a few of the students joined in.

"Class of Summer 1939, I am proud of your future, I am *sure* of your future. I send you out now to your great *adventure!*"

Most of them were headed over to U.S.C. to live the non-working life for at least four more years.

"And I send my prayers and blessings with you!"

The honor students received their diplomas first. Out they came. Abe Mortenson was called. He got his. I applauded.

"Where's he gonna end up?" Jimmy asked.

"Cost accountant in an auto parts manufacturing concern. Somewhere near Gardena, California."

"A lifetime job . . ." said Jimmy.

"A lifetime wife," I added.

"Abe will never be miserable . . ."

"Or happy."

"An obedient man . . ."

"A broom."

"A stiff . . ."

"A wimp."

When the honor students had been taken care of they began on us. I felt uncomfortable sitting there. I felt like walking out.

"Henry Chinaski!" I was called.

"Public servant," I told Jimmy.

I walked up to and across the stage, took the diploma, shook the principal's hand. It felt slimy like the inside of a dirty fish bowl. (Two years later he would be exposed as an embezzler of school funds; he was to be tried, convicted and jailed.)

I passed Mortenson and the honor group as I went back to my seat. He looked over and gave me the finger, so only I could see it. That got me. It was so unexpected.

I walked back and sat down next to Jimmy.

"Mortenson gave me the *finger!*"

"No, I don't *believe* it!"

"Son-of-a-bitch! He's spoiled my day! Not that it was worth a fuck anyhow but he's really greased it over now!"

"I can't believe he had the guts to *finger* you."

"It's not like him. You think he's getting some coaching?"

"I don't know what to think."

"He knows that I can bust him in half without even inhaling!"

"Bust him!"

"But don't you see, he's won? It's the way he surprised me!"

"All you gotta do is kick his ass all up and down."

"Do you think that son-of-a-bitch learned something reading all those books? I know there's nothing in them because I read every fourth page."

"Jimmy Hatcher!" His name was called.

"Priest," he said.

"Poultry farmer," I said.

Jimmy went up and got his. I applauded loudly. Anybody who could live with a mother like his deserved some accolade. He came back and we sat watching all the golden boys and girls go up and get theirs.

"You can't blame them for being rich," Jimmy said.

"No, I blame their fucking parents."

"And their grandparents," said Jimmy.

"Yes, I'd be happy to take their new cars and their pretty girlfriends and I wouldn't give a fuck about anything like social justice."

"Yeah," said Jimmy. "I guess the only time most people think about injustice is when it happens to them."

The golden boys and girls went on parading across the stage. I sat there wondering whether to punch Abe out or not. I could see him flopping on the sidewalk still in his cap and gown, the victim of my right cross, all the pretty girls screaming, thinking, my god, this Chinaski guy must be a *bull* on the springs!

On the other hand, Abe wasn't much. He was hardly there. It wouldn't take anything to punch him out. I decided not to do it. I had already broken his arm and his parents hadn't sued mine, finally. If I busted his head they would surely go ahead and sue. They would take my old man's last copper. Not that I would mind. It was my mother: she would suffer in a fool's way: senselessly and without reason.

Then, the ceremony was over. The students left their seats and filed out. Students met with parents, relatives on the front lawn. There was much hugging, embracing. I saw my parents waiting. I walked up to them, stood about four feet away.

"Let's get out of here," I said.

My mother was looking at me.

"Henry, I'm so proud of you!"

Then my mother's head turned. "Oh, there goes Abe and his parents! They're such *nice* people! *Oh, Mrs. Mortenson!*"

They stopped. My mother ran over and threw her arms about Mrs. Mortenson. It was Mrs. Mortenson who had decided not to sue after many, many hours of conversation upon the telephone with my mother. It had been decided that I was a confused individual and that my mother had suffered enough that way.

My father shook hands with Mr. Mortenson and I walked over to Abe.

"O.K., cocksucker, what's the idea of giving me the finger?"

"What?"

"The *finger!*"

"I don't know what you're talking about!"

"The finger!"

"Henry, I really don't know what you're talking about!"

"All right, Abraham, it's time to go!" said his mother.

The Mortenson family walked off together. I stood there watching them. Then we started walking to our old car. We walked west to the corner and turned south.

"Now that Mortenson boy really knows how to *apply* himself!" said my father. "How are *you* ever going to make it? I've never even seen you look *at* a schoolbook, let alone *inside* of one!"

"Some books are dull," I said.

"Oh, they're *dull*, are they? So you don't *want* to study? What *can* you do? What *good* are you? What can you *do*? It has cost me thousands of dollars to raise you, feed you, clothe you! Suppose I left you here on the street? Then what would you do?"

"Catch butterflies."

My mother began to cry. My father pulled her away and down the block to where their ten-year-old car was parked. As I stood there, the other families roared past in their new cars, going somewhere.

Then Jimmy Hatcher and his mother walked by. She stopped. "Hey, wait a minute," she told Jimmy, "I want to congratulate Henry."

Jimmy waited and Clare walked over. She put her face close to mine. She spoke softly so Jimmy wouldn't hear. "Listen, Honey, any time you *really* want to graduate, I can arrange to give you your diploma."

"Thanks, Clare, I might be seeing you."

"I'll rip your balls off, Henry!"

"I don't doubt it, Clare."

She went back to Jimmy and they walked away down the street.

A very old car rolled up, stopped, the engine died. I could see my mother weeping, big tears were running down her cheeks.

"Henry, get in! *Please* get in! Your father is right but I love you!"

"Forget it. I've got a place to go."

"No, Henry, get in!" she wailed. "Get in or I'll *die!*"

I walked over, opened the rear door, climbed into the rear seat. The engine started and we were off again. There I sat, Henry Chinaski, Class of Summer '39, driving into the bright future. No, being driven. At the first red light the car stalled. As the signal turned green my father was still trying to start the engine. Somebody behind us honked. My father got the car started and we were in motion again. My mother had stopped crying. We drove along like that, each of us silent.

46

Times were still hard. Nobody was any more surprised than I when Mears-Starbuck phoned and asked me to report to work the next Monday. I had gone all around town putting in dozens of applications. There was nothing else to do. I didn't want a job but I didn't want to live with my parents either. Mears-Starbuck must have had thousands of applications on hand. I couldn't believe they had chosen me. It was a department store with branches in many cities.

The next Monday, there I was walking to work with my lunch in a brown paper bag. The department store was only a few blocks away from my former high school.

I still didn't understand why I had been selected. After filling out the application, the interview had lasted only a few minutes. I must have given all the right answers.

First paycheck I get, I thought, I'm going to get myself a room near the downtown L.A. Public Library.

As I walked along I didn't feel so alone and I wasn't. I noticed a starving mongrel dog following me. The poor creature was terribly thin; I could see his ribs poking through his skin. Most of his fur had fallen off. What remained clung in dry, twisted patches. The dog was beaten, cowed, deserted, frightened, a victim of Homo sapiens.

I stopped and knelt, put out my hand. He backed off.

"Come here, fellow, I'm your friend . . . Come on, come on . . ."

He came closer. He had such sad eyes.

"What have they done to you, boy?"

He came still closer, creeping along the sidewalk, trembling, wagging his tail quite rapidly. Then he leaped at me. He was large, what was left of him. His forelegs pushed me backwards and I was flat on the sidewalk and he was licking my face, mouth, ears, forehead, everywhere. I pushed him off, got up and wiped my face.

"Easy now! You need something to *eat!* FOOD!"

I reached into my bag and took out a sandwich. I unwrapped it and broke off a portion.

"Some for you and some for me, old boy!"

I put his part of the sandwich on the sidewalk. He came up, sniffed at it, then walked off, slinking, staring back at me over his shoulder as he walked down the street away from me.

"Hey, wait, buddy! That was *peanut butter!* Come here, have some *bologna!* Hey, boy, come here! Come back!"

The dog approached again, cautiously. I found the bologna sandwich, ripped off a chunk, wiped the cheap watery mustard off, then placed it on the sidewalk.

The dog walked up to the bit of sandwich, put his nose to it, sniffed, then turned and walked off. This time he didn't look back. He accelerated down the street.

No wonder I had been depressed all my life. I wasn't getting proper nourishment.

I walked on toward the department store. It was the same street I had walked along to go to high school.

I arrived. I found the employees' entrance, pushed the door open and walked in. I went from bright sunlight into semi-darkness. As my eyes adjusted I could make out a man standing several feet away in front of me. Half of his left ear had been sliced off at some point in the past. He was a tall, very thin man with needlepoint grey pupils centered in otherwise colorless eyes. A very tall thin man, yet right above his belt, sticking out over his belt—suddenly—was a sad and hideous and strange pot belly. All his fat had settled there while the remainder of him had wasted away.

"I'm Superintendent Ferris," he said. "I presume that you're Mr. Chinaski?"

"Yes, sir."

"You're five minutes late."

"I was delayed by . . . Well, I stopped to try to feed a starving dog," I grinned.

"That's one of the lousiest excuses I've ever heard and I've been here thirty-five years. Couldn't you come up with a better one than that?"

"I'm just starting, Mr. Ferris."

"And you're almost finished. Now," he pointed, "the timeclock is over there and the card rack is over there. Find your card and punch in."

I found my card. Henry Chinaski, employee #68754. Then I walked up to the timeclock but I didn't know what to do.

Ferris walked over and stood behind me, staring at the timeclock.

"You're now six minutes late. When you are ten minutes late we dock you an hour."

"I guess it's better to be an hour late."

"Don't be funny. If I want a comedian I listen to Jack Benny. If you're an hour late you're docked your whole god-damned job."

"I'm sorry, but I don't know how to use a timeclock. I mean, how do I punch in?"

Ferris grabbed the card out of my hand. He pointed at it.

"See this slot?"

"Yeah."

"What?"

"I mean, 'yes.'"

"O.K., that slot is for the first day of the week. Today."

"Ah."

"You slip the timecard into here like this . . ."

He slipped it in, then pulled it out.

"Then when your timecard is in there you hit this lever."

Ferris hit the lever but the timecard wasn't in there.

"I understand. Let's begin."

"No, wait."

He held the timecard in front of me.

"Now, when you punch out for lunch, you hit this slot."

"Yes, I understand."

"Then when you punch back in, you hit the next slot. Lunch is thirty minutes."

"Thirty minutes, I've got it."

"Now, when you punch out, you hit the last slot. That's four punches a day. Then you go home, or to your room or wherever, sleep, come back and hit it four more times each working day until you get fired, quit, die or retire."

"I've got it."

"And I want you to know that you've delayed my indoctrination speech to our new employees, of which you, at the moment, are one. I am in charge here. My word is law and your wishes mean nothing. If I dislike anything about you—the way you tie your shoes, comb your hair or fart, you're back on the streets, get it?"

"Yes, sir!"

A young girl came flouncing in, running on her high heels, long brown hair flowing behind her. She was dressed in a tight red dress. Her lips were large and expressive with excessive lipstick. She theatrically pulled her card out of the rack, punched in, and breathing with minor excitement, she put her card back in the rack.

She glanced over at Ferris.

"Hi, Eddie!"

"Hi, Diana!"

Diana was obviously a salesgirl. Ferris walked over to her. They stood talking. I couldn't hear the conversation but I could hear them laughing. Then they broke off. Diana walked over and waited for the elevator to take her to her work. Ferris walked back toward me holding my timecard.

"I'll punch in now, Mr. Ferris," I told him.

"I'll do it for you. I want to start you out right."

Ferris inserted my timecard into the clock and stood there. He waited. I heard the clock tick, then he hit it. He put my card in the rack.

"How late was I, Mr. Ferris?"

"Ten minutes. Now follow me."

I followed along behind him.

I saw the group waiting.

Four men and three women. They were all old. They seemed to have salivary problems. Little clumps of spittle had formed at the corners of their mouths; the spittle had dried and turned white and then been coated by new wet spittle. Some of them were too thin, others too fat. Some were near-sighted; others trembled. One old fellow in a brightly colored shirt had a hump on his back. They all smiled and coughed, puffing at cigarettes.

Then I got it. The message.

Mears-Starbuck was looking for *stayers*. The company didn't care for employee turnover (although these new recruits obviously weren't going anywhere but to the grave—until then they'd remain grateful and loyal employees). And I had been chosen to work alongside of them. The lady in the employment office had evaluated me as belonging with this pathetic group of losers.

What would the guys in high school think if they saw me? Me, one of the toughest guys in the graduating class.

I walked over and stood with my group. Ferris sat on a table facing us. A shaft of light fell upon him from an overhead transom. He inhaled his cigarette and smiled at us.

"Welcome to Mears-Starbuck . . ."

Then he seemed to fall into a reverie. Perhaps he was thinking about when he had first joined the department store thirty-five years ago. He blew a few smoke rings and watched them rise into the air. His half-sliced ear looked impressive in the light from above.

The guy next to me, a little pretzel of a man, knifed his sharp little elbow into my side. He was one of those individuals whose glasses always seem ready to fall off. He was uglier than I was.

"Hi!" he whispered. "I'm Mewks. Odell Mewks."

"Hello, Mewks."

"Listen, kid, after work let's you and me make the bars. Maybe we can pick up some girls."

"I can't, Mewks."

"Afraid of girls?"

"It's my brother, he's sick. I've got to watch over him."

"Sick?"

"Worse. Cancer. He has to piss through a tube into a bottle strapped to his leg."

Then Ferris began again. "Your starting salary is forty-four-and-a-half cents an hour. We are non-union here. Management believes that what is fair for the company is fair for you. We are like a family, dedicated to serve and to profit. You will each receive a ten-percent discount on all merchandise you purchase from Mears-Starbuck . . ."

"OH, BOY!" Mewks said in a loud voice.

"Yes, Mr. Mewks, it's a good deal. You take care of us, we'll take care of you."

I could stay with Mears-Starbuck for forty-seven years, I thought. I could live with a crazy girlfriend, get my left ear sliced off and maybe inherit Ferris' job when he retired.

Ferris talked about which holidays we could look forward to and then the speech was over. We were issued our smocks and our lockers and then we were directed to the underground storage facilities.

Ferris worked down there too. He manned the phones. Whenever he answered the phone he would hold it to his sliced left ear with his left hand and clamp his right hand under his left armpit. "Yes? Yes? Yes. Coming right up!"

"Chinaski!"

"Yes, sir."

"Lingerie department . . ."

Then he would pick up the order pad, list the items needed and how many of each. He never did this while on the phone, always afterwards.

"Locate these items, deliver them to the lingerie department, obtain a signature and return."

His speech never varied.

My first delivery *was* to lingerie. I located the items, placed them in my little green cart with its four rubber wheels and pushed it toward the elevator. The elevator was at an upper floor and I pressed the button and waited. After some time I could see the bottom of the elevator as it came down. It was very slow. Then it was at basement level. The doors opened and an albino with one eye stood at the controls. Jesus.

He looked at me.

"New guy, huh?" he asked.

"Yeah."

"What do you think of Ferris?"

"I think he's a great guy."

They probably lived together in the same room and took turns manning the hotplate.

"I can't take you up."

"Why not?"

"I gotta take a shit."

He left the elevator and walked off.

There I stood in my smock. This was the way things usually worked. You were a governor or a garbageman, you were a tight-rope walker or a bank robber, you were a dentist or a fruit picker, you were this or you were that. You wanted to do a good job. You manned your station and then you stood and waited for some asshole. I stood there in my smock next to my green cart while the elevator man took a shit.

It came to me then, clearly, why the rich, golden boys and girls were always laughing. They knew.

The albino returned.

"It was great. I feel thirty pounds lighter."

"Good. Can we go now?"

He closed the doors and we rose to the sales floor. He opened the doors.

"Good luck," said the albino.

I pushed my green cart down through the aisles looking for the lingerie department, a Miss Meadows.

Miss Meadows was waiting. She was slender and classy-looking. She looked like a model. Her arms were folded. As I approached her I noticed her eyes. They were an emerald green, there was depth, a knowledge there. I should know somebody like that. Such eyes, such class. I stopped my cart in front of her counter.

"Hello, Miss Meadows," I smiled.

"Where the hell have you been?" she asked.

"It just took this long."

"Do you realize I have customers waiting? Do you realize that I'm attempting to run an efficient department here?"

The salesclerks got ten cents an hour more than we did, plus commissions. I was to discover that they never spoke to us in a friendly way. Male or female, the clerks were the same. They took any familiarity as an affront.

"I've got a good mind to phone Mr. Ferris."

"I'll do better next time, Miss Meadows."

I placed the goods on her counter and then handed her the form to sign. She scratched her signature furiously on the paper, then instead of handing it back to me she threw it into my green cart.

"Christ, I don't know where they *find* people like you!"

I pushed my cart over to the elevator, hit the button and waited. The doors opened and I rolled on in.

"How'd it go?" the albino asked me.

"I feel thirty pounds heavier," I told him.

He grinned, the doors closed and we descended.

Over dinner that night my mother said, "Henry, I'm so proud of you that you have a job!"

I didn't answer.

My father said, "Well, aren't you glad to have a job?"

"Yeah."

"Yeah? Is *that* all you can say? Do you realize how many men are unemployed in this nation now?"

"Plenty, I guess."

"Then you should be grateful."

"Look, can't we just eat our food?"

"You should be grateful for your food, too. Do you know how much this meal cost?"

I shoved my plate away. "Shit! I can't eat this stuff!"

I got up and walked to my bedroom.

"I've got a good mind to come back there and teach you what is what!"

I stopped. "I'll be waiting, old man."

Then I walked away. I went in and waited. But I knew he wasn't coming. I set the alarm to get ready for Mears-Starbuck. It was only 7:30 p.m. but I undressed and went to bed. I switched off the light and was in the dark. There was nothing else to do, nowhere to go. My parents would soon be in bed with the lights out.

My father liked the slogan, "Early to bed and early to rise, makes a man healthy, wealthy and wise."

But it hadn't done any of that for him. I decided that I might try to reverse the process.

208

I couldn't sleep.
Maybe if I masturbated to Miss Meadows?
Too cheap.
I wallowed there in the dark, waiting for something.

47

The first three or four days at Mears-Starbuck were identical. In fact, similarity was a very dependable thing at Mears-Starbuck. The caste system was an accepted fact. There wasn't a single salesclerk who spoke to a stockclerk outside of a perfunctory word or two. And it affected me. I thought about it as I pushed my cart about. Was it possible that the salesclerks were more intelligent than the stockclerks? They certainly dressed better. It bothered me that they assumed that their station meant so much. Perhaps if I had been a salesclerk I would have felt the same way. I didn't much care for the other stockclerks. Or the salesclerks.

Now, I thought, pushing my cart along, I have this job. Is this to be it? No wonder men robbed banks. There were too many demeaning jobs. Why the hell wasn't I a superior court judge or a concert pianist? Because it took training and training cost money. But I didn't want to be anything anyhow. And I was certainly succeeding.

I pushed my cart to the elevator and hit the button.

Women wanted men who made money, women wanted men of mark. How many classy women were living with skid row bums? Well, I didn't want a woman anyhow. Not to live with. How could men live with women? What did it mean? What I wanted was a cave in Colorado with three-years' worth of foodstuffs and drink. I'd wipe my ass with sand. Anything, anything to stop drowning in this dull, trivial and cowardly existence.

The elevator came up. The albino was still at the controls. "Hey, I hear you and Mewks made the bars last night!"

"He bought me a few beers. I'm broke."

"You guys get laid?"

"I didn't."

"Why don't you guys take me along next time? I'll show you how to get some snatch."

"What do you know?"

"I've been around. Just last week I had a Chinese girl. And you know, it's just like they say."

"What's that?"

We hit the basement and the doors opened.

"Their snatch doesn't run up and down, it runs from side to side."

Ferris was waiting for me.

"Where the hell you been?"

"Home gardening."

"What did you do, fertilize the fuchsias?"

"Yeah, I drop one turd in each pot."

"Listen, Chinaski . . ."

"Yes?"

"The punchlines around here belong to me. Got it?"

"Got it."

"Well, get this. I've got an order here for Men's Wear."

He handed me the order slip.

"Locate these items, deliver them, obtain a signature and return."

Men's Wear was run by Mr. Justin Phillips, Jr. He was well-bred, he was polite, around twenty-two. He stood very straight, had dark hair, dark eyes, brooding lips. There was an unfortunate absence of cheekbones but it was hardly noticeable. He was pale and wore dark clothing with beautifully starched shirts. The salesgirls loved him. He was sensitive, intelligent, clever. He was also just a bit nasty as if some forebear had passed down that right to him. He had only broken with tradition once to speak to me. "It's a shame, isn't it, those rather ugly scars on your face?"

As I rolled my cart up to Men's Wear, Justin Phillips was

standing very straight, head tilted a bit, staring, as he did most of the time, looking off and up as if he was seeing things we were not. He saw things out there. Maybe I just didn't recognize breeding when I saw it. He certainly appeared to be above his surroundings. It was a good trick if you could do it and get paid at the same time. Maybe that's what management and the salesgirls liked. Here was a man truly too good for what he was doing, but he was doing it anyhow.

I rolled up. "Here's your order, Mr. Phillips."

He appeared not to notice me, which hurt in a sense, and was a good thing in another. I stacked the goods on the counter as he stared off into space, just above the elevator door.

Then I heard golden laughter and I looked. It was a gang of guys who had graduated with me from Chelsey High. They were trying on sweaters, hiking shorts, various items. I knew them by sight only, as we had never spoken during our four years of high school. The leader was Jimmy Newhall. He had been the halfback on our football team, undefeated for three years. His hair was a beautiful yellow, the sun always seemed to be highlighting parts of it, the sun or the lights in the schoolroom. He had a thick, powerful neck and above it sat the face of a perfect boy sculpted by some master sculptor. Everything was exactly as it should be: nose, forehead, chin, the works. And the body likewise, perfectly formed. The others with Newhall were not exactly as perfect as he was, but they were close. They stood around and tried on sweaters and laughed, waiting to go to U.S.C. or Stanford.

Justin Phillips signed my receipt. I was on my way back to the elevator when I heard a voice:

"HEY, SKI! SKI, YOU LOOK GREAT IN YOUR LITTLE OUTFIT!"

I stopped, turned, gave them a casual wave of the left hand.

"Look at him! Toughest guy in town since Tommy Dorsey!"

"Makes Gable look like a toilet plunger."

I left my wagon and walked back. I didn't know what I was going to do. I stood there and looked at them. I didn't like them, never had. They might look glorious to others but not to me. There was something about their bodies that was like a woman's body. They were soft, they had never faced any fire. They were beautiful nothings. They made me sick. I hated them. They were part of the nightmare that always haunted me in one form or another.

Jimmy Newhall smiled at me. "Hey, stockboy, how come you never tried out for the team?"

"It wasn't what I wanted."

"No guts, eh?"

"You know where the parking lot on the roof is?"

"Sure."

"See you there . . ."

They strolled out toward the parking lot as I took my smock off and threw it into the cart. Justin Phillips, Jr. smiled at me, "My dear boy, you are going to get your ass whipped."

Jimmy Newhall was waiting, surrounded by his buddies.

"Hey, look, the stockboy!"

"You think he's wearing ladies' underwear?"

Newhall was standing in the sun. He had his shirt off and his undershirt too. He had his gut sucked in and his chest pushed out. He looked good. What the hell had I gotten into? I felt my underlip trembling. Up there on the roof, I felt fear. I looked at Newhall, the golden sun highlighting his golden hair. I had watched him many times on the football field. I had seen him break off many 50 and 60 yard runs while I rooted for the other team.

Now we stood looking at each other. I left my shirt on. We kept standing. I kept standing.

Newhall finally said, "O.K., I'm going to take you now." He started to move forward. Just then a little old lady dressed in black came by with many packages. She had on a tiny green felt hat.

"Hello, boys!" she said.

"Hello, ma'am."

"Lovely day . . ."

The little old lady opened her car door and loaded in the packages. Then she turned to Jimmy Newhall.

"Oh, what a *fine* body you have, my boy! I'll bet you could be Tarzan of the Apes!"

"No, ma'am," I said. "Pardon me, but he's the *ape* and those with him are his tribe."

"Oh," she said. She got into her car, started it and we waited as she backed out and drove off.

"O.K., Chinaski," said Newhall, "all through school you were famous for your sneer and your big god-damned mouth. And *now* I'm going to put the cure on you!"

Newhall bounded forward. He was ready. I wasn't quite ready. All I saw was a backdrop of blue sky and a flash of body and fists. He was quicker than an ape, and bigger. I couldn't seem to throw a punch, I only felt his fists and they were rock hard. Squinting through punched eyes I could see his fists, swinging, landing, my god, he had power, it seemed endless and there was no place to go. I began to think, maybe you are a sissy, maybe you should be, maybe you should quit.

But as he continued to punch, my fear vanished. I felt only astonishment at his strength and energy. Where did he get it? A swine like him? He was loaded. I couldn't see anymore—my eyes were blinded by flashes of yellow and green light, purple light— then a terrific shot of RED . . . I felt myself going down.

Is this the way it happens?

I fell to one knee. I heard an airplane passing overhead. I wished I was on it. I felt something run over my mouth and chin . . . it was warm blood running from my nose.

"Let him go, Jimmy, he's finished . . ."

I looked at Newhall. "Your mother sucks cock," I told him.

"I'LL KILL YOU!"

Newhall rushed me before I could quite get up. He had me by the throat and we rolled over and over, under a Dodge. I heard his head hit something. I didn't know what it hit but I heard the sound. It happened quite quickly and the others were not as aware of it as I was.

I got up and then Newhall got up.

"I'm going to kill you," he said.

Newhall windmilled in. This time it wasn't nearly so bad. He punched with the same fury, but something was missing. He was weaker. When he hit me I didn't see flashes of color, I could see the sky, the parked cars, the faces of his friends, and him. I had always been a slow starter. Newhall was still trying but he was definitely weaker. And I had my small hands, I was blessed with small hands, lousy weapons.

214

What a weary time those years were—to have the desire and the need to live but not the ability.

I dug a hard right to his belly and I heard him gasp so I grabbed him behind the neck with my left and dug another right to his belly. Then I pushed him off and cracked him with a one-two, right into that sculpted face. I saw his eyes and it was great. I was bringing something to him that he had never felt before. He was terrified. Terrified because he didn't know how to handle defeat. I decided to finish him slowly.

Then someone slugged me on the back of the head. It was a good hard shot. I turned and looked.

It was his red-headed friend, Cal Evans.

I yelled, pointing at him. "Stay the fuck away from me! I'll take all of you one at a time! As soon as I'm done with this guy, you're next!"

It didn't take much to finish Jimmy. I even tried some fancy footwork. I jabbed a bit, played around and then I moved in and started punching. He took it pretty good and for a while I thought I couldn't finish it but all of a sudden he gave me this strange look which said, hey, look, maybe we ought to be buddies and go have a couple of beers together. Then he dropped.

His friends moved in and picked him up, they held him up, talked to him, "Hey, Jim, you O.K.?"

"What'd the son-of-a-bitch do to you, Jim? We'll clean his drawers, Jim. Just give us the word."

"Take me home," Jim said.

I watched them go down the stairway, all of them trying to hold him up, one guy carrying his shirt and undershirt . . .

I went downstairs to get my cart. Justin Phillips was waiting.

"I didn't think you'd be back," he smiled disdainfully.

"Don't fraternize with the unskilled help," I told him.

I pushed off. My face, my clothes—I was pretty badly messed up. I walked to the elevator and hit the button. The albino came in due time. The doors opened.

"The word's out," he said. "I hear you're the new heavyweight champion of the world."

News travels fast in places where nothing much ever happens.

215

Ferris of the sliced ear was waiting.

"You just don't go around beating the shit out of our customers."

"It was only one."

"We have no way of knowing when you might start in on the others."

"This guy baited me."

"We don't give a damn about that. That's what happens. All we know is that you were out of line."

"How about my check?"

"It'll be mailed."

"O.K., see you . . ."

"Wait, I'll need your locker key."

I got out my key chain which only had one other key on it, pulled off the locker key and handed it to Ferris.

Then I walked to the employees' door, pulled it open. It was a heavy steel door which worked awkwardly. As it opened, letting in the daylight, I turned and gave Ferris a small wave. He didn't respond. He just looked straight at me. Then the door closed on him. I liked him, somehow.

48

"So you couldn't hold a job for a week?"

We were eating meatballs and spaghetti. My problems were always discussed at dinner time. Dinner time was almost always an unhappy time.

I didn't answer my father's question.

"What happened? Why did they can your ass?"

I didn't answer.

"Henry, answer your father when he speaks to you!" my mother said.

"He couldn't hack it, that's all!"

"Look at his face," said my mother, "it's all bruised and cut. Did your boss beat you up, Henry?"

"No, Mother . . ."

"Why don't you eat, Henry? You never seem to be hungry."

"He can't eat," said my father, "he can't work, he can't do anything, he's not worth a fuck!"

"You shouldn't talk that way at the dinner table, Daddy," my mother told him.

"Well, it's true!" My father had an immense ball of spaghetti rolled on his fork. He jammed it into his mouth and started chewing and while chewing he speared a large meatball and plunged it into his mouth, then worked in a piece of French bread.

I remembered what Ivan had said in *The Brothers Karamazov*, "Who doesn't want to kill the father?"

As my father chewed at the mass of food, one long string of spaghetti dangled from a corner of his mouth. He finally noticed it and sucked it in noisily. Then he reached, put two large teaspoons

of white sugar into his coffee, lifted the cup and took a giant
mouthful, which he immediately spit out across his plate and onto
the tablecloth.

"That shit's too *hot!*"

"You should be more careful, Daddy," said my mother.

I combed the job market, as they used to say, but it was a dreary
and useless routine. You had to know somebody to get a job even
as a lowly bus boy. Thus everybody was a dishwasher, the whole
town was full of unemployed dishwashers. I sat with them in
Pershing Square in the afternoons. The evangelists were there
too. Some had drums, some had guitars, and the bushes and
restrooms crawled with homosexuals.

"Some of them have money," a young bum told me. "This guy
took me to his apartment for two weeks. I had all I could eat and
drink and he bought me some clothes but he sucked me dry, I
couldn't stand up after a while. One night when he was asleep I
crawled out of there. It was horrible. He kissed me once and I
knocked him across the room. 'You ever do that again,' I told him,
'and I'll kill you!'"

Clifton's Cafeteria was nice. If you didn't have much money,
they let you pay what you could. And if you didn't have any
money, you didn't have to pay. Some of the bums went in there
and ate well. It was owned by some very nice rich old man, a very
unusual person. I could never make myself go in there and load
up. I'd go in for a coffee and an apple pie and give them a nickel.
Sometimes I'd get a couple of weenies. It was quiet and cool in
there and clean. There was a large waterfall and you could sit next
to it and imagine that everything was quite all right. Philippe's was
nice too. You could get a cup of coffee for three cents with all the
refills you wanted. You could sit in there all day drinking coffee
and they never asked you to leave no matter how bad you looked.
They just asked the bums not to bring in their wine and drink it
there. Places like that gave you hope when there wasn't much
hope.

The men in Pershing Square argued all day about whether
there was a God or not. Most of them didn't argue very well but
now and then you got a Religionist and an Atheist who were

well-versed and it was a good show.

When I had a few coins I'd go to the underground bar beneath the big movie house. I was 18 but they served me. I looked like I could be almost any age. Sometimes I looked 25, sometimes I felt like 30. The bar was run by Chinese who never spoke to anyone. All I needed was the first beer and then the homosexuals would start buying. I'd switch to whiskey sours. I'd bleed them for whiskey sours and when they started closing in on me, I'd get nasty, push off and leave. After a while they caught on and the place wasn't any good anymore.

The library was the most depressing place I went. I had run out of books to read. After a while I would just grab a thick book and look for a young girl somewhere. There were always one or two about. I'd sit three or four chairs away, pretending to read the book, trying to look intelligent, hoping some girl would pick me up. I knew that I was ugly but I thought if I looked intelligent enough I might have some chance. It never worked. The girls just made notes on their pads and then they got up and left as I watched their bodies moving rhythmically and magically under their clean dresses. What would Maxim Gorky have done under such circumstances?

At home it was always the same. The question was never asked until after the first few bites of dinner were partaken. Then my father would ask, "Did you find a job today?"

"No."

"Did you try anywhere?"

"Many places. I've gone back to some of the same places for the second or third time."

"I don't believe it."

But it was true. It was also true that some companies put ads in the papers every day when there were no jobs available. It gave the employment department in those companies something to do. It also wasted the time and screwed up the hopes of many desperate people.

"You'll find a job tomorrow, Henry," my mother would always say . . .

49

I looked for a job all summer and couldn't find one. Jimmy
Hatcher caught on at an aircraft plant. Hitler was acting up in
Europe and creating jobs for the unemployed. I had been with
Jimmy that day when we had turned in our applications. We filled
them out in similar fashion, the only difference being where it said
Place of Birth, I put down Germany and he put down Reading, Pa.

"Jimmy got a job. He came from the same school and he's your
age," said my mother. "Why couldn't you get a job at the aircraft
plant?"

"They can tell a man who doesn't have a taste for work," said
my father. "All he wants to do is to sit in the bedroom on his dead
ass and listen to his symphony music!"

"Well, the boy likes music. That's something."

"But he doesn't DO anything with it! He doesn't make it
USEFUL!"

"What should he do?"

"He should go to a radio station and tell them he likes that kind
of music and get a job broadcasting."

"Christ, it's not done like that, it's not that easy."

"What do you know? Have you tried it?"

"I tell you, it can't be done."

My father put a large piece of pork chop into his mouth. A
greasy portion hung out from between his lips as he chewed. It
was as if he had three lips. Then he sucked it in and looked at my
mother. "You see, mama, the boy doesn't want to work."

220

My mother looked at me. "Henry, why don't you eat your food?"

It was finally decided that I would enroll at L.A. City College. There was no tuition fee and second-hand books could be purchased at the Co-op Book Store. My father was simply ashamed that I was unemployed and by going to school I would at least earn some respectability. Eli LaCrosse (Baldy) had already been there a term. He counseled me.

"What's the easiest fucking thing to take?" I asked him.

"Journalism. Those journalism majors don't do anything."

"O.K., I'll be a journalist."

I looked through the school booklet.

"What's this Orientation Day they speak of here?"

"Oh, you just skip that, that's bullshit."

"Thanks for telling me, buddy. We'll go instead to that bar across from campus and have a couple of beers."

"Damn right!"

"Yeah."

The day after Orientation Day was the day you signed up for classes. People were running about frantically with papers and booklets. I had come over on the streetcar. I took the "W" to Vermont and then took the "V" north to Monroe. I didn't know where everybody was going, or what I should do. I felt sick.

"Pardon me . . ." I asked a girl.

She turned her head and kept walking briskly. A guy came running by and I grabbed him by the back of his belt and stopped him.

"Hey, what the hell are you doing?" he asked.

"Shut up. I want to know what's going on! I want to know what to do!"

"They explained everything to you in Orientation."

"Oh . . ."

I let him go and he ran off. I didn't know what to do. I had imagined that you just went somewhere and told them you wanted to take Journalism, Beginning Journalism, and they'd give you a card with a schedule of your classes. It was nothing like that. These people knew what to do and they wouldn't talk. I felt as if I was in grammar school again, being mutilated by the crowd who knew more than I did. I sat down on a bench and watched them running back and forth. Maybe I'd fake it. I'd just tell my parents I was going to L.A. City College and I'd come every day and lay on the lawn. Then I saw this guy running along. It was Baldy. I got him from behind by the collar.

"Hey, hey, Hank! What's happening?"

"I ought to cream you right now, you little asshole!"

"What's wrong? What's wrong?"

"How do I get a fucking class? What do I do?"

"I thought you knew!"

"How? *How* would I know? Was I born with this knowledge inside of me, fully indexed, ready to consult when needed?"

I walked him over to a bench, still holding him by his shirt collar. "Now, lay it out, nice and clear, everything that needs to be done and how to do it. Do a good job and I might not cream you at this moment!"

So Baldy explained it all. I had my own Orientation Day right there. I still held him by the collar. "I'm going to let you go now. But some day I'm going to even this thing out. You're going to pay for fucking me over. You won't know when, but it's going to happen."

I let him go. He went running off with the rest of them. There was no need for me to worry or hurry. I was going to get the worst classes, the worst teachers and the worst hours. I strolled about leisurely signing up for classes. I appeared to be the only unconcerned student on campus. I began to feel superior.

Until my first 7 a.m. English class. It was 7:30 a.m. and I was hungover as I stood there outside the door, listening. My parents had paid for my books and I had sold them for drinking money. I had slid out of the bedroom window the night before and had closed the neighborhood bar. I had a throbbing beer hangover. I still felt drunk. I opened the door and walked in. I stood there. Mr. Hamilton, the English instructor, was standing before the class, singing. A record player was on, loud, and the class was singing along with Mr. Hamilton. It was Gilbert and Sullivan.

222

*Now I am the ruler
of the Queen's Navy . . .*

*I copied all the letters
in a big round hand . . .*

*Now I am the ruler
of the Queen's Navy . . .*

*Stick close to your desks
and never go to sea . . .*

*And you all may be rulers
of the Queen's Navy . . .*

I walked to the rear of the class and found an empty seat. Hamilton walked over and shut off the record player. He was dressed in a black-and-white pepper suit with a shirt-front of bright orange. He looked like Nelson Eddy. Then he faced the class, glanced at his wrist watch and addressed me:

"You must be Mr. Chinaski?"

I nodded.

"You are thirty minutes late."

"Yes."

"Would you be thirty minutes late to a wedding or a funeral?"

"No."

"Why not, pray tell?"

"Well, if the funeral was mine I'd have to be on time. If the wedding was mine it would be my funeral." I was always quick with the mouth. I would never learn.

"My dear sir," said Mr. Hamilton, "we have been listening to Gilbert and Sullivan in order to learn proper enunciation. Please stand up."

I stood up.

"Now, please sing, *Stick close to your desks and never go to sea and you'll always be the ruler of the Queen's Navy.*"

I stood there.

"Well, go ahead, please!"

I went through it and sat down.

"Mr. Chinaski, I could barely hear you. Couldn't you sing with just a bit more verve?"

I stood up again. I sucked in a giant sea of air and let go. "IF YA WANNA BE DA RULLER OF DEY QUEEN'S NABY STICK CLOSE TA YUR DESKS AN NEVA GO TA SEA!"

I had gotten it backwards.

"Mr. Chinaski," said Mr. Hamilton, "please sit down."

I sat down. It was Baldy's fault.

50

Everybody had gym period at the same time. Baldy's locker was about four or five down from mine in the same row. I went to my locker early. Baldy and I had a similar problem. We hated wool pants because the wool itched our legs but our parents just loved for us to wear wool. I had solved the problem, for Baldy and myself, by letting him in on a secret. All you had to do was to wear your pajamas underneath the wool pants.

I opened my locker and undressed. I got my pants and pajamas off and then I took the pajamas and hid them on top of the locker. I got into my gym suit. The other guys were starting to walk in.

Baldy and I had some great pajama stories but Baldy's was the best. He had been out with his girlfriend one night, they had gone to some dance. In between dances his girlfriend had said, "What's that?"

"What's what?"

"There's something sticking out of your pant cuff."

"What?"

"My goodness! You're wearing your *pajamas* underneath your pants!"

"Oh? Oh, that . . . I must have forgotten . . ."

"I'm leaving right now!"

She never dated him again.

All the guys were changing into their gym clothes. Then Baldy walked in and opened his locker.

"How ya doing, pal?" I asked him.

"Oh, hello, Hank . . ."

"I've got a 7 a.m. English class. It really starts the day out right. Only they ought to call it *Music Appreciation I.*"

"Oh yeah. Hamilton. I've heard of him. Hee hee hee . . ."

I walked over to him.

Baldy had unbuckled his pants. I reached over and yanked his pants down. Underneath were green striped pajamas. He tried to yank his pants back up but I was too strong for him.

"HEY, FELLOWS, LOOK! JESUS CHRIST, HERE'S A GUY WHO WEARS HIS PAJAMAS TO SCHOOL!"

Baldy was struggling. His face was florid. A couple of guys walked over and looked. Then I did the worst. I yanked his pajamas down.

"AND LOOKY HERE! THE POOR FUCKER IS NOT ONLY BALD BUT HE DOESN'T HARDLY HAVE A COCK! WHAT IS THIS POOR FUCKER GOING TO DO WHEN HE CONFRONTS A WOMAN?"

Some big guy standing nearby said, "Chinaski, you're really a piece of shit!"

"Yeah," said a couple of other guys. "Yeah . . . yeah . . ." I heard other voices.

Baldy pulled his pants up. He was actually crying. He looked at the guys. "Well, Chinaski wears pajamas too! *He* was the guy who started me doing it! Look in his locker, just look in his locker!"

Baldy ran down to my locker and ripped the door open. He pulled all my clothing out. The pajamas weren't in there.

"He's hidden them! He's hidden them somewhere!"

I left my clothes on the floor and walked out on the field for roll call. I stood in the second row. I did a couple of deep knee bends. I noticed another big guy behind me. I'd heard his name around, Sholom Stodolsky.

"Chinaski," he said, "you're a piece of shit."

"Don't mess with me, man, I've got an edgy nature."

"Well, I'm messing with you."

"Don't push me too far, fat boy."

"You know the place between the Biology Building and the tennis courts?"

"I've seen it."

226

"I'll meet you there after gym."
"O.K.," I said.

I didn't show up. After gym I cut the rest of my classes and took the streetcars down to Pershing Square. I sat on a bench and waited for some action. It seemed a long time coming. Finally a Religionist and an Atheist got into it. They weren't much good. I was an Agnostic. Agnostics didn't have much to argue about. I left the park and walked down to 7th and Broadway. That was the center of town. There didn't seem to be much doing there, just people waiting for the signals to change so they could cross the street. Then I noticed my legs were starting to itch. I had left my pajamas on top of the locker. What a fucking lousy day it had been from beginning to end. I hopped a "W" streetcar and sat in the back as it rolled along carrying me back toward home.

51

I only met one student at City College that I liked, Robert Becker. He wanted to be a writer. "I'm going to learn everything there is to learn about writing. It will be like taking a car apart and putting it back together again."

"Sounds like work," I said.

"I'm going to do it."

Becker was an inch or so shorter than I was but he was stocky, he was powerfully built, with big shoulders and arms.

"I had a childhood disease," he told me. "I had to lay in bed one time for a year squeezing two tennis balls, one in each hand. Just from doing that, I got to be like this."

He had a job as a messenger boy at night and was putting himself through college.

"How'd you get your job?"

"I knew a guy who knew a guy."

"I'll bet I can kick your ass."

"Maybe, maybe not. I'm only interested in writing."

We were sitting in an alcove overlooking the lawn. Two guys were staring at me.

Then one of them spoke. "Hey," he asked me, "do you mind if I ask you something?"

"Go ahead."

"Well, you used to be a sissy in grammar school, I remember you. And now you're a tough guy. What happened?"

"I don't know."

"Are you a cynic?"

"Probably."

"Are you happy being a cynic?"

"Yes."

"Then you're not a cynic because cynics aren't happy!"

The two guys did a little vaudeville handshake act and ran off, laughing.

"They made you look bad," said Becker.

"No, they were trying too hard."

"*Are* you a cynic?"

"I'm unhappy. If I was a cynic it would probably make me feel better."

We hopped down from the alcove. Classes were over. Becker wanted to put his books in his locker. We walked there and he dumped them in. He handed me five or six sheets of paper.

"Here read this. It's a short story."

We walked down to my locker. I opened it and handed him a paper bag.

"Take a hit . . ."

It was a bottle of port.

Becker took a hit, then I took one.

"You always keep one of these in your locker?" he asked.

"I try to."

"Listen, tonight's my night off. Why don't you come meet some of my friends?"

"People don't do me much good."

"These are different people."

"Yeah? Where at? Your place?"

"No. Here, I'll write down the address . . ." He began writing on a piece of paper.

"Listen, Becker, what do these people do?"

"Drink," said Becker.

I put the slip into my pocket . . .

That night after dinner I read Becker's short story. It was good and I was jealous. It was about riding his bike at night and then delivering a telegram to a beautiful woman. The writing was objective and clear, there was a gentle decency about it. Becker claimed Thomas Wolfe as an influence but he didn't wail and ham

229

it up like Wolfe did. The emotion was there but it wasn't spelled out in neon. Becker could write, he could write better than I could.

My parents had gotten me a typewriter and I had tried some short stories but they had come out very bitter and ragged. Not that that was so bad but the stories seemed to beg, they didn't have their own vitality. My stories were darker than Becker's, stranger, but they didn't work. Well, one or two of them had worked—for me—but it was more or less as if they had fallen into place instead of being guided there. Becker was clearly better. Maybe I'd try painting.

I waited until my parents were asleep. My father always snored loudly. When I heard him I opened the bedroom screen and slid out over the berry bush. That put me into the neighbor's driveway and I walked slowly in the dark. Then I walked up Longwood to 21st Street, took a right, then went up the hill along Westview to where the "W" car ended its route. I dropped my token in and walked to the rear of the car, sat down and lit a cigarette. If Becker's friends were anywhere as good as Becker's short story it was going to be one hell of a night.

Becker was already there by the time I found the Beacon Street address. His friends were in the breakfast nook. I was introduced. There was Harry, there was Lana, there was Gobbles, there was Stinky, there was Marshbird, there was Ellis, there was Dogface and finally there was The Ripper. They all sat around a large breakfast table. Harry had a legitimate job somewhere, he and Becker were the only ones employed. Lana was Harry's wife, Gobbles their baby was sitting in a highchair. Lana was the only woman there. When we were introduced she had looked right at me and smiled. They were all young, thin, and puffed at rolled cigarettes.

"Becker told us about you," said Harry. "He says you're a writer."

"I've got a typewriter."

"You gonna write about us?" asked Stinky.

"I'd rather drink."

230

"Fine. We're going to have a drinking contest. Got any money?" Stinky asked.

"Two dollars . . ."

"O.K., the ante is two dollars. Everybody up!" Harry said.

That made eighteen dollars. The money looked good laying there. A bottle appeared and then shot glasses.

"Becker told us you think you're a tough guy. Are you a tough guy?"

"Yeah."

"Well, we're gonna see . . ."

The kitchen light was very bright. It was straight whiskey. A dark yellow whiskey. Harry poured the drinks. Such beauty. My mouth, my throat, couldn't wait. The radio was on. *Oh, Johnny, oh Johnny, how you can love!* somebody sang.

"Down the hatch!" said Harry.

There was no way I could lose. I could drink for days. I had never had enough to drink.

Gobbles had a tiny shot glass of his own. As we raised ours and drank them, he raised his and drank. Everybody thought it was funny. I didn't think it was so funny for a baby to drink but I didn't say anything.

Harry poured another round.

"You read my short story, Hank?" Becker asked.

"Yeah."

"How'd you like it?"

"It was good. You're ready now. All you need is some luck."

"Down the hatch!" said Harry.

The second round was no problem, we all got it down, including Lana.

Harry looked at me. "You like to duke it, Hank?"

"No."

"Well, in case you do, we got Dogface here."

Dogface was twice my size. It was so wearisome being in the world. Every time you looked around there was some guy ready to take you on without even inhaling. I looked at Dogface. "Hi, buddy!"

"Buddy, my ass," he said. "Just get your next drink down."

Harry poured them all around. He skipped Gobbles in the highchair, though, which I appreciated. All right, we raised them, we all got that round down. Then Lana dropped out.

"Somebody's got to clean up this mess and get Harry ready for work in the morning," she said.

The next round was poured. Just as it was the door banged open and a large good-looking kid of around 22 came running into the room. "*Shit, Harry*," he said, "*hide me! I just held up a fucking gas station!*"

"My car's in the garage," Harry said. "Get down on the floor in the back seat and stay there!"

We drank up. The next round was poured. A new bottle appeared. The eighteen dollars was still in the center of the table. We were still all hanging in there except Lana. It was going to take plenty of whiskey to do us in.

"Hey," I asked Harry, "aren't we going to run out of drinks?"

"Show him, Lana . . ."

Lana pulled open some upper cupboard doors. I could see bottles and bottles of whiskey lined up, all the same brand. It looked like the loot from a truck hijack and it probably was. And these were the gang members: Harry, Lana, Stinky, Marshbird, Ellis, Dogface and The Ripper, maybe Becker, and most likely the young guy now on the floor in the back seat of Harry's car. I felt honored to be drinking with such an active part of the population of Los Angeles. Becker not only knew how to write, Becker knew his people. I would dedicate my first novel to Robert Becker. And it would be a better novel than *Of Time and the River*.

Harry kept pouring the rounds and we kept drinking them down. The kitchen was blue with cigarette smoke.

Marshbird dropped out first. He had a very large nose, he just shook his head, no more, no more, and all you could see was this long nose waving "no" in the blue smoke.

Ellis was the next to drop out. He had a lot of hair on his chest but evidently not much on his balls.

Dogface was next. He just jumped up and ran to the crapper and puked. Listening to him Harry got the same idea and leaped up and puked in the sink.

That left me, Becker, Stinky and The Ripper.

Becker quit next. He just folded his arms on the table, put his head down in his arms and that was it.

"The night's so young," I said. "I usually drink until the sun comes up."

232

"Yeah," said The Ripper, "you shit in a basket too!"

"Yeah, and it's shaped like your head."

The Ripper stood up. "You son-of-a-bitch, I'll bust your ass!"

He swung at me from across the table, missed and knocked over the bottle. Lana got a rag and mopped it up. Harry opened a bottle.

"Sit down, Rip, or you forfeit your bet," Harry said.

Harry poured a new round. We drank them down.

The Ripper stood up, walked to the rear door, opened it and looked out into the night.

"Hey, Rip, what the hell you doing?" Stinky asked.

"I'm checking to see if there's a full moon."

"Well, is there?"

There was no answer. We heard him fall through the door, down the steps and into the bushes. We left him there.

That left me and Stinky.

"I've never seen anybody take Stinky yet," said Harry.

Lana had just put Gobbles to bed. She walked back into the kitchen. "Jesus, there are dead bodies all over the place."

"Pour 'em, Harry," I said.

Harry filled Stinky's glass, then mine. I knew there was no way I could get that drink down. I did the only thing I could do. I pretended it was easy. I grabbed the shot glass and belted it down. Stinky just stared at me. "I'll be right back. I gotta go to the crapper."

We sat and waited.

"Stinky's a nice guy," I said. "You shouldn't call him Stinky. How'd he get that name?"

"I dunno," said Harry, "somebody just laid it on him."

"That guy in the back of your car. He ever going to come out?"

"Not till morning."

We sat and waited. "I think," said Harry, "we better take a look."

We opened the bathroom door. Stinky didn't appear to be in there. Then we saw him. He had fallen into the bathtub. His feet stuck up over the edge. His eyes were closed, he was down in there, and out. We walked back to the table. "The money's yours," said Harry.

"How about letting me pay for some of those bottles of whiskey?"

"Forget it."

"You mean it?"

"Yes, of course."

I picked up the money and put it in my right front pocket. Then I looked at Stinky's drink.

"No use wasting this," I said.

"You mean you're going to drink that?" asked Lana.

"Why not? One for the road . . ."

I gulped it down.

"O.K., see you guys, it's been great!"

"Goodnight, Hank . . ."

I walked out the back door, stepping over The Ripper's body. I found a back alley and took a left. I walked along and I saw a green Chevy sedan. I staggered a bit as I approached it. I grabbed the rear door handle to steady myself. The god-damned door was unlocked and it swung open, knocking me sideways. I fell hard, skinning my left elbow on the pavement. There was a full moon. The whiskey had hit me all at once. I felt as if I couldn't get up. I had to get up. I was supposed to be a tough guy. I rose, fell against the half-open door, grabbed at it, held it. Then I had the inside handle and was steadying myself. I got myself into the back seat and then I just sat there. I sat there for some time. Then I started to puke. It really came. It came and it came, it covered the rear floorboard. Then I sat for a while. Then I managed to get out of the car. I didn't feel as dizzy. I took out my handkerchief and wiped the vomit off my pant legs and off of my shoes as best I could. I closed the car door and walked on down the alley. I had to find the "W" streetcar. I would find it.

I did. I rode it in. I made it down Westview Street, walked down 21st Street, turned south down Longwood Avenue to 2122. I walked up the neighbor's driveway, found the berry bush, crawled over it, through the open screen and into my bedroom. I undressed and went to bed. I must have consumed over a quart of whiskey. My father was still snoring, just as he had been when I had left, only at the moment it was louder and uglier. I slept anyhow.

As usual I approached Mr. Hamilton's English class thirty minutes late. It was 7:30 a.m. I stood outside the door and listened. They were at Gilbert and Sullivan again. And it was still all about going to the sea and the Queen's Navy. Hamilton couldn't get enough of that. In high school I'd had an English teacher and it had been Poe, Poe, Edgar Allan Poe.

I opened the door. Hamilton went over and lifted the needle from the record. Then he announced to the class, "When Mr. Chinaski arrives we always know that it is 7:30 a.m. Mr. Chinaski is *always* on time. The only problem being that it is the *wrong* time."

He paused, glancing at the faces in his class. He was very, very dignified. Then he looked at me.

"Mr. Chinaski, whether you arrive at 7:30 a.m. or whether you arrive at all will not matter. I am assigning you a 'D' for *English I*."

"A 'D,' Mr. Hamilton?" I asked, flashing my famous sneer. "Why not an 'F'?"

"Because 'F,' at times, equates with 'Fuck.' And I don't think you're worth a 'Fuck.'"

The class cheered and roared and stomped and stamped. I turned around, walked out, closed the door behind me. I walked down the hallway, still hearing them going at it in there.

52

The war was going very well in Europe, for Hitler. Most of the students weren't very vocal on the matter. But the instructors were, they were almost all left-wing and anti-German. There seemed to be no right-wing faction among the instructors except for Mr. Glasglow, in Economics, and he was very discreet about it.

It was intellectually popular and proper to be for going to war with Germany, to stop the spread of fascism. As for me, I had no desire to go to war to protect the life I had or what future I might have. I had no Freedom. I had nothing. With Hitler around, maybe I'd even get a piece of ass now and then and more than a dollar a week allowance. As far as I could rationalize, I had nothing to protect. Also, having been born in Germany, there was a natural loyalty and I didn't like to see the whole German nation, the people, depicted everywhere as monsters and idiots. In the movie theatres they speeded up the newsreels to make Hitler and Mussolini look like frenetic madmen. Also, with all the instructors being anti-German I found it personally impossible to simply agree with them. Out of sheer alienation and a natural contrariness I decided to align myself against their point of view. I had never read *Mein Kampf* and had no desire to do so. Hitler was just another dictator to me, only instead of lecturing me at the dinner table he'd probably blow my brains out or my balls off if I went to war to stop him.

Sometimes as the instructors talked on and on about the evils of nazism (we were told always to spell "nazi" with a small "n" even at the beginning of a sentence) and fascism I would leap to my feet and make something up:

"The survival of the human race depends upon selective accountability!"

Which meant, watch out who you go to bed with, but only I knew that. It really pissed everybody off.

I don't know where I got my stuff:

"One of the failures of Democracy is that the common vote guarantees a common leader who then leads us to a common apathetic predictability!"

I avoided any direct reference to Jews and Blacks, who had never given me any trouble. All my troubles had come from white gentiles. Thus, I wasn't a nazi by temperament or choice; the teachers more or less forced it on me by being so much alike and thinking so much alike and with their anti-German prejudice. I had also read somewhere that if a man didn't truly believe or understand what he was espousing, somehow he could do a more convincing job, which gave me a considerable advantage over the teachers.

"Breed a plow horse to a race horse and you get an offspring that is neither swift nor strong. A new Master Race will evolve from purposeful breeding!"

"There are no good wars or bad wars. The only thing bad about a war is to lose it. All wars have been fought for a so-called good Cause on both sides. But only the victor's Cause becomes history's Noble Cause. It's not a matter of who is right or who is wrong, it's a matter of who has the best generals and the better army!"

I loved it. I could make up anything I liked.

Of course, I was talking myself further and further away from any chance with the girls. But I had never been that close anyhow. I figured because of my wild speeches I was alone on campus but it wasn't so. Some others had been listening. One day, walking to my Current Affairs class, I heard somebody walking up behind me. I never liked anybody walking behind me, not close. So I turned as I walked. It was the student body president, Boyd Taylor. He was very popular with the students, the only man in the history of the college to have been elected president twice.

"Hey, Chinaski, I want to talk to you."

I'd never cared too much for Boyd, he was the typical good-

237

looking American youth with a guaranteed future, always properly dressed, casual, smooth, every hair of his black mustache trimmed. What his appeal was to the student body, I had no idea. He walked along beside me.

"Don't you think it looks bad for you, Boyd, to be seen walking with me?"

"I'll worry about that."

"All right. What is it?"

"Chinaski, this is just between you and me, got it?"

"Sure."

"Listen, I don't believe in what guys like you stand for or what you're trying to do."

"So?"

"But I want you to know that if you win here and in Europe I'm willing to join your side."

I could only look at him and laugh.

He stood there as I walked on. Never trust a man with a perfectly-trimmed mustache . . .

Other people had been listening as well. Coming out of Current Affairs I ran into Baldy standing there with a guy five feet tall and three feet wide. The guy's head was sunk down into his shoulders, he had a very round head, small ears, cropped hair, pea eyes, tiny wet round mouth.

A nut, I thought, a killer.

"HEY, HANK!" Baldy hollered.

I walked over. "I thought we were finished, LaCrosse."

"Oh no! There are *great* things still to do!"

Shit! Baldy was one too!

Why did the Master Race movement draw nothing but mental and physical cripples?

"I want you to meet Igor Stirnov."

I reached out and we shook hands. He squeezed mine with all his strength. It really hurt.

"Let go," I said, "or I'll bust your fucking missing neck!"

Igor let go. "I don't trust men with limp handshakes. Why do you have a limp handshake?"

"I'm weak today. They burned my toast for breakfast and at

lunch I spilled my chocolate milk."

Igor turned to Baldy. "What's with this guy?"

"Don't worry about him. He's got his own ways."

Igor looked at me again.

"My grandfather was a White Russian. During the Revolution the Reds killed him. I must get even with those bastards!"

"I see."

Then another student came walking toward us. "Hey, Fenster!" Baldy hollered.

Fenster walked up. We shook hands. I gave him a limp one. I didn't like to shake hands. Fenster's first name was Bob. There was to be a meeting at a house in Glendale, the Americans for America Party. Fenster was the campus representative. He walked off. Baldy leaned over and whispered into my ear, "They're Nazis!"

Igor had a car and a gallon of rum. We met in front of Baldy's house. Igor passed the bottle. Good stuff, it really burned the membranes of the throat. Igor drove his car like a tank, right through stop signals. People blew their horns and slammed on their brakes and he waved a fake black pistol at them.

"Hey, Igor," said Baldy, "show Hank your pistol."

Igor was driving. Baldy and I were in the back. Igor passed me his pistol. I looked at it.

"It's great!" Baldy said. "He carved it out of wood and stained it with black shoe polish. Looks real, doesn't it?"

"Yeah," I said. "He's even drilled a hole in the barrel."

I handed the gun back to Igor. "Very nice," I said.

He handed back the jug of rum. I took a hit and handed the bottle to Baldy. He looked at me and said, "Heil Hitler!"

We were the last to arrive. It was a large handsome house. We were met at the door by a fat smiling boy who looked like he had spent a lifetime eating chestnuts by the fire. His parents didn't seem to be about. His name was Larry Kearny. We followed him through the big house and down a long dark stairway. All I could see was Kearny's shoulders and head. He was certainly a well-fed fellow and looked to be far saner than Baldy, Igor or myself. Maybe there would be something to learn here.

Then we were in the cellar. We found some chairs. Fenster nodded to us. There were seven others there whom I didn't know. There was a desk on a raised platform. Larry walked up and stood behind the desk. Behind him on the wall was a large American flag. Larry stood very straight. "We will now pledge allegiance to the flag of the United States of America!"

My god, I thought, I am in the wrong place!

We stood and took the pledge, but I stopped after "I pledge allegiance . . ." I didn't say to what.

We sat down. Larry started talking from behind the desk. He explained that since this was the first meeting, he would preside. After two or three meetings, after we got to know one another, a president could be elected if we wished. But meanwhile . . .

"We face here, in America, two threats to our liberty. We face the communist scourge and the black takeover. Most often they work hand in hand. We true Americans will gather here in an attempt to counter this scourge, this menace. It has gotten so that no decent white girl can walk the streets anymore without being accosted by a black male!"

Igor leaped up. "We'll kill them!"

"The communists want to divide the wealth for which we have worked so long, which our fathers labored for, and *their* fathers before them worked for. The communists want to give our money to every black man, homo, bum, murderer and child molester who walks our streets!"

"We'll kill them!"

"They must be stopped."

"We'll arm!"

"Yes, we'll arm! And we'll meet here and formulate a master plan to save America!"

The fellows cheered. Two or three of them yelled, "Heil Hitler!" Then the get-to-know-each-other time arrived.

Larry passed out cold beers and we stood around in little groups talking, not much being said, except we reached a general agreement that we needed target practice so that we would be expert with our guns when the time came.

When we got back to Igor's house his parents didn't seem to be about, either. Igor got out a frying pan, put in four cubes of butter, and began to melt them. He took the rum, put it in a large pot and warmed it up.

"This is what men drink," he said. Then he looked at Baldy. "Are you a man, Baldy?"

Baldy was already drunk. He stood very straight, hands down at his sides. "YES, I'M A MAN!" He started to weep. The tears came rolling down. "I'M A MAN!" He stood very straight and yelled, "HEIL HITLER!" the tears rolling.

Igor looked at me. "Are you a man?"

"I don't know. Is that rum ready?"

"I'm not sure I trust you. I'm not so sure that you are one of us. Are you a counter-spy? Are you an enemy agent?"

"No."

"Are you one of us?"

"I don't know. Only one thing I'm sure of."

"What's that?"

"I don't like you. Is the rum ready?"

"You *see?*" said Baldy. "I told you he was mean!"

"We'll see who is the meanest before the night is ended," said Igor.

Igor poured the melted butter into the boiling rum, then shut off the flame and stirred. I didn't like him but he certainly was different and I liked that. Then he found three drinking cups, large, blue, with Russian writing on them. He poured the buttered rum into the cups.

"O.K.," he said, "drink up!"

"Shit, it's about time," I said and I let it slide down. It was a little too hot and it stank.

I watched Igor drink his. I saw his little pea eyes over the rim of his cup. He managed to get it down, driblets of golden buttered rum leaking out of the corners of his stupid mouth. He was looking at Baldy. Baldy was standing, staring down into his cup. I knew from the old days that Baldy just didn't have a natural love of drinking.

Igor stared at Baldy. "Drink up!"

"Yes, Igor, yes . . ."

Baldy lifted the blue cup. He was having a difficult time. It was too hot for him and he didn't like the taste. Half of it ran out of his mouth and over his chin and onto his shirt. His empty cup fell to the kitchen floor.

Igor squared himself in front of Baldy.

"You're not a man!"

"I AM A MAN, IGOR! I AM A MAN!"

"YOU LIE!"

Igor backhanded him across the face and as Baldy's head jumped to one side, he straightened him up with a slap to the other side of his face. Baldy stood at attention with his hands rigidly at his sides.

"I'm . . . a man . . ."

Igor continued to stand in front of him.

"I'll *make* a man out of you!"

"O.K.," I said to Igor, "leave him alone."

Igor left the kitchen. I poured myself another rum. It was dreadful stuff but it was all there was.

Igor walked back in. He was holding a gun, a real one, an old six-shooter.

"We will now play Russian roulette," he announced.

"Your mother's ass," I said.

"I'll play, Igor," said Baldy, "I'll play! I'm a *man!*"

"All right," said Igor, "there is one bullet in the gun. I will spin the chamber and hand the gun to you."

Igor spun the chamber and handed the gun to Baldy. Baldy took it and pointed it at his head. "I'm a man . . . I'm a man . . . I'll do it!"

He began crying again. "I'll do it . . . I'm a man . . ."

Baldy let the muzzle of the gun slip away from his temple. He pointed it away from his skull and pulled the trigger. There was a click.

Igor took the gun, spun the chamber and handed it to me. I handed it back.

"You go first."

Igor spun the chamber, held the gun up to the light and looked through the chamber. Then he put the gun to his temple and pulled the trigger. There was a click.

"Big deal," I said. "You checked the chamber to see where the bullet was."

242

Igor spun the chamber and handed the gun to me. "Your turn . . ."

I handed the gun back. "Stuff it," I told him.

I walked over to pour myself another rum. As I did there was a shot. I looked down. Near my foot, in the kitchen floor, there was a bullet hole.

I turned around.

"You ever point that thing at me again and I'll kill you, Igor."

"Yeah?"

"Yeah."

He stood there smiling. He slowly began to raise the gun. I waited. Then he lowered the gun. That was about it for the night. We went out to the car and Igor drove us home. But we stopped first at Westlake Park and rented a boat and went out on the lake to finish off the rum. With the last drink, Igor loaded up the gun and shot holes in the bottom of the boat. We were forty yards from shore and had to swim in . . .

It was late when I got home. I crawled over the old berry bush and through the bedroom window. I undressed and went to bed while in the next room my father snored.

53

I was coming home from classes down Westview hill. I never had any books to carry. I passed my exams by listening to the class lectures and by guessing at the answers. I never had to cram for exams. I could get my "C's." And as I was coming down the hill I ran into a giant spider web. I was always doing that. I stood there pulling the sticky web from myself and looking for the spider. Then I saw him: a big fat black son-of-a-bitch. I crushed him. I had learned to hate spiders. When I went to hell I would be eaten by a spider.

All my life, in that neighborhood, I had been walking into spider webs, I had been attacked by blackbirds, I had lived with my father. Everything was eternally dreary, dismal, damned. Even the weather was insolent and bitchy. It was either unbearably hot for weeks on end, or it rained, and when it rained it rained for five or six days. The water came up over the lawns and poured into the houses. Who'd ever planned the drainage system had probably been well paid for his ignorance about such matters.

And my own affairs were as bad, as dismal, as the day I had been born. The only difference was that now I could drink now and then, though never often enough. Drink was the only thing that kept a man from feeling forever stunned and useless. Everything else just kept picking and picking, hacking away. And nothing was interesting, nothing. The people were restrictive and careful, all alike. And I've got to live with these fuckers for the rest of my life, I thought. God, they all had assholes and sexual organs and their mouths and their armpits. They shit and they chattered

244

and they were dull as horse dung. The girls looked good from a distance, the sun shining through their dresses, their hair. But get up close and listen to their minds running out of their mouths, you felt like digging in under a hill and hiding out with a tommy-gun. I would certainly never be able to be happy, to get married, I could never have children. Hell, I couldn't even get a job as a dishwasher.

Maybe I'd be a bank robber. Some god-damned thing. Something with flare, fire. You only had one shot. Why be a window washer?

I lit a cigarette and walked further down the hill. Was I the only person who was distracted by this future without a chance?

I saw another one of those big black spiders. He was about face-high, in his web, right in my path. I took my cigarette and placed it against him. The tremendous web shook and leaped as he jumped, the branches of the bush trembled. He leaped out of the web and fell to the sidewalk. Cowardly killers, the whole bunch of them. I crushed him with my shoe. A worthwhile day, I had killed two spiders, I had upset the balance of nature—now we would all be eaten up by the bugs and the flies.

I walked further down the hill, I was near the bottom when a large bush began to shake. The King Spider was after me. I strode forward to meet it.

My mother leaped out from behind the bush. *"Henry, Henry, don't go home, don't go home, your father will kill you!"*

"How's he going to do that? I can whip his ass."

"No, he's *furious*, Henry! Don't go home, he'll kill you! I've been waiting here for hours!"

My mother's eyes were wide with fear and quite beautiful, large and brown.

"What's he doing home this early?"

"He had a headache, he got the afternoon off!"

"I thought you were working, that you'd found a new job?"

She'd gotten a job as a housekeeper.

"He came and got me! He's *furious!* He'll *kill you!*"

"Don't worry, Mom, if he messes with me I'll kick his god-damned ass, I promise you."

"Henry, he found your short stories and he read them!"

"I never asked him to read them."

"He found them in a drawer! He read them, he read all of them!"

I had written ten or twelve short stories. Give a man a type-writer and he becomes a writer. I had hidden the stories under the paper lining of my shorts-and-stockings drawer.

"Well," I said, "the old man poked around and he got his fingers burned."

"He said that he was going to kill you! He said that no son of his could write stories like that and live under the same roof with him!"

I took her by the arm. "Let's go home, Mom, and see what he does . . ."

"Henry, he's thrown all your clothes out on the front lawn, all your dirty laundry, your typewriter, your suitcase and your stories!"

"My stories?"

"Yes, those too . . ."

"I'll kill him!"

I pulled away from her and walked across 21st Street and toward Longwood Avenue. She went after me.

"Henry, Henry, don't go in there."

The poor woman was yanking at the back of my shirt.

"Henry, listen, get yourself a room somewhere! Henry, I have ten dollars! Take this ten dollars and get yourself a room some-where!"

I turned. She was holding out the ten.

"Forget it," I said. "I'll just go."

"Henry, take the money! Do it for me! Do it for your mother!"

"Well, all right . . ."

I took the ten, put it in my pocket.

"Thanks, that's a lot of money."

"It's all right, Henry. I love you, Henry, but you must go."

She ran ahead of me as I walked toward the house. Then I saw it: everything was strewn across the lawn, all my dirty and clean clothes, the suitcase flung there open, socks, shirts, pajamas, an old robe, everything flung everywhere, on the lawn and into the street. And I saw my manuscripts being blown in the wind, they were in the gutter, everywhere.

My mother ran up the driveway to the house and I screamed after her so he could hear me, "TELL HIM TO COME OUT HERE AND I'LL KNOCK HIS GOD-DAMNED HEAD OFF!"

246

I went after my manuscripts first. That was the lowest of the blows, doing that to me. They were the one thing he had no right to touch. As I picked up each page from the gutter, from the lawn and from the street, I began to feel better. I found every page I could, placed them in the suitcase under the weight of a shoe, then rescued the typewriter. It had broken out of its case but it looked all right. I looked at my rags scattered about. I left the dirty laundry, I left the pajamas, which were only a handed-down pair of his discards. There wasn't much else to pack. I closed the suitcase, picked it up with the typewriter and started to walk away. I could see two faces peering after me from behind the drapes. But I quickly forgot that, walked up Longwood, across 21st and up old Westview hill. I didn't feel much different than I had always felt. I was neither elated nor dejected; it all seemed to be just a continuation. I was going to take the "W" streetcar, get a transfer, and go somewhere downtown.

54

I found a room on Temple Street in the Filipino district. It was
$3.50 a week, upstairs on the second floor. I paid the landlady—a
middle-aged blond—a week's rent. The toilet and tub were down
the hall but there was a wash basin to piss in.

My first night there I discovered a bar downstairs just to the
right of the entrance. I liked that. All I had to do was climb the
stairway and I was home. The bar was full of little dark men but
they didn't bother me. I'd heard all the stories about Filipinos—
that they liked white girls, blonds in particular, that they carried
stilettoes, that since they were all the same size, seven of them
would chip in and buy one expensive suit, with all the accessories,
and they would take turns wearing the suit one night a week.
George Raft had said somewhere that Filipinos set the style
trends. They stood on street corners and swung golden chains
around and around, thin golden chains, seven or eight inches long,
each man's chain-length indicating the length of his penis.

The bartender was Filipino.
"You're new, huh?" he asked.
"I live upstairs. I'm a student."
"No credit."
I put some coins down.
"Give me an Eastside."

248

He came back with the bottle.

"Where can a fellow get a girl?" I asked.

He picked up some of the coins.

"I don't know anything," he said and walked to the register.

That first night I closed the bar. Nobody bothered me. A few blond women left with the Filipinos. The men were quiet drinkers. They sat in little groups with their heads close together, talking, now and then laughing in a very quiet manner. I liked them. When the bar closed and I got up to leave the bartender said, "Thank you." That was never done in American bars, not to me anyhow.

I liked my new situation. All I needed was money.

I decided to keep going to college. It would give me some place to be during the daytime. My friend Becker had dropped out. There wasn't anybody that I much cared for there except maybe the instructor in Anthropology, a known Communist. He didn't teach much Anthropology. He was a large man, casual and likeable.

"Now the way you fry a porterhouse steak," he told the class, "you get the pan red hot, you drink a shot of whiskey and then you pour a thin layer of salt in the pan. You drop the steak in and sear it but not for too long. Then you flip it, sear the other side, drink another shot of whiskey, take the steak out and eat it immediately."

Once when I was stretched out on the campus lawn he had come walking by and had stopped and stretched out beside me.

"Chinaski, you don't believe all that Nazi hokum you're spreading around, do you?"

"I'm not saying. Do you believe your crap?"

"Of course I do."

"Good luck."

"Chinaski, you're nothing but a wienerschnitzel."

He got up, brushed off the grass and leaves and walked away . . .

I had been at the Temple Street place only for a couple of days when Jimmy Hatcher found me. He knocked on the door one night and I opened it and there he was with two other guys, fellow aircraft workers, one called Delmore, the other, Fastshoes.

"How come he's called 'Fastshoes'?"

"You ever lend him money, you'll know."

"Come on in . . . How in Christ's name did you find me?"

"Your folks had you traced by a private dick."

"Damn, they know how to take the joy out of a man's life."

"Maybe they're worried?"

"If they're worried all they have to do is send money."

"They claim you'll drink it up."

"Then let them worry . . ."

The three of them came in and sat around on the bed and the floor. They had a fifth of whiskey and some paper cups. Jimmy poured all around.

"Nice place you've got here."

"It's great. I can see the City Hall every time I stick my head out the window."

Fastshoes pulled a deck of cards from his pocket. He was sitting on the rug. He looked up at me.

"You gamble?"

"Every day. You got a marked deck?"

"Hey, you son-of-a-bitch!"

"Don't curse me or I'll hang your wig on my mantlepiece."

"Honest, man, these cards are straight!"

"All I play is poker and 21. What's the limit?"

"Two bucks."

"We'll split for the deal."

I got the deal and called for draw poker, regular. I didn't like wild cards, too much luck was needed that way. Two bits for the kitty. As I dealt, Jimmy poured another round.

"How are you making it, Hank?"

"I'm writing term papers for the other people."

"Brilliant."

"Yeah . . ."

"Hey, you guys," said Jimmy, "I told you this guy was a genius."

"Yeah," said Delmore. He was to my right. He opened.

250

"Two bits," he said.

We followed him in.

"Three cards," said Delmore.

"One," said Jimmy.

"Three," said Fastshoes.

"I'll stand," I said.

"Two bits," said Delmore.

We all stayed in and then I said, "I'll see your two bits and raise you two bucks."

Delmore dropped out, Jimmy dropped out. Fastshoes looked at me. "What else do you see besides City Hall when you stick your head out the window?"

"Just play your hand. I'm not here to chat about gymnastics or the scenery."

"All right," he said, "I'm out."

I scooped up the pot and gathered in their cards, leaving mine face down.

"What did ya have?" asked Fastshoes.

"Pay to see or weep forever," I said sweeping my cards into the deck and mixing them together, shuffling them, feeling like Gable before he got weakened by God at the time of the San Francisco earthquake.

The deck changed hands but my luck held, most of the time. It had been payday at the aircraft plant. Never bring a lot of money to where a poor man lives. He can only lose what little he has. On the other hand it is mathematically possible that he might win whatever you bring with you. What you must do, with money and the poor, is never let them get too close to one another.

Somehow I felt that the night was to be mine. Delmore soon tapped out and left.

"Fellows," I said, "I've got an idea. Cards are too slow. Let's just match coins, ten bucks a toss, odd man wins."

"O.K.," said Jimmy.

"O.K.," said Fastshoes.

The whiskey was gone. We were into a bottle of my cheap wine.

"All right," I said, "flip the coins high! Catch them on your palms. And when I say 'lift,' we'll check the result."

We flipped them high. Caught them.

"Lift!" I said.

I was odd man. Shit. Twenty bucks, just like that.

I jammed the tens into my pocket.

"Flip!" I said. We did.

"Lift!" I said.

I won again.

"Flip!" I said.

"Lift!" I said.

Fastshoes won.

I got the next.

Then Jimmy won.

I got the next two.

"Wait," I said, "I've got to piss!"

I walked over to the sink and pissed. We had finished the bottle of wine. I opened the closet door. "I got another bottle of wine in here," I told them.

I took most of the bills out of my pocket and threw them into the closet. I came out, opened the bottle, poured drinks all around.

"Shit," said Fastshoes looking into his wallet, "I'm almost broke."

"Me too," said Jimmy.

"I wonder who's got the money?" I asked.

They weren't very good drinkers. Mixing the wine and the whiskey was bad for them. They were weaving a bit.

Fastshoes fell back against the dresser knocking an ashtray to the floor. It broke in half.

"Pick it up," I said.

"I won't pick up shit," he said.

"I said, 'pick it up'!"

"I won't pick up shit."

Jimmy reached and picked up the broken ashtray.

"You guys get out of here," I said.

"You can't make me go," said Fastshoes.

"All right," I said, "just open your mouth *one* more time, say *one* word and you won't be able to separate your head from your asshole!"

"Let's go, Fastshoes," said Jimmy.

I opened the door and they filed past unsteadily. I followed them down the hall to the head of the stairway. We stood there.

"Hank," said Jimmy, "I'll see you again. Take it easy."

"All right, Jim . . ."

"Listen," Fastshoes said to me, "You . . ."

I shot a straight right into his mouth. He fell backward down the stairway, twisting and bouncing. He was about my size, six feet and one-eighty, and you could hear the sound of him for a block. Two Filipinos and the blond landlady were in the lobby. They looked at Fastshoes laying there but they didn't move toward him.

"You killed him!" said Jimmy.

He ran down the stairway and turned Fastshoes over. Fastshoes had a bloody nose and mouth. Jimmy held his head. Jimmy looked up at me.

"That wasn't right, Hank . . ."

"Yeah, what ya gonna do?"

"I think," said Jimmy, "that we're going to come back and get you . . ."

"Wait a minute," I said.

I walked back to my room and poured myself a wine. I hadn't liked Jimmy's paper cups and I had been drinking out of a used jelly glass. The paper label was still on the side, stained with dirt and wine. I walked back out.

Fastshoes was reviving. Jimmy was helping him to his feet. Then he put Fastshoes' arm around his neck. They were standing there.

"Now what did you say?" I asked.

"You're an ugly man, Hank. You need to be taught a lesson."

"You mean I'm not pretty?"

"I mean, you *act* ugly . . ."

"Take your friend out of here before I come down there and finish him off!"

Fastshoes raised his bloody head. He had on a flowered Hawaiian shirt, only now many of the colors were stained with red.

He looked at me. Then he spoke. I could barely hear him. But I heard it. He said, "I'm going to kill you . . ."

"Yeah," said Jimmy, "we'll get you."

"YEAH, FUCKERS?" I screamed. "I'M NOT GOING ANYWHERE! ANYTIME YOU WANT TO FIND ME I'LL BE IN ROOM 5! I'LL BE WAITING! ROOM 5, GOT IT? AND THE DOOR WILL BE OPEN!"

I lifted the jelly glass full of wine and drained it. Then I hurled that jelly glass at them. I threw the son-of-a-bitch, hard. But my aim was bad. It hit the side of the stairway wall, glanced off and shot into the lobby between the landlady and her two Filipino friends.

Jimmy turned Fastshoes toward the exit door and began slowly walking him out. It was a tedious, agonizing journey. I heard Fastshoes again, half moaning, half weeping, "I'll kill him . . . I'll kill him . . ."

Then Jimmy had him out the doorway. They were gone.

The blond landlady and the two Filipinos were still standing in the lobby, looking up at me. I was barefooted, and had gone five or six days without a shave. I needed a haircut. I only combed my hair once, in the morning, then didn't bother again. My gym teachers were always after me about my posture: "Pull your *shoulders* back! Why are you looking at the *ground?* What's down *there?*"

I would never set any trends or styles. My white t-shirt was stained with wine, burned, with many cigarettes and cigar holes, spotted with blood and vomit. It was too small, it rode up exposing my gut and belly button. And my pants were too small. They gripped me tightly and rose well above my ankles.

The three of them stood and looked at me. I looked down at them. "Hey, you guys, come on up for a little drink!"

The two little men looked up at me and grinned. The landlady, a faded Carole Lombard type, looked on impassively. Mrs. Kansas, they called her. Could she be in love with me? She was wearing pink shoes with high heels and a black sparkling sequinned dress. Little chips of light flashed at me. Her breasts were something that no mere mortal would ever see—they were only for kings, dictators, rulers, Filipinos.

"Anybody got a smoke?" I asked. "I'm out of smokes."

The little dark fellow standing to one side of Mrs. Kansas made a slight motion with one hand toward his jacket pocket and a pack of Camels jumped in the lobby air. Deftly he caught the pack in

254

his other hand. With the invisible tap of a finger on the bottom of the pack a smoke leaped up, tall, true, singular and exposed, ready to be taken.

"Hey, shit, thanks," I said.

I started down the stairway, made a mis-step, lunged, almost fell, grabbed the bannister, righted myself, readjusted my perceptions, and walked on down. Was I drunk? I walked up to the little guy holding the pack. I bowed slightly.

I lifted out the Camel. Then I flipped it in the air, caught it, stuck it into my mouth. My dark friend remained expressionless, the grin having vanished when I had begun down the stairway. My little friend bent forward, cupped his hands around the flame and lit my smoke.

I inhaled, exhaled. "Listen, why don't you all come up to my place and we'll have a couple of drinks?"

"No," said the little guy who had lit my cigarette.

"Maybe we can catch the Bee or some Bach on my radio! I'm *educated*, you know. I'm a student . . ."

"No," said the other little guy.

I took a big drag on my smoke, then looked at Carole Lombard—Mrs. Kansas.

Then I looked at my two friends.

"She's *yours*. I don't want her. She's yours. Just come on up. We'll drink a little wine. In good old room 5."

There was no answer. I rocked on my heels a bit as the whiskey and the wine fought for possession. I let my cigarette dangle a bit from the right side of my mouth as I sent up a plume of smoke. I continued letting the cigarette dangle like that.

I knew about stilettoes. In the little time I had been there I had seen two enactments of the stiletto. From my window one night, looking out at the sound of sirens, I saw a body there just below my window on the Temple Street sidewalk, in the moonlight, under the streetlight. Another time, another body. Nights of the stiletto. Once a white man, the other time one of them. Each time, blood running on the pavement, real blood, just like that, moving across the pavement and into the gutter, you could see it going along in the gutter, meaningless, dumb . . . that so *much* blood could come from just one man.

"All right, my friends," I said to them, "no hard feelings. I'll drink alone . . ."

I turned and started to walk toward the stairway.

"Mr. Chinaski," I heard Mrs. Kansas' voice.

I turned and looked at her flanked by my two little friends.

"Just go to your room and sleep. If you cause any more distur-
bance I will phone the Los Angeles Police Department."

I turned and walked back up the stairway.

*No life anywhere, no life in this town or this place or in this weary
existence . . .*

My door was open. I walked in. There was one-third of a cheap
bottle of wine left.

Maybe there was another bottle in the closet?

I opened the closet door. No bottle. But there were tens and
twenties everywhere. There was a rolled twenty lying between a
pair of dirty socks with holes in the toes; and there from a shirt
collar, a ten dangling; and here from an old jacket, another ten
caught in a side pocket. Most of the money was on the floor.

I picked up a bill, slipped it into the side pocket of my pants,
went to the door, closed and locked it, then went down the
stairway to the bar.

55

A couple of nights later Becker walked in. I guess my parents gave him my address or he located me through the college. I had my name and address listed with the employment division at the college, under "unskilled labor." "I will do anything honest or otherwise," I had written on my card. No calls.

Becker sat in a chair as I poured the wine. He had on a Marine uniform.

"I see they sucked you in," I said.

"I lost my Western Union job. It was all that was left."

I handed him his drink. "You're not a patriot then?"

"Hell no."

"Why the Marines?"

"I heard about boot camp. I wanted to see if I could get through it."

"And you did."

"I did. There are some crazy guys there. There's a fight almost every night. Nobody stops it. They almost kill each other."

"I like that."

"Why don't you join?"

"I don't like to get up early in the morning and I don't like to take orders."

"How are you going to make it?"

"I don't know. When I get down to my last dime I'll just walk over to skid row."

"There are some real weirdos down there."

"They're everywhere."

257

I poured Becker another wine.

"The problem is," he said, "that there's not much time to write."

"You still want to be a writer?"

"Sure. How about you?"

"Yeah," I said, "but it's pretty hopeless."

"You mean you're not good enough?"

"No, they're not good enough."

"What do you mean?"

"You read the magazines? The 'Best Short Stories of the Year' books? There are at least a dozen of them."

"Yeah, I read them . . ."

"You read *The New Yorker? Harper's? The Atlantic?*"

"Yeah . . ."

"This is 1940. They're still publishing 19th Century stuff, heavy, labored, pretentious. You either get a headache reading the stuff or you fall asleep."

"What's wrong?"

"It's a trick, it's a con, a little inside game."

"Sounds like you've been rejected."

"I knew I *would* be. Why waste the stamps? I need wine."

"I'm going to break through," said Becker. "You'll see my books on the library shelves one day."

"Let's not talk about writing."

"I've read your stuff," said Becker. "You're too bitter and you hate everything."

"Let's not talk about writing."

"Now you take Thomas Wolfe . . ."

"God damn Thomas Wolfe! He sounds like an old woman on the telephone!"

"O.K., who's your boy?"

"James Thurber."

"All that upper-middle-class folderol . . ."

"He *knows* that everyone is crazy."

"Thomas Wolfe is of the earth . . ."

"Only assholes talk about writing . . ."

"You calling me an asshole?"

"Yes . . ."

I poured him another wine and myself another wine.

258

"You're a fool for getting into that uniform."

"You call me an asshole and you call me a fool. I thought we were friends."

"We are. I just don't think you're protecting yourself."

"Every time I see you you have a drink in your hand. You call *that* protecting yourself?"

"It's the best way I know. Without drink I would have long ago cut my god-damned throat."

"That's bullshit."

"Nothing's bullshit that works. The Pershing Square preachers have their God. I have the blood of my god!"

I raised my glass and drained it.

"You're just hiding from reality," Becker said.

"Why not?"

"You'll never be a writer if you hide from reality."

"What are you talking about? That's what writers *do!*"

Becker stood up. "When you talk to me, don't raise your voice."

"What do you want to do, raise my dick?"

"You don't have a dick!"

I caught him unexpectedly with a right that landed behind his ear. The glass flew out of his hand and he staggered across the room. Becker was a powerful man, much stronger than I was. He hit the edge of the dresser, turned, and I landed another straight right to the side of his face. He staggered over near the window which was open and I was afraid to hit him then because he might fall into the street.

Becker gathered himself together and shook his head to clear it.

"All right now," I said, "let's have a little drink. Violence nauseates me."

"O.K.," said Becker.

He walked over and picked up his glass. The cheap wine I drank didn't have corks, the tops just unscrewed. I unscrewed a new bottle. Becker held out his glass and I poured him one. I poured myself one, set the bottle down. Becker emptied his. I emptied mine.

"No hard feelings," I said.

"Hell, no, buddy," said Becker, putting down his glass. Then he dug a right into my gut. I doubled over and as I did he pushed down on the back of my head and brought his knee up into my face. I dropped to my knees, blood running from my nose all over my shirt.

"Pour me a drink, buddy," I said, "let's think this thing over."

"Get up," said Becker, "that was just chapter one."

I got up and moved toward Becker. I blocked his jab, caught his right on my elbow, and punched a short straight right to his nose. Becker stepped back. We both had bloody noses.

I rushed him. We were both swinging blindly. I caught some good shots. He hit me with another good right to the belly. I doubled over but came up with an uppercut. It landed. It was a beautiful shot, a lucky shot. Becker lurched backwards and fell against the dresser. The back of his head hit the mirror. The mirror shattered. He was stunned. I had him. I grabbed him by the shirt front and hit him with a hard right behind his left ear. He dropped on the rug, and knelt there on all fours. I walked over and unsteadily poured myself a drink.

"Becker," I told him, "I kick ass around here about twice a week. You just showed up on the wrong day."

I emptied my glass. Becker got up. He stood a while looking at me. Then he came forward.

"Becker," I said, "listen . . ."

He started a right lead, pulled it back and slammed a left to my mouth. We started in again. There wasn't much defense. It was just punch, punch, punch. He pushed me over a chair and the chair flattened. I got up, caught him coming in. He stumbled backwards and I landed another right. He crashed backwards into the wall and the whole room shook. He bounced off and landed a right high on my forehead and I saw lights: green, yellow, red . . . Then he landed a left to the ribs and a right to the face. I swung and missed.

God damn, I thought, doesn't anybody *hear* all this noise? Why don't they come and stop it? Why don't they call the police?

Becker rushed me again. I missed a roundhouse right and then that was it for me . . .

When I regained consciousness it was dark, it was night. I was under the bed, just my head was sticking out. I must have crawled under there. I was a coward. I had puked all over myself. I crawled out from under the bed.

260

I looked at the smashed dresser mirror and the chair. The table was upside down. I walked over and tried to set it upright. It fell over. Two of the legs wouldn't hold. I tried to fix them as best I could. I set the table up. It stood a moment, then fell over again. The rug was wet with wine and puke. I found a wine bottle lying on its side. There was a bit left. I drank that down and then looked around for more. There was nothing. There was nothing to drink. I put the chain on the door. I found a cigarette, lit it and stood in the window, staring down at Temple Street. It was a nice night out.

Then there was a knock on the door. "Mr. Chinaski?" It was Mrs. Kansas. She wasn't alone. I heard other voices whispering. She was with her little dark friends.

"Mr. Chinaski?"

"Yes?"

"I want to come into your room."

"What for?"

"I want to change the sheets."

"I'm sick now. I can't let you in."

"I just want to change the sheets. I'll be just a few minutes."

"No, I can't let you in. Come in the morning."

I heard them whispering. Then I heard them walking down the hall. I went over and sat on the bed. I needed a drink, bad. It was a Saturday night, the whole town was drunk.

Maybe I could sneak out?

I walked to the door and opened it a crack, leaving the chain on, and I peeked out. At the top of the stairway there was a Filipino, one of Mrs. Kansas' friends. He had a hammer in his hand. He was down on his knees. He looked up at me, grinned, and then pounded a nail into the rug. He was pretending to fix the rug. I closed the door.

I really needed a drink. I paced the floor. Why could everybody in the world have a drink but me? How long was I going to have to stay in that god-damned room? I opened the door again. It was the same. He looked up at me, grinned, then hammered another nail into the floor. I closed the door.

I got out my suitcase and began throwing my few clothes in there.

I still had quite a bit of money I had won gambling but I knew that I could never pay for the damages to that room. Nor did I want to. It really hadn't been my fault. They should have stopped the fight. And Becker had broken the mirror . . .

I was packed. I had the suitcase in one hand and my portable typewriter in its case in the other. I stood in front of the door for some time. I looked out again. He was still there. I slipped the chain off the door. Then I pulled the door open and burst out. I ran toward the stairway.

"HEY! *Where you go?*" the little guy asked. He was still down on one knee. He started to raise his hammer. I swung the portable typewriter hard against the side of his head. It made a horrible sound. I was down the steps and through the lobby and out the door.

Maybe I had killed the guy.

I started running down Temple Street. Then I saw a cab. He was empty. I leaped in.

"Bunker Hill," I said, "*fast!*"

56

I saw a vacancy sign in the window in front of a rooming-house, had the cabby pull up. I paid him and walked up on the front porch, rang the bell. I had one black eye from the fight, another cut eye, a swollen nose, and my lips were puffed. My left ear was bright red and every time I touched it, an electric shock ran through my body.

An old man came to the door. He was in his undershirt and it looked like he had spilled chili and beans across the front of it. His hair was grey and uncombed, he needed a shave and he was puffing on a wet cigarette that stank.

"You the landlord?" I asked.

"Yep."

"I need a room."

"You workin'?"

"I'm a writer."

"You don't look like a writer."

"What do they look like?"

He didn't answer.

Then he said, "$2.50 a week."

"Can I see it?"

He belched, then said, "Foller me . . ."

We walked down a long hall. There was no hall rug. The boards creaked and sank as we walked on them. I heard a man's voice from one of the rooms.

"Suck me, you piece of shit!"

"Three dollars," I heard a woman's voice.

"Three dollars? I'll give you a bloody asshole!"

He slapped her hard, she screamed. We walked on.

"The place is in back," the guy said, "but you are allowed to use the house bathroom."

There was a shack in back with four doors. He walked up to #3 and opened it. We walked in. There was a cot, a blanket, a small dresser and a little stand. On the stand was a hotplate.

"You got a hotplate here," he said.

"That's nice."

"$2.50 in advance."

I paid him.

"I'll give you your receipt in the morning."

"Fine."

"What's your name?"

"Chinaski."

"I'm Connors."

He slipped a key off his key ring and gave it to me.

"We run a nice quiet place here. I want to keep it that way."

"Sure."

I closed the door behind him. There was a single light overhead, unshaded. Actually the place was fairly clean. Not bad. I got up, went outside and locked the door behind me, walked through the back yard to an alley.

I shouldn't have given that guy my real name, I thought. I might have killed my little dark friend over on Temple Street.

There was a long wooden stairway which went down the side of a cliff and led to the street below. Quite romantic. I walked along until I saw a liquor store. I was going to get my drink. I bought two bottles of wine and I felt hungry too so I purchased a large bag of potato chips.

Back at my place, I undressed, climbed onto my cot, leaned against the wall, lit a cigarette and poured a wine. I felt good. It was quiet back there. I couldn't hear anybody in any of the other rooms in my shack. I had to take a piss, so I put on my shorts, went around the back of the shack and let go. From up there I could see the lights of the city. Los Angeles was a good place, there were many poor people, it would be easy to get lost among them. I went back inside, climbed back on the cot. As long as a man had wine

264

and cigarettes he could make it. I finished off my glass and poured another.

Maybe I could live by my wits. The eight-hour day was impossible, yet almost everybody submitted to it. And the war, everybody was talking about the war in Europe. I wasn't interested in world history, only my own. What crap. Your parents controlled your growing-up period, they pissed all over you. Then when you got ready to go out on your own, the others wanted to stick you into a uniform so you could get your ass shot off.

The wine tasted great. I had another.

The war. Here I was a virgin. Could you imagine getting your ass blown off for the sake of history before you even knew what a woman was? Or owned an automobile? What would I be protecting? Somebody else. Somebody else who didn't give a shit about me. Dying in a war never stopped wars from happening.

I could make it. I could win drinking contests, I could gamble. Maybe I could pull a few holdups. I didn't ask much, just to be left alone.

I finished the first bottle of wine and started in on the second.

Halfway through the second bottle, I stopped, stretched out. My first night in my new place. It was all right. I slept.

I was awakened by the sound of a key in the door. Then the door pushed open. I sat up on the cot. A man started to step in.

"GET THE FUCK OUT OF HERE!" I screamed.

He left fast. I heard him running off.

I got up and slammed the door.

People did that. They rented a place, stopped paying rent and kept the key, sneaking back to sleep there if it was vacant or robbing the place if the occupant was out. Well, *he* wouldn't be back. He knew if he tried it again that I'd bust his sack.

I went back to my cot and had another drink.

I was a little nervous. I was going to have to pick up a knife.

I finished my drink, poured another, drank that and went back to sleep.

57

After English class one day Mrs. Curtis asked me to stay.

She had great legs and a lisp and there was something about the legs and the lisp together that heated me up. She was about 32, had culture and style, but like everybody else, she was a god-damned liberal and that didn't take much originality or fight, it was just more Franky Roosevelt worship. I liked Franky because of his programs for the poor during the Depression. He had style too. I didn't think he really gave a damn about the poor but he was a great actor, great voice, and he had a great speech writer. But he wanted us in the war. It would put him into the history books. War presidents got more power and, later, more pages. Mrs. Curtis was just a chip off old Franky only she had much better legs. Poor Franky didn't have any legs but he had a wonderful brain. In some other country he would have made a powerful dictator.

When the last student left I walked up to Mrs. Curtis' desk. She smiled up at me. I had watched her legs for many hours and she knew it. She knew what I wanted, that she had nothing to teach me. She had only said one thing which I remembered. It wasn't her own idea, obviously, but I liked it:

"You can't overestimate the stupidity of the general public."

"Mr. Chinaski," she looked up at me, "we have certain students in this class who think they are very smart."

"Yeh?"

"Mr. Felton is our smartest student."

"O.K."

266

"What is it that troubles you?"

"What?"

"There's something . . . troubling you."

"Maybe."

"This is your last semester, isn't it?"

"How did you know?"

I'd been giving those legs a goodbye look. I'd decided the campus was just a place to hide. There were some campus freaks who stayed on forever. The whole college scene was soft. They never told you what to expect out there in the real world. They just crammed you with theory and never told you how hard the pavements were. A college education could destroy an individual for life. Books could make you soft. When you put them down, and really went *out* there, then you needed to know what they never told you. I had decided to quit after that semester, hang around Stinky and the gang, maybe meet somebody who had guts enough to hold up a liquor store or better yet, a bank.

"I knew you were going to quit," she said softly.

"'Begin' is a better word."

"There's going to be a war. Did you read 'Sailor Off The Bremen'?"

"That *New Yorker* stuff doesn't work for me."

"You've got to read things like that if you want to understand what is happening today."

"I don't think so."

"You just rebel against *everything*. How are you going to survive?"

"I don't know. I'm already tired."

Mrs. Curtis looked down at her desk for a long time. Then she looked up at me.

"We're going to get drawn into the war, one way or the other. Are you going to go?"

"That doesn't matter. I might, I might not."

"You'd make a good sailor."

I smiled, thought about being a sailor, then discarded that idea.

"If you stay another term," she said, "you can have anything you want."

She looked up at me and I knew exactly what she meant and she knew that I knew exactly what she meant.

"No," I said, "I'm leaving."

I walked toward the door. I stopped there, turned, gave her a little nod goodbye, a slight and quick goodbye. Outside I walked along under the campus trees. Everywhere, it seemed, there was a boy and a girl together. Mrs. Curtis was sitting alone at her desk as I walked alone. What a great triumph it would have been. Kissing that lisp, working those fine legs open, as Hitler swallowed up Europe and peered toward London.

After a while I walked over toward the gym. I was going to clean out my locker. No more exercising for me. People always talked about the good clean smell of fresh sweat. They had to make excuses for it. They never talked about the good clean smell of fresh shit. There was nothing really as glorious as a good beer shit—I mean after drinking twenty or twenty-five beers the night before. The odor of a beer shit like that spread all around and stayed for a good hour-and-a-half. It made you realize that you were really alive.

I found the locker, opened it and dumped my gym suit and shoes into the trash. Also two empty wine bottles. Good luck to the next one who got my locker. Maybe he'd end up mayor of Boise, Idaho. I threw the combo lock into the trash too. I'd never liked that combination: 1, 2, 1, 1, 2. Not very mental. The address of my parents' house had been 2122. Everything was minimal. In the R.O.T.C. it had been 1, 2, 3, 4; 1, 2, 3, 4. Maybe some day I'd move up to 5.

I walked out of the gym and took a shortcut through the playing field. There was a game of touch football going on, a pick-up game. I cut to one side to avoid it.

Then I heard Baldy: "Hey, Hank!"

I looked up and he was sitting in the stands with Monty Ballard. There wasn't much to Ballard. The nice thing about him was that he never talked unless you asked him a question. I never asked him any questions. He just looked at life out from underneath his dirty yellow hair and yearned to be a biologist.

I waved to them and kept walking.

"Come on up here, Hank!" Baldy yelled. "It's important."

I walked over. "What is it?"

268

"Sit down and watch that stocky guy in the gym suit."

I sat down. There was only one guy in a gym suit. He had on track choes with spikes. He was short but wide, very wide. He had amazing biceps, shoulders, a thick neck, heavy short legs. His hair was black; the front of his face almost flat; small mouth, not much nose, and the eyes, the eyes were there somewhere.

"Hey, I heard about this guy," I said.

"Watch him," said Baldy.

There were four guys on each team. The ball was snapped. The quarterback faded to pass. King Kong, Jr. was on defense. He played about halfway back. One of the guys on the offensive team ran deep, the other ran short. The center blocked. King Kong, Jr. lowered his shoulders and sped toward the guy playing short. He smashed into him, burying a shoulder into his side and gut and dumped him hard. Then he turned and trotted away. The pass was completed to the deep man for a TD.

"You see?" said Baldy.

"King Kong . . ."

"King Kong isn't playing football at all. He just hits some guy as hard as he can, play after play."

"You can't hit a pass receiver before he catches the ball," I said. "It's against the rules."

"Who's going to tell him?" Baldy asked.

"You going to tell him?" I asked Ballard.

"No," said Ballard.

King Kong's team took the kickoff. Now he could block legally. He came down and savaged the littlest guy on the field. He knocked the guy completely over, his head went between his legs as he flipped. The little guy was slow getting up.

"That King Kong is a subnormal," I said. "How did he ever pass his entrance exam?"

"They don't have them here."

King Kong's team lined up. Joe Stapen was the best guy on the other team. He wanted to be a shrink. He was tall, six foot two, lean, and he had guts. Joe Stapen and King Kong charged each other. Stapen did pretty good. He didn't get dumped. The next play they charged each other again. This time Joe bounced off and gave a little ground.

"Shit," said Baldy, "Joe's giving up."

The next time Kong hit Joe even harder, spinning him around, then running him 5 or 6 yards back up the field, his shoulder buried in Joe's back.

"This is really disgusting! That guy's nothing but a fucking *sadist!*" I said.

"Is he a sadist?" Baldy asked Ballard.

"He's a fucking sadist," said Ballard.

The next play Kong shifted back to the smallest guy. He just ran over him and piled on top of him, dropping him hard. The little guy didn't move for a while. Then he sat up and held his head. It looked like he was finished. I stood up.

"Well, here I go," I said.

"*Get* that son-of-a-bitch!" said Baldy.

"Sure," I said.

I walked down to the field.

"Hey, fellas. Need a player?"

The little guy stood up, started to walk off the field. He stopped as he reached me.

"Don't go in there. All that guy wants is to kill somebody."

"It's just touch football," I said.

It was our ball. I got into the huddle with Joe Stapen and the other two survivors.

"What's the game plan?" I asked.

"Just to stay the fuck alive," said Joe Stapen.

"What's the score?"

"I think they're winning," said Lenny Hill, the center.

We broke out of the huddle. Joe Stapen stood back and waited for the ball. I stood looking at Kong. I'd never seen him around campus. He probably hung around the men's crapper in the gym. He looked like a shit-sniffer. He also looked like a fetus-eater.

"Time!" I called.

Lenny Hill straightened up over the ball. I looked at Kong.

"My name's Hank. Hank Chinaski. Journalism."

Kong didn't answer. He just stared at me. He had dead white skin. There was no glitter or life in his eyes.

"What's your name?" I asked him.

He just kept staring.

"What's the matter? Got some placenta caught in your teeth?"

Kong slowly raised his right arm. Then he straightened it out

270

and pointed a finger at me. Then he lowered his arm.

"Well, suck my weenie," I said, "what's *that* mean?"

"Come on, let's play ball," one of Kong's mates said.

Lenny bent over the ball and snapped it. Kong came at me. I couldn't seem to focus on him. I saw the grandstand and some trees and part of the Chemistry Building shake as he crashed into me. He knocked me over backwards and then circled around me, flapping his arms like wings. I got up, feeling dizzy. First Becker K.O.'s me, then this sadistic ape. He smelled; he stank; a real evil son-of-a-bitch.

Stapen had thrown an incomplete pass. We huddled.

"I got an idea," I said.

"What's that?" asked Joe.

"I'll throw the ball. You block."

"Let's leave it the way it is," said Joe.

We broke out of the huddle. Lenny bent over the ball, snapped it back to Stapen. Kong came at me. I lowered a shoulder and rushed at him. He had too much strength. I bounced off him, straightened up, and as I did Kong came again, knifing his shoulder into my belly. I fell. I leaped up right away but I didn't feel like getting up. I was having breathing problems.

Stapen had thrown a short complete pass. Third down. No huddle. When the ball snapped Kong and I ran at each other. At the last moment I left my feet and hurled myself at him. The weight of my body hit his neck and his head, knocking him off balance. As he fell I kicked him as hard as I could and caught him right on the chin. We were both on the ground. I got up first. As Kong rose there was a red blotch on the side of his face and blood at the corner of his mouth. We trotted back to our positions.

Stapen had thrown an incomplete pass. Fourth down. Stapen dropped back to punt. Kong dropped back to protect his safety man. The safety man caught the punt and they came pounding up the field, Kong leading the way for his runner. I ran at them. Kong was expecting another high hurdle. This time I dove and clipped him at the ankles. He went down hard, his face hitting the ground. He was stunned, he stayed there, his arms spread out. I ran up and kneeled down. I grabbed him by the back of the neck, hard. I squeezed his neck and rammed my knee into his backbone and dug it in. "Hey, Kong, buddy, are you all right?"

The others came running up. "I think he's hurt," I said. "Come on, somebody help me get him off the field."

Stapen got him on one side and I got Kong on the other and we walked him to the sideline. Near the sideline I pretended to stumble and ground my left shoe into his ankle.

"Oh," said Kong, "please leave me alone . . ."

"I'm just helpin' ya, buddy."

When we got him to the sideline we dropped him. Kong sat and rubbed the blood from his mouth. Then he reached down and felt his ankle. It was skinned and would soon begin to swell. I bent over him. "Hey, Kong, let's finish the game. We're behind 42-7 and need a chance to catch up."

"Naw, I gotta make my next class."

"I didn't know they taught dog-catching here."

"It's *English Lit I.*"

"That figures. Well, look, I'll help you over to the gym and I'll put you under a hot shower, what you say?"

"No, you stay away from me."

Kong got up. He was pretty busted. The great shoulders sagged, there was dirt and blood on his face. He limped a few steps. "Hey, Quinn," he said to one of his buddies, "gimme a hand . . ."

Quinn took one of Kong's arms and they walked slowly across the field toward the gym.

"Hey, Kong!" I yelled, "I hope you make your class! Tell Bill Saroyan I said 'hello'!"

The other fellows were standing around, including Baldy and Ballard who had come down from the stands. Here I had done my best ever god-damned act and not a pretty girl around for miles.

"Anybody got a smoke?" I asked.

"I got some Chesterfields," Baldy said.

"You still smoking pussy cigarettes?" I asked.

"I'll take one," said Joe Stapen.

"All right," I said, "since that's all there is."

We stood around, smoking.

"We still have enough guys around to play a game," somebody said.

"Fuck it," I said. "I hate sports."

"Well," said Stapen, "you sure took care of Kong."

272

"Yeah," said Baldy, "I watched the whole thing. There's only one thing that confuses me."

"What's that?" asked Stapen.

"I wonder which guy is the sadist?"

"Well," I said, "I gotta go. There's a Cagney movie showing tonight and I'm taking my cunt."

I began to walk across the field.

"You mean you're taking your right hand to the movie?" one of the guys yelled after me.

"Both hands," I said over my shoulder.

I walked off the field, down past the Chemistry Building and then out on the front lawn. There they were, boys and girls with their books, sitting on benches, under the trees, or on the lawn. Green books, blue books, brown books. They were talking to each other, smiling, laughing at times. I cut over to the side of the campus where the "V" car line ended. I boarded the "V," got my transfer, went to the back of the car, took the last seat in back, as always, and waited.

58

I made practice runs down to skid row to get ready for my future. I didn't like what I saw down there. Those men and women had no special daring or brilliance. They wanted what everybody else wanted. There were also some obvious mental cases down there who were allowed to walk the streets undisturbed. I had noticed that both in the very poor and very rich extremes of society the mad were often allowed to mingle freely. I knew that I wasn't entirely sane. I still knew, as I had as a child, that there was something strange about myself. I felt as if I were destined to be a murderer, a bank robber, a saint, a rapist, a monk, a hermit. I needed an isolated place to hide. Skid row was disgusting. The life of the sane, average man was dull, worse than death. There seemed to be no possible alternative. Education also seemed to be a trap. The little education I had allowed myself had made me more suspicious. What were doctors, lawyers, scientists? They were just men who allowed themselves to be deprived of their freedom to think and act as individuals. I went back to my shack and drank . . .

Sitting there drinking, I considered suicide, but I felt a strange fondness for my body, my life. Scarred as they were, they were mine. I would look into the dresser mirror and grin: if you're going to go, you might as well take eight, or ten or twenty of them with you . . .

It was a Saturday night in December. I was in my room and I drank much more than usual, lighting cigarette after cigarette, thinking of girls and the city and jobs, and of the years ahead. Looking ahead I liked very little of what I saw. I wasn't a misanthrope and I wasn't a misogynist but I liked being alone. It felt good to sit alone in a small space and smoke and drink. I had always been good company for myself.

Then I heard the radio in the next room. The guy had it on too loud. It was a sickening love song.

"Hey, buddy!" I hollered, "turn that thing down!"
There was no response.
I walked to the wall and pounded on it.
"I SAID, 'TURN THAT FUCKING THING DOWN!'"
The volume remained the same.
I walked outside to his door. I was in my shorts. I raised my leg and jammed my foot into the door. It burst open. There were two people on the cot, an old fat guy and an old fat woman. They were fucking. There was a small candle burning. The old guy was on top. He stopped and turned his head and looked. She looked up from underneath him. The place was very nicely fixed-up with curtains and a little rug.
"Oh, I'm sorry . . ."
I closed their door and went back to my place. I felt terrible. The poor had a right to fuck their way through their bad dreams. Sex and drink, and maybe love, was all they had.
I sat back down and poured a glass of wine. I left my door open. The moonlight came in with the sounds of the city: juke boxes, automobiles, curses, dogs barking, radios . . . We were all in it together. We were all in one big shit pot together. There was no escape. We were all going to be flushed away.
A small cat walked by, stopped at my door and looked in. The eyes were lit by the moon: pure red like fire. Such wonderful eyes.
"Come on, kitty . . ." I held my hand out as if there were food in it. "Kitty, kitty . . ."

The cat walked on by.

I heard the radio in the next room shut off.

I finished my wine and went outside. I was in my shorts as before. I pulled them up and tucked in my parts. I stood before the other door. I had broken the lock. I could see the light from the candle inside. They had the door wedged closed with something, probably a chair.

I knocked quietly.

There was no answer.

I knocked again.

I heard something. Then the door opened.

The old fat guy stood there. His face was hung with great folds of sorrow. He was all eyebrows and mustache and two sad eyes.

"Listen," I said, "I'm very sorry for what I did. Won't you and your girl come over to my place for a drink?"

"No."

"Or maybe I can bring you both something to drink?"

"No," he said, "please leave us alone."

He closed the door.

I awakened with one of my worst hangovers. I usually slept until noon. This day I couldn't. I dressed and went to the bathroom in the main house and made my toilet. I came back out, went up the alley and then down the stairway, down the cliff and into the street below.

Sunday, the worst god-damned day of them all.

I walked over to Main Street, past the bars. The B-girls sat near the doorways, their skirts pulled high, swinging their legs, wearing high heels.

"Hey, honey, come on in!"

Main Street, East 5th, Bunker Hill. Shitholes of America.

There was no place to go. I walked into a Penny Arcade. I walked around looking at the games but had no desire to play any of them. Then I saw a Marine at a pinball machine. Both his hands gripped the sides of the machine, as he tried to guide the ball with body-English. I walked up and grabbed him by the back of his collar and his belt.

"Becker, I demand a god-damned rematch!"

276

I let go of him and he turned.

"No, nothing doing," he said.

"Two out of three."

"Balls," he said, "I'll buy you a drink."

We walked out of the Penny Arcade and down Main Street. A B-girl hollered out from one of the bars, "Hey, Marine, come on in!"

Becker stopped. "I'm going in," he said.

"Don't," I said, "they are human roaches."

"I just got paid."

"The girls drink tea and they water your drinks. The prices are double and you never see the girl afterwards."

"I'm going in."

Becker walked in. One of the best unpublished writers in America, dressed to kill and to die. I followed him. He walked up to one of the girls and spoke to her. She pulled her skirt up, swung her high heels and laughed. They walked over to a booth in a corner. The bartender came around the bar to take their order. The other girl at the bar looked at me.

"Hey, honey, don't you wanna play?"

"Yeah, but only when it's my game."

"You scared or queer?"

"Both," I said, sitting at the far end of the bar.

There was a guy between us, his head on the bar. His wallet was gone. When he awakened and complained, he'd either be thrown out by the bartender or handed over to the police.

After serving Becker and the B-girl the bartender came back behind the bar and walked over to me.

"Yeh?"

"Nothing."

"Yeh? What ya want in here?"

"I'm waiting for my friend," I nodded at the corner booth.

"You sit here, you gotta drink."

"O.K. Water."

The bartender went off, came back, set down a glass of water.

"Two bits."

I paid him.

The girl at the bar said to the bartender, "He's queer or scared."

The bartender didn't say anything. Then Becker waved to him

and he went to take their order.

The girl looked at me. "How come you ain't in uniform?"

"I don't like to dress like everybody else."

"Are there any other reasons?"

"The other reasons are my own business."

"Fuck you," she said.

The bartender came back. "You need another drink."

"O.K.," I said, slipping another quarter toward him.

Outside, Becker and I walked down Main Street.

"How'd it go?" I asked.

"There was a table charge, plus the two drinks. It came to $32."

"Christ, I could stay drunk for two weeks on that."

"She grabbed my dick under the table, she rubbed it."

"What did she say?"

"Nothing. She just kept rubbing my dick."

"I'd rather rub my own dick and keep the thirty-two bucks."

"But she was so beautiful."

"God damn, man, I'm walking along in step with a perfect idiot."

"Someday I'm going to write all this down. I'll be on the library shelves: BECKER. The 'B's' are very weak, they need help."

"You talk too much about writing," I said.

We found another bar near the bus depot. It wasn't a hustle joint. There was just a barkeep and five or six travelers, all men. Becker and I sat down.

"It's on me," said Becker.

"Eastside in the bottle."

Becker ordered two. He looked at me.

"Come on, be a man, join up. Be a Marine."

"I don't get any thrill trying to be a man."

"Seems to me you're always beating up on somebody."

"That's just for entertainment."

"Join up. It'll give you something to write about."

"Becker, there's always something to write about."

"What are you gonna do, then?"

I pointed at my bottle, picked it up.

"How are ya gonna make it?" Becker asked.

"Seems like I've heard that question all my life."

"Well, I don't know about you but I'm going to try everything! War, women, travel, marriage, children, the works. The first car I own I'm going to take it completely apart! Then I'm going to put it back together again! I want to know about things, what makes them work! I'd like to be a correspondent in Washington, D.C. I'd like to be where big things are happening."

"Washington's crap, Becker."

"And women? Marriage? Children?"

"Crap."

"Yeah? Well, what do you want?"

"To hide."

"You poor fuck. You need another beer."

"All right."

The beer arrived.

We sat quietly. I could sense that Becker was off on his own, thinking about being a Marine, about being a writer, about getting laid. He'd probably make a good writer. He was bursting with enthusiasms. He probably loved many things: the hawk in flight, the god-damned ocean, full moon, Balzac, bridges, stage plays, the Pulitzer Prize, the piano, the god-damned Bible.

There was a small radio in the bar. There was a popular song playing. Then in the middle of the song there was an interruption. The announcer said, "A bulletin has just come in. The Japanese have bombed Pearl Harbor. I repeat: The Japanese have just bombed Pearl Harbor. All military personnel are requested to return immediately to their bases!"

We looked at each other, hardly able to understand what we'd just heard.

"Well," said Becker quietly, "that's it."

"Finish your beer," I told him.

Becker took a hit.

"Jesus, suppose some stupid son-of-a-bitch points a machine gun at me and pulls the trigger?"

"That could well happen."

"Hank . . ."

"What?"

"Will you ride back to the base with me on the bus?"

"I can't do that."

The bartender, a man about 45 with a watermelon gut and fuzzy eyes walked over to us. He looked at Becker. "Well, Marine, it looks like you gotta go back to your base, huh?"

That pissed me. "Hey, fat boy, let him finish his drink, O.K.?"

"Sure, sure . . . Want a drink on the house, Marine? How about a shot of good whiskey?"

"No," said Becker, "it's all right."

"Go ahead," I told Becker, "take the drink. He figures you're going to die to save his bar."

"All right," said Becker, "I'll take the drink."

The barkeep looked at Becker.

"You got a nasty friend . . ."

"Just give him his drink," I said.

The other few customers were babbling wildly about Pearl Harbor. Before, they wouldn't speak to each other. Now they were mobilized. The Tribe was in danger.

Becker got his drink. It was a double shot of whiskey. He drank it down.

"I never told you this," he said, "but I'm an orphan."

"God damn," I said.

"Will you at least come to the bus depot with me?"

"Sure."

We got up and walked toward the door.

The barkeep was rubbing his hands all over his apron. He had his apron all bunched up and was excitedly rubbing his hands on it.

"Good luck, Marine!" he hollered.

Becker walked out. I paused inside the door and looked back at the barkeep.

"World War I, eh?"

"Yeh, yeh . . ." he said happily.

I caught up with Becker. We half-ran to the bus depot together. Servicemen in uniform were already beginning to arrive. The whole place had an air of excitement. A sailor ran past.

"I'M GOING TO KILL ME A JAP!" he screamed.

Becker stood in the ticket line. One of the servicemen had his girlfriend with him. The girl was talking, crying, holding onto

280

him, kissing him. Poor Becker only had me. I stood to one side, waiting. It was a long wait. The same sailor who had screamed earlier came up to me. "Hey, fellow, aren't you going to help us? What're you standing there for? Why don't you go down and sign up?"

There was whiskey on his breath. He had freckles and a very large nose.

"You're going to miss your bus," I told him.

He went off toward the bus departure point.

"*Fuck the god-damned fucking Japs!*" he said.

Becker finally had his ticket. I walked him to his bus. He stood in another line.

"Any advice?" he asked.

"No."

The line was filing slowly into the bus. The girl was weeping and talking rapidly and quietly to her soldier.

Becker was at the door. I punched him on the shoulder. "You're the best I've known."

"Thanks, Hank . . ."

"Goodbye . . ."

I walked out of there. Suddenly there was traffic on the street. People were driving badly, running stoplights, screaming at each other. I walked back over to Main Street. America was at war. I looked into my wallet: I had a dollar. I counted my change: 67¢.

I walked along Main Street. There wouldn't be much for the B-girls today. I walked along. Then I came to the Penny Arcade. There wasn't anybody in there. Just the owner standing in his high-perched booth. It was dark in that place and it stank of piss.

I walked along in the dark aisles among the broken machines. They called it a Penny Arcade but most of the games cost a nickel and some a dime. I stopped at the boxing machine, my favorite. Two little steel men stood in a glass cage with buttons on their chins. There were two hand grips, like pistol grips, with triggers, and when you squeezed the triggers the arms of your fighter would uppercut wildly. You could move your fighter back and forth and from side to side. When you hit the button on the chin of the other fighter he would go down hard on his back, K.O.'d. When I was a kid and Max Schmeling K.O.'d Joe Louis, I had run out into the street looking for my buddies, yelling *"Hey, Max Schmeling K.O.'d Joe Louis!"* And nobody answered me, nobody said anything, they had just walked away with their heads down.

It took two to play the boxing game and I wasn't going to play with the pervert who owned the place. Then I saw a little Mexican boy, eight or nine years old. He came walking down the aisle. A nice-looking, intelligent Mexican boy.

"Hey, kid?"

"Yes, Mister?"

"Wanna play this boxing game with me?"

"Free?"

"Sure. I'm paying. Pick your fighter."

He circled around, peering through the glass. He looked very serious. Then he said, "O.K., I'll take the guy in the red trunks. He looks best."

"All right."

The kid got on his side of the game and stared through the glass. He looked at his fighter, then he looked up at me.

"Mister, don't you know that there's a war on?"

"Yes."

We stood there.

"You gotta put the coin in," said the kid.

"What are you doing in this place?" I asked him. "How come you're not in school?"

"It's Sunday."

I put the dime in. The kid started squeezing his triggers and I started squeezing mine. The kid had made a bad choice. The left arm of his fighter was broken and only reached up halfway. It could never hit the button on my fighter's chin. All the kid had was a right hand. I decided to take my time. My guy had blue trunks. I moved him in and out, making sudden flurries. The Mexican kid was great, he kept trying. He gave up on the left arm and just squeezed the trigger for the right arm. I rushed blue trunks in for the kill, squeezing both triggers. The kid kept pumping the right arm of red trunks. Suddenly blue trunks dropped. He went down hard, making a clanking sound.

282

"I got ya, Mister," said the kid.

"You won," I said.

The kid was excited. He kept looking at blue trunks flat on his ass.

"You wanna fight again, Mister?"

I paused, I don't know why.

"You out of money, Mister?"

"Oh, no."

"O.K., then, we'll fight."

I put in another dime and blue trunks sprang to his feet. The kid started squeezing his one trigger and the right arm of red trunks pumped and pumped. I let blue trunks stand back for a while and contemplate. Then I nodded at the kid. I moved blue trunks in, both arms flailing. I felt I had to win. It seemed very important. I didn't know why it was important and I kept thinking, why do I think this is so important?

And another part of me answered, just because it is.

Then blue trunks dropped again, hard, making the same iron clanking sound. I looked at him laying on his back down there on his little green velvet mat.

Then I turned around and walked out.

An internationally famous figure in contemporary poetry and prose, Charles Bukowski was born in Andernach, Germany in 1920, and brought to the United States at the age of three. He was raised in Los Angeles and presently lives in San Pedro, California. He published his first story when he was twenty-four and began writing poetry at the age of thirty-five. He has now published forty books of poetry and prose, the most recent of which were his highly acclaimed novel *Ham on Rye* (Black Sparrow, 1982), a book of stories *Hot Water Music* (Black Sparrow, 1983), a book of poetry *You Get So Alone at Times That It Just Makes Sense* (Black Sparrow, 1986), an original screenplay *The Movie: "Barfly"* (Black Sparrow, 1987) and most recently *The Roominghouse Madrigals: Early Selected Poems 1946-1966* (Black Sparrow, 1988). Most of his books have now been published in translation in over a dozen languages, and his poems and stories continue to appear in magazines and newspapers throughout the world.